Jane Stays Dreaming

Also by Britnee Meiser

All My Bests

Jane Stays DREAMING

Britnee Meiser

Aladdin
New York   Amsterdam/Antwerp   London
Toronto   Sydney/Melbourne   New Delhi

This book is a work of fiction. Any references to historical events, real people, or real places are used fictitiously. Other names, characters, places, and events are products of the author's imagination, and any resemblance to actual events or places or persons, living or dead, is entirely coincidental.

ALADDIN
An imprint of Simon & Schuster Children's Publishing Division
1230 Avenue of the Americas, New York, New York 10020
For more than 100 years, Simon & Schuster has championed authors and the stories they create. By respecting the copyright of an author's intellectual property, you enable Simon & Schuster and the author to continue publishing exceptional books for years to come. We thank you for supporting the author's copyright by purchasing an authorized edition of this book.
No amount of this book may be reproduced or stored in any format, nor may it be uploaded to any website, database, language-learning model, or other repository, retrieval, or artificial intelligence system without express permission. All rights reserved. Inquiries may be directed to Simon & Schuster, 1230 Avenue of the Americas, New York, NY 10020 or permissions@simonandschuster.com.
First Aladdin hardcover edition September 2025
Text © 2025 by Britnee Meiser
Jacket illustration © 2025 by Ana Hard
Jacket design by Heather Palisi
Interior design by Mike Rosamilia
Also available in an Aladdin paperback edition.
All rights reserved, including the right of reproduction in whole or in part in any form.
ALADDIN and related logo are registered trademarks of Simon & Schuster, LLC.
For information about special discounts for bulk purchases, please contact Simon & Schuster Special Sales at 1-866-506-1949 or business@simonandschuster.com.
Simon & Schuster strongly believes in freedom of expression and stands against censorship in all its forms. For more information, visit BooksBelong.com.
The Simon & Schuster Speakers Bureau can bring authors to your live event. For more information or to book an event, contact the Simon & Schuster Speakers Bureau at 1-866-248-3049 or visit our website at www.simonspeakers.com.
The text of this book was set in Adobe Caslon Pro.
Manufactured in the United States of America 0825 BVG
2 4 6 8 10 9 7 5 3 1
Library of Congress Cataloging-in-Publication Data
Names: Meiser, Britnee author
Title: Jane stays dreaming / by Britnee Meiser.
Description: First Aladdin paperback edition. | New York : Aladdin, 2025. | Audience term: Teenagers | Audience: Ages 10 and Up | Summary: Shy high school freshman Jane secretly runs a popular blog, but her real and online lives collide when she realizes that her childhood friend Leo is interested in the same girl Jane's been helping through her advice column.
Identifiers: LCCN 2024059154 (print) | LCCN 2024059155 (ebook) | ISBN 9781665978859 paperback | ISBN 9781665978866 hardcover | ISBN 9781665978873 ebook
Subjects: CYAC: Blogs—Fiction | Interpersonal relations—Fiction | Friendship—Fiction | Family life—Fiction | High schools—Fiction | Schools—Fiction | LCGFT: Novels
Classification: LCC PZ7.1.M46914 Jan 2025 (print) | LCC PZ7.1.M46914 (ebook) | DDC [Fic]—dc23/eng/20250423
LC record available at https://lccn.loc.gov/2024059154
LC ebook record available at https://lccn.loc.gov/2024059155

For all the girls in their rooms,
dreaming of something bigger

Jane Stays Dreaming

New post from AnaStaysDreaming
Sunday, March 30, 6:48 p.m.

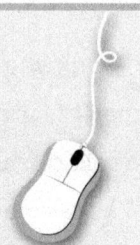

Hi from Birthday Land

Yesterday I was in New York City, sitting outside at a café on a cute little cobblestone street. It was the perfect temperature, mid-sixties, light-jacket weather. The sun was setting, casting a warm glow over everything. Izzy, Leo, and I had just eaten the most delicious meal. Then Leo said something funny, and we all laughed, the kind of all-encompassing laughter that made my eyes burn and my stomach hurt. All of a sudden, a flicker of light caught my eye. I turned and spotted a candle sticking out of a piece of raspberry cheesecake (my favorite!). The server put it down in front of me, and just like that, my friends started singing. *Happy birthday to you . . .* I was embarrassed, of course, but still, I couldn't stop smiling. I just felt so happy. I took a deep breath, made a wish, and blew out the candle. When I looked up—at my friends, the city, the golden sky—I realized my wish had already come true.

At the risk of sounding braggy, my birthday weekend has been a real-life fairy tale. Seriously, Cinderella's got NOTHING on me. I want to tell you all about it, but I don't have much time. In a few minutes, Miles is picking me up and taking me out to dinner. He wants to surprise me, so he won't say where we're going, but he told me to wear something nice. I know, I know. He's the best boyfriend ever.

Thank you all SO much for the birthday wishes. Even though I can't respond to them all, I read every single one and am truly feeling the love. I got a few birthday-related questions too, that I'll try to answer on (Talk to Me) Tuesday. In related news I hit 100k followers yesterday (!!!), which is, without a doubt, the best present I could've asked for. It means so much that you're all here right now, reading this, and that you continue to stick by me while I regale you with the details of my silly little life.

So, happy birthday to me, but you can have my wish. I already have everything I need :)

There's the doorbell. Gotta go! xoxo

Stay dreaming,
Anastasia

Chapter 1

"Happy birthday to you . . ."

A wave of dread washes over me. "Mom, please—"

"Happy birthday to you," Mom continues singing a little more forcefully. The rest of the table joins in, including the random couple who got seated at our hibachi table. I sink down in my seat, embarrassed. *"Happy birthday, dear Jane. Happy birthday to you!"*

"Blow out the candle!" Mom says, leaning around my dad so she can see. I frown down at the plate in front of me. It's just one candle sticking out of a mound of fried rice. But I do what she says. I blow without bothering to make a wish—if you ask me, a wish requires a cake—the flame dies out, and everybody claps. *Ta-da.*

There's a flash of light to my left. I look at Leo. He takes another picture.

"Oh yeah." He pulls the camera away from his face and turns it around to show me. "That's a keeper."

My scowling face takes up most of the screen. Yep, that's

my pale skin, dark green eyes, and dirty-blond hair that washes me out whenever a flash gets involved. The shot is so tight, I can clearly see the wings of my eyeliner flicking out at different angles. I groan and push the camera away. I spent half an hour in front of the mirror trying to get them to match.

"I can't believe our girl is fifteen," says Leo's mom, Ava, seated on Leo's other side. Her parents moved to the US from Brazil when she was fifteen, and she still has a slight Portuguese accent. She looks at my mom. "Charli, remember when the kids were little enough to take bubble baths together? They had those adorable rubber duckies—"

"And Leo wouldn't get in without his Spider-Man doll," Mom says. She and Ava are always talking over each other, like their friendship has surpassed the need for complete sentences. "He said Spider-Man would save him if the bubbles got too high."

"Leo the lion." Roman, Leo's very Italian father, reaches out and ruffles up his son's already unruly dark hair. They call him that because he was scared of everything when he was little, like the Cowardly Lion. Once, on the playground in kindergarten, a little bird landed on his shoulder, and he got so freaked out, he wet his pants. I had to give him my jacket to wrap around himself before anybody could see. To this day, he still has a phobia of birds.

Ava throws her head back and laughs. I look at Leo, horrified. He has an equally uncomfortable expression on his face. Neither of us says anything, though. We're used to these mortifying little trips down memory lane.

Our parents have been best friends since practically forever. Ava and Roman actually introduced my parents at a St. Patrick's Day party when they were all in college. My dad took one look at my mom, wearing a sparkly green top hat and a fake red beard, and was instantly smitten. They started dating two weeks later, and the four of them have been inseparable ever since.

"Leo the lion and Clumsy Cat," Dad says, smiling at me in that nostalgic way of his, and I worry for a second he might get emotional. "Best friends forever."

Leo and I were born four weeks apart, and to this day, those four weeks are probably the longest we've ever *been* apart. It was our parents' doing at first, lumping us together for playdates, signing us up for the same day care centers and swim lessons, but eventually we gravitated toward each other on our own. Now Leo's like a brother. He's more like a brother than my *actual* brother, who, by the way, couldn't even be bothered to show up tonight.

"Dad, please." I tug on the sleeves of my purple cardigan. Mom bought it for me as a birthday gift. I wore it to make her happy, even though I think it makes me look boxy. "No Clumsy Cat. It's my birthday."

"Fine, fine," Dad says. Then his eyes widen, and he points at the hibachi chef. "Ooh, Janie! Shrimp toss!"

I look at the chef. Sure enough, he's standing on the other side of the grill with a freshly cooked shrimp on the end of his spatula. He's smiling at me expectantly. "Birthday girl goes first?"

"Uh . . ." I don't want to be rude, but the last thing I want for my birthday is shrimp flying at my face. Unfortunately, the hibachi chef must look at my open mouth and see a target, because he launches the shrimp right at me. My reflexes aren't quick enough, and it hits me in the eye.

"Ow." I cover my eye with my hand, just as the flash on Leo's camera goes off again. I whip my head around to yell at him.

"Sorry," he says, quickly putting the camera down. "I figured you'd catch it. You know, since you're no longer Clumsy Cat."

"If you don't cut it out with the embarrassing pictures, *Leopold*—"

And then the sentence dies in my throat. Past Leo's head, sitting at a table near the front of the restaurant, I see broad shoulders, a blue-and-white varsity jacket, a familiar swoop of light blond hair. Ethan Gray.

My heart contracts in my chest.

I've been in love with Ethan Gray ever since I sat behind him in English class in the seventh grade. One time, a pencil fell out of his desk without him realizing, and I picked it up and kept it. I'd wrap my fingers around it, imagining the places where he touched it and pretending that my hand was touching his. I still have the pencil. I even use it sometimes, but only on special occasions.

Ethan Gray is sitting at a table with an older couple—his parents?—holding chopsticks, popping a piece of sushi into his mouth. He seems engrossed in whatever the man is saying to him. Hopefully that means he didn't see me get hit in the eye with a shrimp. Not that he'd even recognize me if he did. In the two years I've known him, we've said exactly two words to each other. "Sorry," when he bumped into me once, and "um," when I tried to respond but forgot how to speak English.

"Earth to Jane," Leo says, snapping me out of it.

"Huh?" I blink at him, taking in his hazel eyes, the amused smirk on his face.

"You went to Mars again."

Leo is used to my dissociative tendencies. Since I was a kid, I've had the ability to zone out anywhere, anytime. He calls it going to Mars.

"What was I saying?"

"You were threatening me. Maybe trying to glare me to death." He turns around, tries to follow my eyeline. "What were you looking at?"

"Nothing," I say, but it's no use. I see recognition cross Leo's features when he spots Ethan Gray.

"Him?" There's disbelief in his voice, and something else, too. Disappointment?

"No."

"Jane," Leo says, as if reading my mind. "Please tell me you're staring because he's got something in his teeth, and not because you like him."

I don't know what to say at first. Talking about crushes with Leo has always felt weirdly off-limits, like such a conversation would cross some sort of invisible line. That's why I never told him about Ethan Gray. It's not just that I assumed he wouldn't want to hear it. It's that *I* wouldn't want him to hear it.

"So what if I do?"

Leo shakes his head. Disappointment, definitely.

"He's bad news," Leo says. "You know the rumors."

I put my hand over my eye again. It's starting to throb. "They're just rumors. You don't know him." It was never confirmed that he broke up Kelsey Welles and Pete Cunningham. Not everything you hear in high school is true. In fact, most things probably aren't.

He gives me a skeptical look. "Neither do you."

I frown at him. *Not yet,* I want to say. But one day, things will be different. I just have to figure out how to get him to notice me.

The hibachi chef waves to get Leo's attention. "Shrimp?"

I shake my head on Leo's behalf. "He doesn't like seafood." The chef frowns and moves down the line.

"Where's Jeremiah tonight?" I hear Ava ask my mom. "I haven't seen that kid in forever."

"He's at home writing a paper," Mom says. "He had all spring break to do it, so naturally, he put it off until the last day." She turns to look at Dad, who's in the middle of his own shrimp toss. "Marty, give him a call. Make sure he's not on the PlayStation."

"He's definitely on the PlayStation," I say. "What's the point in calling? He's just going to lie and say he's not."

But Dad, chewing his shrimp, pulls out his phone anyway. Of course we can't make it through my birthday dinner without discussing Jeremiah. He's a year older than me, but my parents are always so worried about him, Mom especially. I want to tell her that maybe if she stopped babying him so much, he'd be forced to grow up. But I know what she'd say. It's what she always says. *Your brother isn't like you, Jane. He needs guidance.*

The chef finishes the shrimp toss, and everyone catches theirs except me. Then he gets to work chopping and grilling our main course. While our parents delight in the theatrics of the onion volcano—I can't help but smile at the sincerity of their oohs and aahs every time the chef does one of his tricks—and Leo scrolls through the photos on his camera, I let my gaze drift toward Ethan again. A new Netzine post starts to take shape in my mind.

Miles took me to a sushi restaurant. He wore his varsity jacket, of course, but I didn't mind, because he looked so handsome in it. I wore a new lilac dress I got at a boutique in SoHo on my birthday trip. Izzy insisted *that I buy it. She said lilac was my color. When Miles saw me in it, he spun me around and told me I was the most beautiful girl he'd ever seen. And then...*

On the walk back to the car, while our parents work out the details of their next double-date night, Leo pulls me aside.

"I got you something," he says, not quite meeting my eye. If I didn't know any better, I'd think he was nervous. "Hang on."

He runs ahead to his parents' Audi and opens the back door. He leans inside and, a moment later, emerges with a present. It's small and rectangular, wrapped in sparkly silver paper and tied with a pink bow.

"Wow." I take the present from him and examine it. "It's so pretty."

"You haven't even opened it yet."

"I don't need to," I tell him, hugging the gift to my chest. "I already love it."

He laughs. "I think you'll love what's inside even more."

"Oh yeah?" I hold it up to my ear and shake it a little. "Is it a puppy?"

He rolls his eyes and nudges me playfully. "Just *open* it."

I do as he says, carefully untying the bow and tearing the edge of the paper so I don't make a mess. Underneath is a little purple picture frame with thick, rounded edges, like the kind you'd get from a cool antique shop. Inside the frame: a selfie of me and Leo that he took last year. His hair is shorter, and

I'm holding out my hand to block the camera because I didn't want my picture taken. *I look ugly,* I remember saying to him. *You could never look ugly,* he replied, and took it anyway. Now it's one of my favorite pictures of us. It's candid—real.

"You're right." I smile up at him. "I love it even more."

He smiles too, and I throw my arms around him and pull him into a hug. "Thank you."

"Happy birthday," he says softly, hugging me back.

His arms are familiar and warm, a cozy shield against the chilly night air. I rest my cheek on his chest and close my eyes, not wanting to let go yet, and he must sense it, because he squeezes me tighter. I breathe a sigh of relief, feeling completely at ease, the way I always do with Leo. If I had a candle, I think I'd wish this feeling could last forever.

Chapter 2

When we get home from the restaurant, I shut myself in my room with my laptop, lie on my bed, and log into my Netzine. There are already hundreds of notifications reacting to my last post, plus dozens of comments—people wishing me happy birthday, or asking me the name of the café, or telling me they have a crush on Leo (I get those a lot). As usual, there are a few people asking for pictures, too, but I delete those comments. Anastasia doesn't post pictures of herself or her friends. She values her privacy.

I write up my newest post, going into more detail about Anastasia's birthday weekend, and schedule it for tomorrow. Since I started *AnaStaysDreaming* two years ago, I've tried to make a post every day, even if it's something small. I've learned that subscribers appreciate consistency. They like to feel like they're living Anastasia's life right alongside her. That means no breaks, not even on my birthday.

I look at my profile in preview mode, which shows me how the newest post will look on my page when it's uploaded.

The diary posts are offset with pretty photos of her (my) favorite places and things, quotes from books and movies she (I) loves, and anything else she (I) deems inspiring. Nothing can be out of order. When people visit this profile, I want them to be transported away from reality and into dreamland. After all, that's where it takes me.

I remember the first post I ever wrote as Anastasia. It was Valentine's Day, seventh grade. The student council had hosted a fundraiser where you could pay five dollars and they'd deliver a little teddy bear to your Valentine during homeroom. That morning, as I watched other girls get their bears from friends or crushes, I was overcome with an awful mix of jealousy and sadness. I wanted a bear—they were pink, and *so* cute—but more than that, I wanted what the bear represented: someone who cared enough to pay five dollars to tell the whole school you're their Valentine.

I got home that afternoon and logged into Netzine. I'd made my own profile a few weeks before, and my posts were an endless cycle of movie nights with my friends and pictures of my basset hound Maggie in Mom's garden. I was starting to bore even myself. I opened up a new draft, intending to write about how much I hated Valentine's Day, but something else came out instead. It was a story about a girl who got two teddy bears and had to choose, over a dramatic lunchtime showdown, which boy would be her Valentine. In the end, she chose neither and then spent the night eating chocolate hearts with her best friends. When I finished writing, I wasn't sad about not getting a bear anymore. I didn't *need* one. In this dreamland I'd created, I could have whatever I wanted.

It all happened quickly after that. I created my new identity, archived all my old posts, and changed the name of my Netzine from *xoxojane5* to *AnaStaysDreaming*. When I published my first post as Anastasia, I had three followers. Now, two years later, I have over a hundred thousand. I can write about the things I love under the guise of someone with a much more interesting life. It's a win-win—for my followers and for me.

I scan my profile page for eyesores. It's a light pink background with my blog name written in sketched cursive at the top. Underneath are navigation tabs that read *Home*, *About*, and *Ask*. My unpublished diary post appears first, next to a sunny photo of a café on a cobblestone street, a bouquet of peonies, and a quote from the movie *Breakfast at Tiffany's*: "Okay, life's a fact, people do fall in love, people do belong to each other, because that's the only chance anybody's got for real happiness."

I smile, satisfied. That's the movie that made me fall in love with New York City. The first time I saw it, with my best friend Camila in my basement when we were thirteen, I knew I wanted to grow up and live a life as glamorous as Holly Golightly's.

In the distance, the doorbell rings, followed by Maggie's bellowing howl. I don't think much of it—Sunday nights at our house are a revolving door of Jeremiah's friend Danny,

Mom's book club, the neighbors—until there's a knock on my bedroom door.

"Come in," I say, while the door is already opening. I look up from my screen and find Camila standing there with a pastry box in one hand and a gift bag in the other.

"Happy birthday!"

"Ohmigod!" I roll off my bed and run over to hug her. "I didn't think I'd see you until tomorrow."

"We just got back," she says, hugging me even though her hands are full. "But I told my mom she *had* to let me come over. It was the least she could do, making us go on vacation during your birthday."

"How was Myrtle Beach?" I say, letting go. "The pictures looked amazing."

She gestures with her hand in a *whatever* motion. "Same old. Went to the beach during the day, played cards on the porch with my cousins at night. Mom and Aunt Nancy drank a lot of pink wine."

I take in her appearance. She's wearing a light blue lounge set I've never seen before, and her dark hair falls in loose, glossy waves over her shoulders. She does not look like somebody who just spent ten hours in a car. That's Camila, though. Effortlessly glamorous, always.

Just like her online alter ego, Izzy.

"Are you busy?" she says, glancing around me at my laptop.

"Nope." I hurry to shut it before she can see the screen. "Just finishing up the English assignment. *Julius Caesar*, boring."

Camila doesn't know about my Netzine. Nobody does except my parents, who don't have any real concept of what it means to run a popular online blog, and Leo, who doesn't know the specifics but is still sworn to secrecy. Whenever I consider telling Camila, I think about everything I've ever written about her—about Izzy—and decide it would be a horrible idea.

When she had a bad reaction to apples in seventh grade and ended up breaking out in hives on picture day? Wrote about it. The time she did a front handspring during cheerleading tryouts and accidentally kicked the girl next to her in the face? Wrote about that, too. When we weren't speaking for a week because Camila invited Gemma Reeves, cheerleading captain, to see Olivia Rodrigo in concert instead of me, I wrote that Izzy was desperate for attention (too harsh, I know, but Cami only invited Gemma as a thank-you for helping her make the squad, when she *knew* how much I would've loved to have gone to the show). There's lots of good stuff too—of course there is. But in Camila's anxious mind, the good tends to get overshadowed by the bad.

She sits down on the bed. "I can't stay long, anyway. Mom said half an hour, and then I have to go home to unpack."

I sit down next to her, hug my stuffed elephant to my chest. These short visits were becoming more and more common. But Cami and I have been best friends for years. So what if she's been a little busy with the cheer squad lately? At least she came, right?

"What's wrong with your eye?" Camila cocks her head. "It looks puffy. And a little red. Oh no—you don't have pink eye, do you?" She leans back a little, like I'm contagious.

"*No.* I got hit with a flying shrimp."

She raises her eyebrows in surprise.

"Long story."

She gives me a pitying look. "You didn't do anything fun for your birthday?"

I shrug. I had begged my parents to take me to New York City for the day—it's only a couple of hours in the car, and even less by train—but Jeremiah is grounded for failing his math test, and they didn't trust him to stay home alone. "We went to hibachi with the Amatos. Woo-freaking-hoo."

"You love hibachi," she says. "And Leo."

I scrunch up my nose. "Excuse me, I do not *love* Leo."

"You know what I mean," Camila says. And I do, I guess. Leo is my safety net. Nothing is ever completely horrible if he's around.

"Ethan Gray was there," I say, trying to act casual. Camila's jaw drops.

"*What?* For your birthday?"

"Obviously not. He was with his parents, I think. I just saw him there."

"Did he see you?"

"I hope not. If he did, he saw me get hit in the face with a shrimp."

Camila puts a hand up to her mouth to stifle a laugh. She

has a fresh coat of hot pink polish on her nails. I start laughing with her. It *is* kind of funny.

Camila has known about my crush on Ethan since the beginning. For a while she kept trying to get me to talk to him. At the eighth-grade Valentine's Day dance, she actually pushed me in front of him to try to force an interaction. But he didn't even notice me, and I was too chicken to make him. Since then, nothing much has changed.

"Well, maybe this will help." She offers me the packages she came with. "It's not Ethan Gray, but I think it's a suitable consolation prize."

"Ooh." I take the present first. Camila has always been a great gift giver. I remove the tissue paper and pull out a jewelry box the size of a baseball. I open the lid and gasp.

"A necklace!" I squint down at the rectangular silver charm. My excitement dims. "Uh—does that say 'butter'?"

"Yes!" Camila pulls at the chain around her neck, revealing the silver charm hiding underneath her shirt. "And look. I have a croissant. They're best-friend charms!"

"Oh wow. Thank you." I force a smile, but inside I'm confused. Why is she the croissant, and I'm the stick of butter? Croissants are chic—they're Audrey Hepburn walking down Fifth Avenue. Butter is . . . butter.

"Let me put it on you," she says, reaching for the box. I lift my hair off my shoulders while she puts the necklace around me and fastens the clasp.

"There," she says. "It looks perfect! Do you love it?"

I do my best to put on a happy face. I don't want to ruin the moment for her, but I just don't *get* this gift. Croissants and butter aren't really even best-friend charms. They don't say "best" and "friend." They aren't like peanut butter and jelly, which are two obvious halves of a whole. You wouldn't even know they went together unless somebody told you.

"I love it," I say, touching the charm like I could make the words true by wishing on it.

She smiles, obviously pleased. Then she reaches around to the pastry box.

"Part two of your gift." She opens the box, using the lid to hide its contents from my view. "We stopped in the bakery before we got home. I was worried we wouldn't make it in time, but we got there five minutes before closing. How lucky is that?"

She spins the box around to face me. Inside is a little raspberry cheesecake with a single candle sticking out of the top.

I smile for real.

"Happy birthday to—"

I squeal, cutting her off. "Please! No singing!"

"But it's your birthday!" she argues. *"Happy birthday to—"*

"The candle isn't even lit," I say, hoping this obstacle will stop her.

"Good point." She stands up with the box in her hands. "Let's go ask your mom for a lighter."

She's up and out of the room before I can protest any more. I sigh and follow her. We find my mom in the den, sitting at the computer reading a Word document, while Jeremiah stands behind her looking bored.

"Did you copy-paste this whole paragraph?" Mom says, her tired face lit by the glow of the computer screen. "You can't do that, Jeremiah. That's plagiarism."

"I cited it," he says.

"That's not how citations work. You can't just take huge chunks of other people's essays and—"

"Mom," I say. "Camila needs a lighter. She wants to burn the house down."

Jeremiah turns around. His eyes gloss over me and land on Camila. "Hey."

She smiles back at him. "Hey. Want some cheesecake?"

"No!" I snatch the box out of her hands. "It's my birthday cheesecake."

She gives me a chastising look. "There's enough to share."

Without taking her eyes off the screen, Mom reaches into the desk drawer and pulls out a lighter, the kind with a long neck for lighting candles. "Here," she says, holding it out behind her. Jeremiah takes it and hands it to Camila, flipping his dark blond hair out of his eyes in the process. I make a disgusted face. It's a move he does whenever he's trying to look cool.

"Thanks, Mom," I say, grabbing Camila's wrist and pulling her out of the room, into the kitchen.

"Don't stay up too late!" Mom calls out after me. "You've got to wake up for school tomorrow, don't forget."

I groan. It's still spring break for another—I glance at the clock over the stove—three hours and twenty-two minutes. I don't want to think about going back to school yet.

Camila sets the cake box down on the table and walks to the cabinet where we keep the plates. She knows this kitchen like it's her own. We've been best friends since elementary school, when Camila's family moved into a house the next street over, and have spent countless hours raiding each other's pantries.

"Okay." She brings the plate over to the table and uses a spatula to deftly slide the cheesecake onto it. Maggie ambles over curiously, her floppy ears nearly touching the floor. I sit down in front of the cake, put my chin in my hands, and watch as Camila lights the candle. When she starts to sing, I don't ask her to stop. Putting up a fight will only prolong the embarrassment.

"*Happy birthday to youuuuu.*" She finishes the last verse and starts clapping. "Make a wish!"

I look into the candle's flickering flame. There are *so* many things I want. A New York City vacation. That one pair of jeans. Highlights. Ethan Gray. But there's one thing I want more than *anything*. If I had it, then I'd have everything.

I wish my life was more like Anastasia's.

I take a deep breath and blow out the candle.

Chapter 3

The next morning, my hands are full as I'm walking into school. I've got my tote bag, my metal water bottle, the textbooks I have to carry because they don't fit in my bag—when I bought the bag, I definitely chose style over function—and my math homework, which I had to finish in Jeremiah's truck while he drove us to school. Before I can ask Jeremiah to help me carry something, he walks off without so much as a glance back.

"Really nice," I mutter to myself. What if I slipped getting out of the truck and broke my neck or something?

I cross the student parking lot, pausing halfway to adjust the books in my arms. When I'm near the doors, a girl I've never seen before is opening one, heading inside the building.

"Hey," I call out, struggling to balance the water bottle on top of the textbooks. "Can you hold the door?"

She looks back at me. She's got long auburn hair, sort of wavy, and a distant look in her eyes. I meet her gaze and smile. "Thanks, I—"

She steps inside and lets the door swing shut behind her.

My jaw drops in surprise. I forget to balance the water bottle, and it falls out of my arms, hitting the concrete and denting the side.

I walk into third period to find the girl sitting at my desk.

Okay, technically, the newsroom doesn't have assigned seats. People are always coming and going, conducting interviews or typing up stories on the computers or designing page layouts. But generally speaking, everybody on staff at the *Grizzly* has their favorite place to sit. And *my* favorite place to sit is the desk in the back row, second from the left, next to Leo.

But the girl is sitting there now. I *know* it's the same girl—I recognize her wavy auburn hair. She keeps running her fingers through it while she talks to Leo. I feel a twinge of something like betrayal. Why didn't he tell her somebody was already sitting there?

Leo notices me standing by the door, watching him. He makes a face like he knows exactly what I'm thinking, and he's sorry. I try to frown as dramatically as I can. Apology *not* accepted.

"Jane," he says anyway. "Come meet Brynn. She's new. Brynn, this is my Jane." His face gets a little red, and he tries again. "I mean, this is my best friend Jane."

Brynn turns toward me. She's got a heart-shaped face and a mole above her lip that makes her look glamorous, like

Marilyn Monroe. Now I'm even more self-conscious about my eye, which is still bloodshot from getting hit with the shrimp. I'm starting to worry that some seasoning or something got in there, and now it's infected. Maybe Camila was right, and I *do* have pink eye? How do you even get pink eye, anyway?

"Hi." I take a seat at the desk next to her, where Kat usually sits. I wonder if Brynn knows she's created a domino effect that's messing everything up.

"Hi." Her voice is high pitched and sweet with a slight Southern accent. "It's nice to meet you."

"We met this morning. Sort of," I remind her, giving her the opportunity to provide an explanation for what happened. She was about to pee her pants and couldn't wait one more second to get to the bathroom? A wasp was about to fly inside, and she didn't want to risk letting it in and getting stung?

"We did?" Brynn asks. "When?"

"In the parking lot."

Really?" She gives me a small smile. "I'm sorry. I don't remember."

"Brynn just moved here from South Carolina," Leo says. He's looking through pictures on his camera, deleting the bad ones.

Brynn nods in agreement. "My dad's company transferred him. He offered to wait until the end of the school year, but I told him I was fine with it. I think fresh starts are kind of exciting, don't you?"

I hmm in casual agreement and nod. *Now* she wants to talk to me?

Kat appears behind me. She gives me a long, puzzled look and then sits in the empty seat next to me—Daria's seat.

"Aw, who's that?" I hear Brynn ask Leo. She's pointing at a picture on his camera.

"That's Maggie," Leo says. "Jane's dog."

"Kat," Daria says on my other side. "You're in my seat."

Kat looks up from her sketchbook. "Only because Jane is in my seat."

Daria looks at me like I committed the ultimate act of betrayal. "Jane?"

I gesture to Brynn, who's too into her conversation with Leo to notice the chaos she's caused. A look of understanding crosses over Daria's face. "New girl?"

I nod.

Daria sighs. Then she sits down in front of Kat, in Max's seat.

"—really obsessed with dogs," Brynn is saying. "But my dad developed an allergy, so now I have a hermit crab."

"Hey, I had one of those when I was a kid," Leo says. "But it ran away."

I snort. "You don't still believe that."

Leo and Brynn both look at me.

"What do you mean?" he says, and it occurs to me that maybe he does still believe it. Whoops.

"It died? Ava told my mom."

Leo's mouth falls open. "Shelldon died?"

Brynn's bottom lip juts out into a pout. "Oh no."

I let out a little laugh of disbelief. "Come on. Hermit crabs don't run away. How would he have gotten out of the tank?"

"I don't know." Leo actually sounds sad. "Mom said he escaped in the night."

An awkward silence hangs in the air. I feel guilty now. I hate hurting Leo's feelings, even if it is over a hermit crab he had when he was five.

"Sorry," I say to him, meaning it. "I feel like I just told you Santa isn't real."

Brynn puts a hand to her chest. "Santa isn't *real*?" She glances at Leo and smiles playfully, which lightens the mood and makes him laugh. I fight another surge of annoyance. Why do *I* feel like the third wheel right now?

The late bell rings. Halle, the editor in chief of the *Grizzly*, walks to the front of the room and calls for everybody's attention. It's story assignment time.

"I hope you all had a nice spring break," Halle says, sitting on an empty desk. Halle is a junior, the youngest EIC in nearly a decade. She's good at making you feel seen and heard but still doesn't take crap from anybody.

"First, everybody say hey to Brynn." Halle gestures to Brynn with her chin. "She's our newest staff writer, so please make her feel welcome."

The room breaks out into a chorus of "Hi, Brynn" with varying degrees of enthusiasm. She smiles bashfully and waves.

"Okay, let's see." Halle picks up her notepad and starts skimming it. "Daria's got the spring musical feature. Alec's writing the music review. Kat, can you turn in an illustration for that by the end of the week?"

Next to me, without looking up from her sketch pad, Kat gives a thumbs-up.

"Great. Oh—" Halle taps her pencil on the page. "Max is in Mexico until the end of the week, so we're going to need somebody to cover Thursday's baseball game. It's at home." Halle looks up, scans the room. "Any takers?"

I feel a flutter of excitement in my chest. I'm hardly an expert on baseball, or sports in general—Max is sports editor, and he usually covers all the big games—but there's one thing I *do* know.

Ethan Gray is on the baseball team.

Before I realize what's happening, my hand shoots up in the air.

"Jane." Halle uses her pencil to point at me. "Awesome, thanks. And Leo, you'll take photos?"

Leo doesn't hear her at first. He's too busy frowning at me. I avoid his gaze. Now that he knows about my crush on Ethan, he probably thinks that's the only reason I'm volunteering to cover this story. And okay, *yes*, that's a big part of it. But there's something else, too.

I've never really been a risk-taker. Ordinarily I'd keep my hand down and let somebody else do it, but after my birthday last night, I don't know. Something inside me has shifted. I'm thinking about my wish to be more like Anastasia. If I keep doing the same things, how will it ever come true?

I keep my eyes on Halle, firm in my decision. If I'm going to be more like Anastasia, I *have* to take risks. That's kind of her whole thing.

"Leo?"

Leo snaps out of it and looks at Halle. "I've got it covered."

Halle nods. She scribbles something down on her notepad and then says, "Hey, Jane. Why don't you and Brynn cowrite this one? You can show her how we do things around here."

"Oh, that would be great." Brynn looks at me. "If you don't mind."

I bite the inside of my cheek. First the door, then my seat, and now my story? Not to mention she's going way over the top trying to be all sweet and charming in front of Leo. And Leo is falling for it! He's never usually this accommodating to people. Unless he's directing them through his lens, he doesn't talk much at all. What's so special about Brynn?

"Sure," I force out.

While Halle finishes going over story assignments, I push my irritation toward Brynn out of my mind and think about what I'm going to ask Ethan on Thursday. *What's your favorite thing about being on the team? How do you feel about your performance so far this season? Would you say your eyes are more baby blue, or sky blue?*

I sigh. I should probably do some research about baseball so I don't look like a complete fool in front of him.

Halle ends the meeting, and everybody breaks to get started on their assignments. Brynn asks if I want to start prepping for the article, but then Halle pulls her aside to go over AP style rules and other stuff she'll need to know. I take the opportunity to escape to a computer in the back corner of the room, one that isn't visible from the desk of our adviser, Mr. Franklin.

I open a Word document and write a couple of random sentences about the baseball game. That way, if anybody passes by my screen, it will look like I'm brainstorming. Then I open a new incognito tab and log into my Netzine.

I know, I know. It's risky, logging in at school. But Netzine is meant to be used on a computer browser. That's part of its charm. It harkens back to the olden days, when the internet was a place you visited and not something you always had in your pocket. The mobile app only gives you limited access to your home page and profile. I need the computer for the full experience.

My inbox is flooded with questions for Talk to Me Tuesday. I start to skim through them, bookmarking the ones I think are most interesting so I can go back and answer them later. Every Monday it's the same: people submit questions anonymously via the *Ask* box on my profile, I pick ten or twenty to respond to, and then I schedule them to post throughout the day on Tuesday. I've been doing it for a year, and every week the list of questions seems to get longer. People *love* to ask Anastasia for advice on their crushes or their friends or their insecurities. And Anastasia—wise, worldly girl that she is—loves to help them.

When I first started Talk to Me Tuesday, I felt a little bit like an imposter. Who am I to be telling people how to live their lives, when I've barely lived myself? But then I realized something. Nobody has all the answers. We're all just faking it; pulling from movies and books and stories, and whatever else helps us figure out how to be the best versions of ourselves. My answers aren't any more "right" or "wrong" than, say, somebody who writes an advice column for a living. All I can do is try my best, and if that resonates with people, well, what's the harm?

I'm bookmarking a question about the best places to shop for dresses when someone sneaks up behind me and grabs my shoulders.

"Gotcha!" Leo says, making me jump. I minimize the browser, but then, when I realize it's him, I open it up again.

"Max better watch out." He sits down in the empty chair next to me. "He has no idea you're coming for his spot as sports editor."

"I am not," I say. "I'm simply expanding my portfolio."

"You've never cared about expanding your portfolio before."

"Well, things change."

"Uh-huh." He crosses his arms, stiffening a little. "So you volunteering for this story has nothing to do with the fact that Captain America is on the baseball team?"

"Captain America?" I shoot him a look. I should've known this was coming. "Ethan doesn't look like him."

"Yeah he does," Leo says. "But it's not about the way he looks. It's about what he represents."

"Hey, America is a diverse melting pot of cultures and traditions," I retort. "One could argue you being half-Brazilian makes you an even stronger contender for representing America."

"Okay, okay." He leans back in his chair, and I can tell he wants to change the subject. I don't blame him. The only time I've ever confessed a crush to him before was, like, third grade, and it was on Flynn Rider from *Tangled*. If he didn't know what to say then, he definitely doesn't know what to say now.

"What are you working on?" He glances at my screen. "Ah. Blog stuff."

Leo says "blog stuff" the way someone might say "homework." Complete disinterest. That's the way I like it, though. The only reason he even knows about my Netzine is because he saw me working on it once last summer. I told him he could read the diary post I was writing—Anastasia and Izzy meeting cute boys at the boardwalk in Ocean City—and it took him all of five seconds before he chalked it up to fiction and lost interest completely. He doesn't know my username—thank goodness—and he hasn't read it since.

"Shh!" I give him a warning look. "Nobody is supposed to know, remember?"

"That you have a blog? Lots of people have Netzine. It's not like you're doing something illegal."

He's right—lots of people *do* have Netzine now. I was lucky to get in early, when the site was still relatively unknown and it was easier to build a following, but over the last couple years, it's really taken off. Hard to say why—maybe people got sick of the brain rot happening on other social media apps, or maybe they just like having a platform that gives them permission to yap endlessly about themselves. Either way, I don't want anybody to know who I am. For me, the anonymity is the point.

"My identity is a secret," I say, keeping my voice low. "If I'm found out, it would be very, *very* bad."

He makes a serious face and gives me a salute. "Aye, aye, captain."

I turn my attention back to my inbox. "So," I say, scrolling some more. "You and Brynn are all buddy-buddy."

He stuffs his hands into his sweatshirt pockets, stretching out his long legs. "She's nice. And we have algebra together too."

"So what, are you like her unofficial tour guide?"

"What are you, like, jealous?"

I scoff. *Jealous?* What would I be jealous of? Her perfect hair? Her Marilyn mole? Her uninfected eye?

"More like annoyed. She purposely didn't hold the door for me this morning. *And* you gave her my seat."

"Oh come *on*. We barely sit there anyway."

"It's a little thing called loyalty, Leopold."

"It's a little thing called *manners*, Clumsy Cat."

I gasp, stop scrolling to look him in the eye. "Et tu, Brute?"

He gives me a small smile. "Sorry." He starts spinning in his chair. When he goes around a full rotation he says, "Consider it payback for Shelldon."

"I'm going to start calling you Leo the lion in public. See how you like it."

"I don't care," he says, running a hand through his messy brown hair. It hangs to his shoulders now. "It sounds kind of cool if you don't know the context."

"Well, I'll tell *everyone* the context!"

"No you won't," he says. "You talk a big game, but you'd never do anything to hurt me. You care too much."

I roll my eyes and smile into my screen. I don't have a rebuttal. He's right.

New post from AnaStaysDreaming

Tuesday, April 1, 10:00 a.m.

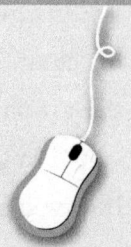

Talk to Me Tuesday

Anonymous asked: Hi Ana!

My boyfriend has been ignoring my texts. Yesterday I stole his phone and found out he's been texting other people WHILE ignoring me. When I confronted him about it, he said he just doesn't see my texts sometimes, and I'm making a big deal out of nothing. What should I do?

Sincerely, Deal or No Deal

AnaStaysDreaming: Dear Deal or No Deal,

In the words of Britney Spears('s T-shirt): DUMP HIM! If he wanted to text you, he would.

Tuesday, April 1, 11:00 a.m.

Anonymous asked: Anastasia! You always recommend the best fashion!! Where should I shop for a prom dress? xoxo!

AnaStaysDreaming: *mwah* thank you! I answered this question a month ago: www.netzine.com/anastaysdreaming/posts/mar/486072 And I'll also add the cute West Village boutique I found on my birthday trip! linked here

Tuesday, April 1, 12:00 p.m.

Anonymous asked: I've always been shy and it's something I wish I could change about myself. What is your advice for being more confident? Love, Shy Guy

AnaStaysDreaming: Dear Shy Guy,

Fake it till you make it! Confidence looks the same to other people whether it's real or not. And if you ever get embarrassed, remember that nobody is thinking about you as much as you're thinking about you.

Tuesday, April 1, 1:00 p.m.

Anonymous asked: Hi Anastasia,

I just started a new school and am kinda crushing on a boy in my class. The problem is, I think he might have a crush on someone else. How can I get him to notice me?

Sincerely, New Girl

AnaStaysDreaming: Dear New Girl,

Boys are simple creatures. They like it when we show an interest, but they don't like it when we try too hard. So do something that shows him you care—ask him about his hobbies, laugh at his jokes (even if they aren't funny), maybe throw in a ~casual~ arm touch—and then back off. Let him come to you. Remember that you're the prize, always.

Chapter 4

The crack of the baseball colliding with the metal bat snaps me out of my thoughts. I look up from my notepad, where I've been going over the questions I want to ask Ethan, just in time to see one of our players slide into first base. When he stands up, his bright-white pants are covered in dirt. I make a face—these players, I'm learning, treat dirt stains like badges of honor—and write down his jersey number.

"Woo-hoo!" Brynn yells, and claps along with everybody else in the bleachers. She's been enthusiastically following this game from the beginning. Smiling like she's having the time of her life, she leans toward me and says, "He's pretty impressive."

I tilt my sunglasses down and crane my neck to get a better look at the dugout. I can just see the edge of Ethan Gray's arm—I know it's him because of the mole above his right elbow.

"So how good are we, anyway?"

I look back at Brynn. The sun shines down on her auburn hair, which seems perfectly windswept, like she got a blowout from Mother Nature. I touch my ponytail self-consciously.

"You mean the team?" I say. "We're one and two." That's what Leo told me when I asked him earlier.

Brynn nods. "Makes sense. We're pretty good at fielding, but batting is lacking. It's like some of these guys are afraid to hit the ball." She shakes her head and returns her gaze to the outfield. "I wonder what the batting averages are."

I pause, surprised. "You know about baseball?"

"Oh." She smiles modestly. "Well, yeah. My dad loves it. He's been taking me to games all my life."

I roll my shoulders back and sit up straighter. Now I feel like I have to start paying attention. I'm supposed to be the one showing *her* the ropes. I can't let her upstage me on her very first story.

Thankfully, that's when Ethan Gray walks out of the dugout. He picks up a bat and starts doing practice swings. Suddenly I don't have any trouble paying attention.

Ethan Gray bats left-handed, I write down. Also: *Butt looks good in uniform.*

"Ethan Gray," Brynn says. "He's the only freshman on varsity, right?"

"Right," I say. "He's super impressive."

"I'll say." Brynn hesitates. "By the way, thanks for letting me work on this article with you. I know it's not, like, *ideal*, having to babysit the new girl. But I appreciate it."

"It's no big deal," I say, watching the muscles in Ethan's arms flex and relax as he swings the bat back and forth, back and forth. *Good form,* I jot down, though I don't know if it is, really. This is my first baseball game. He could be the worst hitter on the team.

"It is, though," Brynn insists. "Not everybody has been as welcoming as you and Leo."

"Talking about me?" says a voice to my right. I tear my gaze from Ethan Gray to find Leo climbing the bleachers, camera in hand. He's got a baseball cap on backward, his go-to accessory for keeping his long hair out of his face when he's shooting sports. He sits down on Brynn's other side.

"I was just thanking Jane for being so welcoming this week," Brynn says, smiling brightly. Her teeth are perfectly straight—I wonder how many years she had braces. "And you, too."

Leo makes a *psh* sound. "You're easy to welcome."

Brynn smiles into her lap while I shoot him a skeptical side-eye. What does that even mean?

"Check this out," Leo says, turning his camera so we can see the screen. It's a picture of the player sliding into first base, the dirt shooting up around him like mist. I nod, impressed but not surprised. Leo's a great photographer—it's why he gets all the big assignments even though he's only a freshman.

"Nice," I say. "Halle's going to love that."

"Oh my gosh." Brynn gapes, leaning in for a better look. "Leo, this is insane. I can't believe you took this!"

Leo's smile is small and humble. "It's okay. I wish the angle was a little lower."

"It's perfect," Brynn says. "How long have you been taking pictures?"

I turn back to the game, tuning them out. Ethan Gray isn't where I left him last—he's walking up to the plate. I scoot forward in my seat. He sort of digs his feet into the dirt before he finds his stance. Then he locks in.

The pitcher throws his first ball, but it goes low. Ethan Gray doesn't swing. My heart swells—he's so *intuitive*. The pitcher tries again. Another low ball. Somebody from the away bleachers shouts out encouragement. It seems to do the trick, because the pitcher's next ball is good. Ethan Gray swings, hits, and sends the ball flying into the outfield.

I stand up, watch the ball arc through the air as Ethan Gray runs to first base. The outfielders rush to catch the ball, but it flies over their heads and lands just short of the fence at the edge of the field. The crowd cheers as Ethan Gray runs past first, then second, sending two other players who were on the bases back to home. Ethan Gray stops at third base. Still, he scored two points for the team, putting us in the lead by one.

"Did you see that?" I turn around to look at Brynn and Leo, but they aren't paying attention. They're huddled around his camera.

"This was Jane's birthday," Leo says, scrolling through pictures. "That's her dad. Our parents are really close. Oh, whoops."

Brynn's hand flies to her mouth to stifle a giggle.

"Pretend you didn't see that," Leo says.

"See what?" I ask, suspicious.

"I can't believe you captured the exact moment the shrimp hit her," Brynn says.

"You didn't delete that?!"

Leo looks guilty. "I might have forgotten."

I lunge for the camera, trying to snatch it out of his hands, but he pulls back, knocking into Brynn.

"Whoa, whoa." Leo hugs the camera to his chest while Brynn giggles nervously. He looks at her. "Sorry. Jane was about to commit a felony."

When it comes to his camera, Leo has one cardinal rule: no touching. It's been that way ever since he got it for Christmas in the eighth grade.

"You've already committed a friendship felony by letting that picture see the light of day," I argue.

"Fine." He flips the screen toward me, and I watch as he presses the trash can button. *Are you sure you want to delete this photo?* He selects *yes*, and all evidence of me nearly getting blinded by a flying shrimp evaporates into the digital ether. "Happy?"

"Yes." I turn back to the field, where the next player is up to bat. "Ooh! Ethan Gray is about to score his third point for the team." I glance back at Leo. "You might want to abandon your trip down Embarrassing Memory Lane and go get this."

He nods once and stands up. *"I'll be back,"* Leo says in a voice like the Terminator, making Brynn laugh.

I watch him climb down the bleachers, shaking my head at his attempt to be funny. Then I look at Brynn. She's watching him too, the ghost of a smile lingering on her face.

When the game ends, and Brynn walks off to interview the coach, I apply a fresh coat of cherry lip gloss and wait by the dugout. Clutching my notepad in both hands, I force myself to take deep, even breaths. Any minute now, Ethan Gray will emerge. When he does, I can't be some fangirl. I have to be serious, a *real* reporter interviewing the MVP about the team's big win. Totally, completely objective.

And then I see him.

The sight of him is so glorious that at first, I can only handle it in pieces. His shoulders, his uniform, his swoop of blond hair, slicked with sweat across his forehead. The way he dabs up one of his teammates, who presumably says something to him like *good game*. He steps out of the shadow of the dugout into the early evening sun, and I swear, it's like the rest of the world dims, as if the angels in the sky are pointing the sun right at him like his own personal spotlight.

All my composure goes right out the window.

"Ethan," I try to say, but my throat is dry and my voice cracks. I clear my throat and try again. "Ethan!"

He turns to look at me—at me! I start to walk toward him even though I can't feel my legs. I can't feel anything except my heartbeat hammering in my chest.

Maybe it's the nerves, or the fact that I'm blinded by his

beauty, but I don't notice the baseball bat lying in the grass. I step on it, and the bat rolls forward, sending my foot flying out from under me. I fall backward and land right on my butt, like a wobbly toddler. Ethan Gray, along with several other guys on the team, sees the whole thing.

I squeeze my eyes shut in embarrassment. *Nice going, Clumsy Cat.*

When I open my eyes, Ethan Gray is standing over me. The sun silhouettes his body, tracing the edges of him in warm, golden light.

"Are you okay?" He holds out his hand to help me up. I take it, dazed.

"Yeah." I stand up. "I think so." I realize I'm still holding on to his hand and quickly let go. "Sorry—uh. I mean, thanks. For helping me."

He smiles. Up close, I see things about him I never noticed before—the faint smattering of freckles over his nose, his long eyelashes, the way his eyes aren't sky blue, or baby blue, but more of a pewter blue with pinprick flecks of green. I will myself to commit every single detail to memory.

"No problem," he says. "Sorry about the bat. Josh should be more careful where he throws his stuff."

"No," I say quickly. "No, I—I'm kind of clumsy. Things like this tend to happen to me. My dad calls me Clumsy Cat."

I wince. *Why* did I just tell him that?

He chuckles. "Clumsy Cat?"

I force a laugh. "Um. I loved *The Aristocats* when I was

little." I feel the need to explain for some reason. "Especially Marie, the little kitten with the pink bow? I think that's where it came from." I press my lips together, silently begging myself to stop talking.

"Ah." He nods. I put my sunglasses on top of my head, and he locks his eyes onto mine. "You're Jane, right? We had English together last year?"

My heart somersaults. He remembers me! Technically we had English together two years ago, not last year, but it doesn't even matter. He *remembers* me.

"That's right," I say, not bothering to correct him. I look at my legs, smooth down my skirt. I'm trying to hide just how much his gaze has unnerved me. "I'm Jane."

He smiles. "Hi, Jane."

My toes curl inside my Mary Janes. I can't *believe* he keeps saying my name.

"Hi."

"If it makes you feel better," he says, brushing his hair off his forehead, "sometimes my dad calls me Wheat Thin."

"Really?" I laugh. "Why?"

"Remember those Wheaties cereal boxes, the ones with the athletes on them?" he says, and I nod. "When I was a kid, I was obsessed with getting on one. My dad started calling me Wheaty, which turned into Wheat Thin. I don't know why—probably because it rhymes with Ethan."

"Makes sense."

"Not really." He laughs. "Oh well."

The conversation tapers off, and an awkward silence hangs in the air. I try to rack my brain for something to say so he doesn't walk away. Then I notice his gaze drift toward the notepad in my hand, and I remember what I'm doing here in the first place.

"Oh," I say. "I'm, um—covering the game for the *Grizzly*? I was hoping I could interview you." I pause, and then add, "It will only take a few minutes."

"Sure," he says. "Let me just get my stuff and tell the guys, and I'll meet you at the bleachers."

"Sounds perfect. Meet you there."

I walk back to the bleachers, cringing at the sound of my own voice. Sounds *perfect*? Sounds desperate, is more like it. I sit down on the bleachers, glancing nervously back at the dugout and hoping I didn't come on too strong and scare him away. That's when I see Brynn.

She's not talking to the coach like she's supposed to be. Instead, she's standing with Leo. I can't hear what he's saying—they're too far away—but whatever it is must be hilarious, because Brynn throws her head back in laughter. Leo smiles, seemingly pleased with himself at having made her laugh. When Brynn composes herself, she puts a hand on his arm. It's quick, casual, and right after she does it, she turns and walks away.

I frown. A strange feeling washes over me, like déjà vu. There's something familiar about what I just witnessed, like I've seen it before. But where?

I look at Leo, who's watching Brynn walk away from him with an unreadable expression on his face. Then I look at Brynn, who's got a small, satisfied smirk on hers.

And then I realize it.

I pull out my cell phone, open up my Netzine app, and click on my profile. I scroll down, down, down, until I get to the most recent batch of Talk to Me Tuesday posts. When I find the one I'm looking for, I stop.

I just started a new school and am kinda crushing on a boy in my class...

I jump to my advice—a compilation of things I've learned from my favorite rom-coms.

...do something that shows him you care—ask him about his hobbies, laugh at his jokes (even if they aren't funny), maybe throw in a ~casual~ arm touch—and then back off. Let him come to you.

Ask him about his hobbies.

"How long have you been taking pictures?"

Laugh at his jokes (even if they aren't funny).

"I'll be back," Leo'd said in a voice like the Terminator, making Brynn laugh.

Throw in a casual arm touch, and then back off.

I blink, stunned. It's a pretty crazy coincidence that my advice to New Girl aligns almost perfectly with Brynn's behavior toward Leo.

It *is* only a coincidence...right?

I push the thoughts away immediately. There's no way. I have over a hundred thousand followers from all over the country—all over the *world*. What are the chances that one of them would be my classmate?

Very, very slim. Practically microscopic.

I watch her walk toward the dugout, where the coach is lingering. She passes by Ethan and says something that makes him smile—*good game*, probably. I look back at Leo. His attention is fixed on his camera once again, as if the whole exchange with Brynn never happened.

As if I imagined the whole thing.

Chapter 5

I get a ride home from the game with Leo. He's quiet most of the time, scrolling through pictures on his camera. At one point I sneak a peek and see one of Brynn on the bleachers, smiling up at him with her hand shielding her eyes from the sun. He studies it for a few long seconds, the way an artist would study a painting in progress, before moving on.

When Ava drops me off, she tells me to say hi to my parents and to remind them about dinner on Saturday night. They're going on a double date to Noodle Star, a fancy new restaurant downtown, which means Jeremiah and I will have the house to ourselves for a few hours. I already told Leo and Camila to come over for a movie night.

I get out of the car and cut across the front yard, side-eyeing Jeremiah's truck along the way. It's this little two-door Ford from the '90s, white with a thick teal stripe cutting across the middle. A total eyesore. But Jeremiah loves it. He saved up all the money he made working at Millie's Ice Cream Parlor last summer to buy it from a guy off Craigslist. More than once, I've caught him sitting inside with no plans to go anywhere, just listening to music.

Inside, the house is quiet. I hear faint shooting sounds coming from the basement, which means Jeremiah is down there on the PlayStation. "Hello?" I call out, but nobody answers, not even Maggie, who's been known to respond with the occasional howl.

I walk through the kitchen, peer out the sliding glass door that leads to the back patio, and there they are. Mom and Dad, sitting around the patio table with a citronella candle between them, each holding a half-empty glass of white wine. Mom's got that telltale crease between her brows that means they're talking about something serious. Past them, in the yard, Maggie is rolling around in the grass with her belly in the air.

I slide open the door, poke my head out. "I'm home."

Maggie jumps up, howls. Mom stops talking abruptly, and she and Dad both turn to look at me.

"Hi there," Dad says. "How was the game?"

I shrug. "We won."

"Oh, that's super!" Dad says, completely seriously. Across from him, Mom takes a sip of her wine. "Get some good interviews?"

"I hope so." Maggie comes up to me, her tongue lolling happily out of her mouth. I crouch down to scratch behind her floppy ears. "Ava says hi and to remind you about Saturday."

"Shoot!" Mom smacks her hand on the table. "Dinner. I forgot."

I look at her. She seems more stressed than usual, which is saying something. She's a landscape gardener, and she's always taking on more clients than she can handle. Part of me wants to ask her what's wrong, but another, bigger part of me doesn't really want to know. Not right now. I've got my own problems.

"'Kay, well." I stand up. Maggie moseys back onto the grass. "I'm going to do some homework."

"Good girl," Dad says.

I start to close the door when Mom adds, "What's Jer doing?"

I hesitate. *My day was great, Mom. Thanks for asking.*

"How should I know?"

"I take it that means he's not at the table, doing his homework?"

"He's in the basement, I think."

Mom leans back in her chair, gives my dad a knowing look. "You see?" she says sharply, and then takes another sip of her wine. Dad stares into the flames of the candle, looking a little bit like he wants to jump into them.

I leave my parents outside, grab some chips from the pantry, and walk back to my room. Same stuff, different day. Why *would* they ask me about school, or the homework I have, or anything at all? Jeremiah is doing something wrong, as Jeremiah is wont to do, and therefore, everything I'm doing right is inconsequential. I think about Anastasia, an only child by design. She's the apple of her parents' eye. She never has to beg them to notice her.

I lock my bedroom door, grab my laptop, and lie down on my bed. Just as I'm logging into Netzine, I get a text from Brynn.

Brynn: Sending you my notes now. We could compile them into a joint doc?

I type back immediately.

Jane: 👍

Jane: I'll create the doc and send you the link

I put my phone down, expecting that to be the end of the conversation, but it buzzes again.

Brynn: This is so fun!

I roll my eyes and lock my phone without replying. She *can't* be serious. I'm tempted to write back to tell her to drop the act—I saw her true colors when she didn't hold the door, and I'd like her a lot more if she stopped pretending to be so nice—but I don't do it. I let my silence speak for itself.

After compiling both of our interview notes into a document, I make it shareable and send the link to her email. She logs on immediately, at which point I log off. I don't like to write with other people watching.

I open up the Netzine home page. I've got ninety-nine-plus notifications and seventy-three new messages. I ignore them all, click on my profile, and find the anonymous message from Talk to Me Tuesday again. I stare at the words, trying to decode them like a cipher to be cracked.

I just started a new school and am kinda crushing on a boy in my class...

Brynn's first day was Monday. This message was delivered to my inbox at 10:12 p.m. on Monday night. That means, if she wrote it, she would've only known Leo for a day. That's a little soon to start crushing on someone, isn't it?

I recall the first time I saw Ethan Gray—English class, seventh grade, the blue T-shirt that made his eyes look like the sky on a sunny day—and I think, *Never mind*.

But Leo is no Ethan Gray. He's goofy and lanky, and his hair is too long, and he's scared of birds. He's . . . Leo.

The problem is, I think he might have a crush on someone else.

Okay, there's no way this part could be about Leo. It would mean that not only does he like someone, but his crush is so obvious that Brynn picked up on it pretty much immediately. Either I'm oblivious—which, come *on*—or this message isn't from Brynn at all.

I stuff a handful of chips into my mouth and go to my home page. Just for fun, I want to see if Brynn has a Netzine, and if I can find her profile. I start by typing her full name into the search bar: Brynn Morgan. This yields hundreds of results, and a quick scroll through them tells me what I already know. This was a long shot. It would take me hours to comb through them all.

I go to my list of followers and type *Brynn Morgan* into the search bar. Zero profiles come up. I delete her last name—not everyone uses last names on Netzine—and just search Brynn.

Twelve results.

I start to go through them. Some of them are easy to discount because they include selfies of girls who are not Brynn, or they're located somewhere that isn't Pennsylvania. Others are harder. They include no personal information, just aesthetic photos, quotes, and songs that tell me a lot about their personalities, but nothing about their identities. In the end, it's all inconclusive.

My thoughts are interrupted by the sound of my mom yelling—at Jeremiah, probably. I hear the words "trespassing," "bad influence," and "consequences." I start to play my music, turning the volume all the way up to tune her out. Then I open up the shared document with the baseball article. Hopefully, Brynn has logged out by now, and I can get started on it before we meet tomorrow.

My jaw drops.

Where there used to be notes, there are now sentences, paragraphs, and quotes. I skim over it quickly, hoping it's not as polished as it seems. But no—the article is done.

She wrote the whole thing.

My phone buzzes with a text.

Brynn: LOL got kind of carried away in the doc and accidentally wrote most of the article. Hope u aren't mad!!! I was feeling inspired! Feel free to change whatever

I stare down at the text, dumbstruck. *Hope u aren't mad.*

Who does she think she is?

I go back to the article to read it for real. By the end, I'm clenching my fists so hard, my nails have imprinted purple crescent moons into my palms. Not because it's bad. Just the opposite—it's good. She clearly knows as much about writing as she does about baseball, which is a lot.

I put my face in my hands. She hasn't just upstaged me. She's juggling flaming swords with one hand and using the other to shove me off the stage altogether.

I can't let this go to print. *Not* because I'm petty, but because this is supposed to be a joint effort. How would it look for both of our names to go on an article that was only written by her? Like I'm lazy? Like she did me a favor? Like she's a stronger candidate to one day become editor in chief?

Not. Freaking. Happening.

I look at my notes again. She used the best stuff, but there are a lot of quotes from Ethan Gray she left out. I get to work right away, restructuring the angle of the article from a team effort to something more Ethan focused. It's not hard to do. Ethan is the only freshman on varsity, and he played a great game. In the end, the article reads like an underdog success story. I finish with a headline: FRESHMAN SHORTSTOP SWINGS FOR THE STARS, by Jane Scott and Brynn Morgan.

I sit up, satisfied, and stretch my arms over my head. This article is just as good as what Brynn wrote. Better, actually. I turned a basic baseball story into a compelling human-interest feature everybody will enjoy. I wonder what Ethan'll think when he reads it. I wonder if he'll think of me.

I email the draft to Halle without bothering to run it by Brynn. Then I open up Netzine, click on *New Post*, and start to type.

New post from AnaStaysDreaming

Friday, April 4, 9:00 a.m.

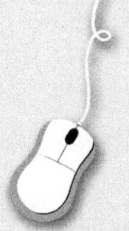

Friyay!

By the time you're reading this, it will be Friday morning, and we will be THISCLOSE to the weekend. And thank goodness for that! This week has been a slog. I don't have any big plans, just a movie night with Izzy and Leo. It'll be our first in a few weeks, since Izzy has been busy (omg—Busy Izzy. I'm going to start calling her that).

Any suggestions on what we should watch? Nothing too scary, for Leo's sake. Last time we watched *The Ring*, and he screamed so loud when the girl crawled out of the well that my neighbor called to make sure we were okay. It was hilarious.

You know what, never mind. Scary suggestions welcome :)

Stay dreaming,
Anastasia

Chapter 6

"We are not watching that," Leo says. He's sitting next to me on the couch with his hands tucked into his sweatshirt pockets and a frown on his face. Maggie lies between us. One of her ears is flopped over Leo's leg.

"Aw come on." I've got the remote hovering over the movie *Signs*, which was suggested by several *AnaStaysDreaming* readers. "It will be fun!"

We're in the basement, which Dad converted into a home theater of sorts a couple of years ago. It's got a big L-couch, a seventy-two-inch TV, and, coolest of all, a movie-theater-style popcorn machine.

"Fun for who? After the last time, I couldn't sleep for days."

I stifle a laugh. Leo the lion, hear him roar.

"Poor wittle baby," I say, reaching out and booping him on the nose.

"Baby?" He catches my hand. "Babies don't have catlike reflexes."

"Baby lions do." I try to pull my hand away, but he holds on tight, making me squeal with laughter. "Let go!"

He's laughing too. "Not until you take it back."

"Leo the baby lion," I say, ignoring him. "That's actually cute."

"I bet a baby lion could still beat you in a fight," he says. "You've got the dexterity of a noodle."

"Well, I wouldn't fight a baby lion. I'd cuddle it."

I stop fighting. He relaxes his grip on my hand but doesn't let go.

"Yeah," he says, his eyes on our hands. "That's way more fun."

I hear the front door open. Maggie's head pops up, and she lets out a howl that makes Leo jump and drop my hand.

"Jeez, Mags," Leo says, rubbing the back of his neck. "Chill."

"You can't tell a basset hound to chill," I say over another howl. "You can't tell them to do anything, really."

I hear voices, plural. Is it our parents, home early, or someone else? Is Jeremiah bringing people over, despite Mom's explicit instructions that he's on social lockdown for the weekend?

The door to the basement opens, and I see a familiar pair of purple Uggs at the top of the stairs. I relax. Camila. Her caramel-colored legs come into view, followed immediately by a pair of baggy black jeans. Jeremiah.

"Sorry I'm late," Camila says, her voice echoing down the stairwell. "I came right from my cheer competition. Mom hardly stopped the car; she just slowed down in front of your house, and I did the ol' tuck-and-roll." She pauses, laughs. "Kidding, obviously."

She gets to the bottom of the stairs, and I take in her appearance. High, slicked-back ponytail, cheer uniform, and about a gallon of body glitter. I must be making a face, because Camila sighs and says, "I didn't have time to go home and change. That would've just made me even later."

"I think you look cool," Jeremiah says, making her smile. I turn my disapproval onto him.

"You can't go on the PlayStation. We're about to watch a movie."

"I know." He looks at me, his green eyes a mirror of my own. "I'm down for a movie."

I scowl. "Who invited you?"

He gestures to his left. "Camila."

"I'm going to change," Camila says quickly, before I can complain. She hoists her gym bag over her shoulder, rounds the corner to the basement bathroom, and shuts herself inside.

Jeremiah looks at the TV screen. "Aw yeah. *Signs?*" He crosses in front of the TV and plops down on the opposite end of the couch. Maggie climbs over Leo to get to him. "Great movie."

I sink into my seat, relenting. There was a time when I would've loved for Jeremiah to crash movie night. As a kid I followed him around everywhere, begging him to play *Wii Sports* or *Mario Party* or any game at all, if it meant he'd hang out with me. But then he got to eighth grade, started listening to a lot of Polar Bear Club and My Chemical Romance, and things changed. *He* changed.

"Is it jumpy?" Leo says. "I don't like movies where stuff jumps out at me."

"No," Jeremiah says, and then tilts his head, considering. "Well, there's this one part—"

"Nope." Leo cuts him off. "I'm good. Look." He points at the screen. *"Shrek 2."*

I groan. "We always watch that. Broaden your horizons!"

"It's not scary, bro," Jeremiah says. Maggie lies down next to him, and he scratches behind her ears. "It's, like, sci-fi."

"Whatever." Leo shrugs and picks up his phone. "You're just going to put on what you want anyway." He looks at his screen, smirks, and starts typing.

I lean over, trying to sneak a glance. "Who are you texting?"

"Nobody."

"That means it's a girl," Jeremiah says, also looking at his phone.

"Is it a girl?" I ask, leaning even farther forward. Leo turns his phone away from me. "Leopold! Tell me!"

"Fine," Leo says. "But don't make it weird." He turns his phone screen so I can see it. The name at the top makes my stomach drop.

Brynn.

"Why are you texting her?" I ask, my tone accusatory. I already told Leo about how she tried to hijack the article we were supposed to write together. That's on top of the door-holding and seat-stealing incidents. In other words: she can't be trusted. "How did you even get her number?"

"I asked for it so I could send her the picture I took of her at the baseball game," Leo says. "It's no big deal."

Jeremiah puts his phone away and starts watching us like we're the entertainment for the evening.

"Let me see." I snatch the phone out of his hands and scroll up to the picture. It's just as I suspected: the one of her smiling on the bleachers. She replied right away: **Omg! You're so talented!!!**

"Leo. Leo, Leo, Leo. *Leo*," I say. "When you send a girl a cute picture you took of her, it's a *very* big deal."

"I send you pictures I take of you all the time," he says, his hazel eyes practically boring into me. "Is that a big deal too?"

"No. That's different."

He raises an eyebrow, looking almost amused. "How?"

"Jane's not cute," Jeremiah pipes in.

I chuck a pillow at his head, but it misses and hits the popcorn machine. Maggie sits up, startled.

"Yo, Big Unit, watch it," Jeremiah says. "If we break that, I'm sure Mom and Dad will blame me."

I make a face. "Big what?"

"Randy Johnson," Leo explains. "He was a pitcher for the Mariners."

"*Ohhh.*" I look back at him. "Did your new best friend Brynn tell you that? I hear she knows *everything* about baseball." I'm trying to keep the conversation light and teasing. Maybe if I manage that, I can *feel* light and teasing too.

Leo just shakes his head and returns his attention to his texts.

I hear the bathroom door open. A second later, Camila turns the corner in sweatpants and an Olivia Rodrigo concert T-shirt. I have to stop myself from saying something bratty about where she got it.

"Movie time!" she says. "Hey, are we making popcorn?"

Jeremiah jumps up. "I got it."

"Such a gentleman," I mumble.

Camila sits on Maggie's other side. "Look at this cutie patootie," she says in a baby voice while she scratches under Maggie's chin. "Did you have a good day today?"

"Oh yeah," Jeremiah says, scooping kernels into the machine. "Me and Mags were straight chillin' all day."

"That's because you're grounded," I say. "Maggie was your babysitter."

Camila turns to look at him over the back of the couch. "Why are you grounded?"

He flips his hair, so obviously trying to play it cool. "I got into some trouble with Danny."

"*Some* trouble?" I say. No way am I letting him off the hook. "Beavis and Butt-Head decided to hop the fence into the Millers' backyard and use their hot tub while they're on vacation."

Camila gasps. "No way."

"It wasn't that big of a deal," Jeremiah says with a shrug. "We've done it before, and they never knew."

"How'd you get caught?" Leo asks.

"I guess they got one of those cameras," Jeremiah says. "With the motion sensor."

"Mrs. Miller got an alert sent to her phone that someone was on their patio," I say, cackling. "She saw footage of them stripping down to their bathing suits, took a screenshot, and immediately sent it to my mom."

"She must've been so proud," Leo says.

"Oh yeah, she's going to hang it on the fridge next to my report card," Jeremiah replies.

"Wait," I say. "I can't believe I never thought of that."

Jeremiah turns on the popcorn machine and sits back down on the couch next to Camila.

"I'd never have the guts to do something like that," Camila says, but she doesn't sound judgmental. She almost sounds like she's in awe. "What did it feel like, hopping over the fence like that?"

He looks at her. "Honestly?" He's got what can only be described as a mischievous twinkle in his eye. Blech. "It was a rush."

I roll my eyes. "Ladies and gentlemen, the baddest boy in Brookhill."

"Don't be jealous just because you never take any risks," Jeremiah says. Behind him, the kernels in the machine start to pop.

"I take plenty of risks," I say, but my voice wavers a little, and they all hear it.

"When's the last time you took a risk?" Jeremiah asks me. "Genuinely. I'm curious."

It was a risk volunteering to cover the baseball story, I think. It was a risk to make it all about Ethan Gray. But I can't say that, because then Jeremiah will also know I like Ethan, and he and Leo will never let me hear the end of it. While I search the depths of my brain for something to say, the popping of the kernels gets louder, more intense.

"That's what I thought," he says, as if it's a confirmation of my perpetual uncoolness. "You're too Goody-Two-Shoes."

I think about Anastasia, hopping on a train to New York City on a whim or sneaking out past curfew to see her friends. Jeremiah would never call Anastasia Goody-Two-Shoes. She always takes risks, and because of it, her life is one big adventure.

"Let's just watch the movie," I say, and press play.

Chapter 7

"Are you sure you can't come?"

Tuesday afternoon, I'm walking with Camila to my locker after the final bell of the day. The hallway is crowded with students pushing past us, rushing to make it to the buses on time. Thankfully, I'm no longer one of them. Jeremiah got his license last month and has been driving me home every day.

Well, except for the days he has detention.

"I'm *sorry*," Camila says. She's clutching her books in her arms like a shield against my disappointment. "The competition is two hours away. I'm going to be beat by the time we get back."

"Just for a little while?" I practically beg. "It's supposed to be nice on Saturday. We can sneak onto the roof and watch my parents' friends make fools of themselves, like we used to."

She gives me a sad smile. "I wish I could. I'm just exhausted, Jane. Cheer has been taking over my life lately."

I nod. *You don't have to tell me.*

Camila used to love coming to my parents' garden parties.

Everyone does. What started as an excuse for my mom to show off her massive lilac bushes has grown into the neighborhood's biggest, fanciest party of the season. Each spring, my parents deck out the backyard with lights and music, set up croquet and serve every type of finger food imaginable, and finish out the night with s'mores around the firepit. There are also my dad's famous mint juleps, which I obviously can't have, but they make some of the adults get real loosey-goosey after the sun goes down. It's funny to watch.

"But we have the day off on Thursday," she continues. "Coach is giving us a rest day. Let's do something." She looks at me. "Ice cream at Millie's?"

"Sure." I shrug. Why not?

"Hey. Where's your necklace?"

Her dark eyes are boring down on the space between my clavicles. It takes me a second to realize she's talking about the butter necklace.

"Oh. Um, I forgot to put it on."

"I'm wearing mine," she says, removing one hand from her stack of books to pull at the croissant charm hanging around her neck. "I wear it every day."

"Me too," I lie, adjusting my grip on my tote bag. "Usually. But I was running late this morning."

Camila nods. I can't tell if she believes me or not, but either way, she doesn't press me on it. I'm relieved. She'd be crushed if she found out I put the necklace back in the box and left it there.

"Oh!" Camila says as we approach my locker. "I forgot

to tell you. You won't *believe* who Gemma saw at the mall with..."

But I don't hear the end of the sentence. Because at that moment, my gaze locks onto the blond, broad-shouldered boy standing there in a varsity baseball jacket, and everything in my periphery dims.

Ethan Gray.

He sees me right after I see him. Then something amazing happens. His eyes don't gloss over me like he's searching for the person he really wants to see. He looks *at* me.

And then he smiles.

And then he waves.

"Ohmigod," Camila says. "I think Ethan Gray is waving at you."

Ethan Gray is waving at me.

My stomach lurches. Is it really hot in here all of a sudden? I'm afraid I'm going to pass out. I try to focus on putting one foot in front of the other, except I can't feel my legs, but they *must* be moving, because in the blink of an eye, I'm standing right in front of him.

"Jane," Ethan Gray says. "Hey."

Camila's eyes widen. She looks at me, waiting for a response that doesn't seem to be coming. She elbows me in the ribs.

"Hi," I force out.

He's holding on to the straps of his book bag with his wide, strong hands. I stare at his hands instead of his face, because his smile is too overwhelming, and his hands are more familiar to me.

"Hi," Camila says too. I know she can sense my nerves and is trying to take some of the pressure off me. "I'm Cami."

"I know," Ethan says. "Cami Mendoza. You cheer, right?"

"I do," Camila says. "In fact, it's what I'm supposed to be doing right now." She gives me a pointed look. "Text me later?"

I nod, knowing what she means is *tell me every single detail about this conversation later*. For a moment: panic. I don't want her to go. Cami has always been supportive of my crush on Ethan, even when other people—cough cough *Leo*—have not. I wish she'd be late to cheer just this once, for me, but it doesn't happen. She walks away.

I dare a glance back at Ethan—*into* the pewter blue of Ethan's eyes. He's still smiling at me.

"I wanted to tell you that I really liked your article," he says.

Article?

I blink. The article. The new issue of the *Grizzly* came out today, distributed to every single homeroom at seven thirty this morning. My baseball article—*fine*, and Brynn's—accompanied by Leo's photo of Ethan sliding into home base, was on the front page.

"You're a great writer," he continues. "You made me seem so cool."

I let out a sound that's somewhere between a cackle and a gasp. Ethan Gray thinks I'm a *great* writer.

"You didn't need my help with that," I say, my eyes bouncing between his face and my black tights. Ugh, is that a run by the knee? "You were the MVP of the game."

He smiles modestly, but he doesn't deny it.

"Yeah, well. It's nice to feel seen, you know?"

I fidget with a loose string on my tote bag. When I glance up at him again, he's sort of ducking down, trying to meet my eyes.

"I don't know," I say. "I'm usually more comfortable behind the scenes."

He nods, but still, I get the feeling that he can't relate, not at all. Meanwhile, the hallway is starting to clear out. Ethan must notice too, because he says, "Do you need to catch the bus?"

I shake my head. "My brother drives." Then I add, "But I should probably hurry up in case he gets sick of waiting."

"I'm sure he wouldn't leave without you," Ethan says, and I smile a little.

"He's done it before," I say, getting to work on my locker combination. It takes all my concentration not to mess up.

Ethan's eyebrows rise in disbelief. "Really?"

My mind flashes back to two days after Jeremiah got his license, when the GameStop at the mall was having a big clearance sale. "Yup. But that's Jeremiah. Too cool for school, and definitely too cool for me."

I open my locker, suddenly hyperaware of the fact that Ethan Gray is standing next to me, looking inside. It's mostly just books and my lunch box and some random makeup scattered on the top shelf, but the door is decorated with dorky middle school pictures of me, Camila, and Leo, plus a whiteboard hanging from a magnet with a few notes scribbled on it. The bottom of the board reads *Leo wuz here.*

"That's messed up," Ethan says, and my embarrassment gives way to something like vindication. *Yes, Ethan Gray. It is.*

I grab the books I'll need for the night and close my locker. Ethan is leaning against the wall with his arms crossed, looking completely perfect and at ease. I imagine he looks that way wherever he goes, the main character in every story.

"Want me to walk you?" he says, looking up at me from under his hair. "I'm going that way anyway."

I smile and look down at the books in my hands. I don't want him to see me blush.

We start toward the student parking lot. I'm an anxious walker, so I naturally move pretty fast, but I force myself to slow down and match his pace. Ethan, I'm learning, walks kind of slow. Usually slow walkers annoy me, but not today. Today, I'm with Ethan Gray, and I will savor this stretch of hallway.

"You should come to the game on Thursday," he says, his arm brushing my elbow. "It's at home."

"I wish I could." My elbow feels like it's on fire. "But Max—our sports editor—is back from Mexico, and I think he's going to cover it."

"Oh," Ethan says. "Well, you don't have to write about it. You can just come."

A tingle shoots down my spine. What does it mean that

Ethan is inviting me to his game? Does he invite a lot of girls, or am I the only one?

"Cool." My mind flashes to Camila, and our plans to go to Millie's. She wouldn't mind a quick stop at a baseball game first, would she? "Yeah, I'll be there."

"Cool," he repeats. I can see him looking at me out of the corner of my eye. "You know, I played my best game of the season last time you were there. You might be my good-luck charm."

My pulse quickens, and nervous laughter escapes my lips. Me, Ethan Gray's good-luck charm?

"This is the first time I've ever had a story on the front page of the *Grizzly*." I tell him. "So maybe you're mine, too."

What I don't say is that really, he's been my good-luck charm for months—ever since Anastasia started dating Miles, my Netzine readership has skyrocketed. Turns out, people love love.

We round the corner toward the doors that lead to the student parking lot. Just past them is the gym, where Ethan will be headed to change for baseball practice. I drag my feet even more. I don't want to say goodbye yet.

"Thanks, um, for walking me," I stumble out. "I mean, walking *with* me. You didn't walk me—I'm not your dog."

I cringe and force myself to stop talking before I can say anything worse.

To my surprise—and relief—Ethan laughs. "Definitely not. My dog doesn't like to go for walks."

I perk up a little. "You have a dog?"

"Yeah. Arnold," he says. "Named after Arnold Palmer. Not nearly as athletic, though."

"The iced tea guy?"

Ethan laughs. I laugh too, even though I'm not sure what's funny. He *is* the iced tea guy, right?

"E-Gray!" someone says behind us. We both turn. It's a guy I recognize from the baseball team.

Ethan gives him a nod. "Coming." Then he looks back at me. "So, Thursday?"

"Yes," I say. "Thursday."

He starts to walk away, and I watch him go, biting the inside of my cheek to keep from grinning like an idiot. Then he turns around.

"By the way," he says, a small smile creeping across his lips. "You can try to hide behind the scenes if you want, but it's not going to work."

My heart starts to pound. What does he mean by that?

"It's not?" My voice sounds wobbly.

"Nope," he says. "I see you. And you look pretty good to me."

He spins back around and jogs to catch up with his friend. I stay where I am. I don't think I could move even if I tried.

You look pretty good to me.

Did Ethan Gray just flirt with me?

I fish my phone out of my tote bag and text Camila. OMG. I wait a few seconds, hoping to see the little dots that mean she's typing. I want to dissect every word—every *syllable*—with the one person who knows how significant this moment is. But the dots don't come. Camila probably won't respond until after cheer practice. Hours from now.

I toss my phone back in the bag and push open the door to the parking lot.

New post from AnaStaysDreaming
Tuesday, April 8, 3:00 p.m.

Talk to Me Tuesday

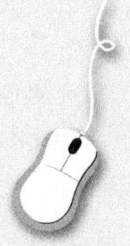

Anonymous asked: Help! Lately it feels like my bestie and I are drifting apart. I don't even know why!? We haven't fought. It's just when we hang out (which is less than we used to), something feels off. You, Izzy, and Leo are friendship goals. How do I fix it? Friend to the End?

AnaStaysDreaming: Dear Friend to the End?,

It seems like maybe all you two need is a chance to reconnect. Watch your favorite movie, go get ice cream, do something fun to remind your bestie of inside jokes and old times. If things still feel off after that, address it head-on. Communication is key in any relationship!

Tuesday, April 8, 4:00 p.m.

Anonymous asked: I wrote to you last week about a crush I had on a boy at my new school, and you gave me advice about how to get him to notice me. Well, you must be a boy whisperer, because everything you said worked perfectly! We've been talking a lot at school, and I think he might be into me.

Now, though, I'm not sure what I should do. I like him, but I don't want to come on too strong and scare him away. Should I back off a little? Tell him how I feel? Wait for him to make the first move? Help me, boy whisperer!!!

Sincerely, New Girl

AnaStaysDreaming: Dear New Girl,

Back off, definitely. If you've been talking a lot, there's a chance you're coming on too strong. He's going to get bored and move on. If he likes you, he'll make the next move. If not, well . . . There's plenty of fish in the school.

Tuesday, April 8, 5:00 p.m.

Anonymous asked: Hey Ana,

My BF and I broke up and I'm devastated. Do you have any tips for healing a broken heart?

Sincerely, Down in the Dumps

AnaStaysDreaming: Dear Down in the Dumps,

Time heals all wounds, which is both good and bad. It's

good, because it means one day you will definitely be over him. But first, you have to get to "one day," which can feel like an agonizing slog of epic proportions. My advice? Distract yourself with friends, trips, and treats. The more you try to distract yourself, the less you'll *have to* try, if you know what I mean.

And when in doubt, remember that you broke up for a reason. He wasn't perfect, and neither was the relationship, so stop pretending otherwise by idealizing it.

Chapter 8

Wednesday morning, in the newsroom, Leo and I are sitting at the computers. He's editing photos, and I'm doing research for my next article, a feature on the food truck festival the Spanish club is hosting on Friday after school.

Well, that's what I'm supposed to be doing. In reality, I'm mostly scrolling Netzine.

"So," Leo says without looking away from his screen. "Your baseball feature was pretty ridiculous."

"What?" I whip my head in his direction. "It was a good article. It got a lot of clicks on the website yesterday."

"You barely even talked about the game. You turned the whole thing into an Ethan Gray puff piece."

"Not a puff piece, a human-interest story." I pick up my dented water bottle and unscrew the cap. "And Ethan Gray loved it."

"I'm sure he did," Leo says dryly. "Considering he's got an ego the size of Canada."

I roll my eyes while I sip my water. "Can't you just be happy my story made the front page? With *your* photo, I might add."

He pushes his long hair back and looks at me in earnest. "I'm just saying. Most guys would feel weird about being singled out for a win that was clearly a team effort."

"Yeah? Well, *I'm* just saying that you're annoying me."

He snorts and turns his attention back to his computer. Just then, Brynn appears in the doorway, looking very *yee-haw* in pigtails and cowboy boots, back from whatever interview she was probably conducting. She walks past us without so much as a glance.

"What's going on there?" I say to him. Leo looks up to see what I'm talking about. When his eyes land on Brynn, his expression is unreadable.

"What do you mean?"

"She hasn't said a word to you all day," I point out. "I thought she was your new bestie."

He shrugs. "She's probably just busy."

I watch her curiously. She puts her notepad down at her desk—my desk—and goes to talk to Halle. I watch Halle's face go from intrigued, to surprised, to—wait, she's looking at me. I avert my gaze back to my screen, minimize the browser that's logged into my Netzine, and open the website for one of the food truck vendors.

"Look," Leo says. "She's coming over."

"Hey, Jane," says a high-pitched, slightly twangy voice behind me. I wince, spin around in my chair.

"Hey, Brynn."

Her smile is wide—too wide, like she's forcing it. All of a sudden I have a bad feeling.

"So, um. It seems like there's been a little bit of a mix-up."

I raise my eyebrows. "A mix-up?"

"Yeah." She starts twirling one of her pigtails around her index finger, like she's purposely trying to look as innocent as possible. It's annoying. "Um, see, I thought I was assigned the food truck story."

I blink at her. *Huh?* "But that's my story."

"I know, and it's completely my mistake. I must've misread the assignment sheet."

I don't know what to say. How could she possibly have misread the assignment sheet? It's alphabetical. Our names aren't even listed next to each other.

"Okay . . . ," I say, wondering why she's bothering to tell me this. "Well, now you know, I guess?"

She doesn't budge, just keeps staring at me with that creepy smile on her face.

"The thing is . . ." I see her eyes flit from me to Leo, and I feel suddenly defensive. *Don't look at Leo*, I want to say. *This is between you and me.*

"The thing is that I already started my interviews," she finishes. "That's where I was just now, interviewing the president of Spanish club."

She pauses like she expects me to say something, but I don't. I'm silent.

Seething.

"So anyway, Halle said that I should probably just take it over, but that I should talk to you first, to make sure you were fine with it."

Still I don't respond. I simply cannot believe the *audacity* of this girl. What if I'm not fine with it? That's what I want to ask her. What if I already started my interviews too? I haven't, but she doesn't know that. For all she knows, I've got a draft ready to show Halle. How *dare* she just assume she can have *my* story?

First she stole my seat. Then the baseball article. And now *this*? That's three strikes. Since Brynn is such a baseball expert, she should know what that means.

She is *out*.

"Fine," I say, already spinning back around in my seat. "Whatever."

I glance at Leo. He's looking at his screen, trying to pretend like he's not paying attention. I want to yell at him to take my side, but of course that's not his style. He's always been a pacifist.

Behind me, Brynn clears her throat. She still isn't leaving. *Why* isn't she leaving?

"I wanted to say," she begins, her voice timid, "that I really liked the changes you made to the baseball feature."

Now Leo's eyes dart toward her.

"Focusing on Ethan Gray instead of the whole team was *genius*," she continues. "It made you want to root for him, you know? Like a real hero's journey type of thing."

I raise my eyebrows suggestively at Leo. *I told you so.*

"You're really talented," Brynn adds.

I glance back at her. She's got a cautious smile on her face. "Thanks," I mumble.

Brynn looks at Leo again. Her expression remains guarded, but there's something else there too. Nerves?

"Hi, Leo," she says, and I swear she pitches her voice up a little.

He nods in her direction. "Hey."

She takes a breath, returns her attention to me. "Okay. I'll, um, let you get back to it."

When she walks away, I clench my jaw and exit out of the food truck's web page. I won't be needing it anymore.

"I can't believe her," I say, mostly to myself, but Leo responds anyway.

"I'm sure it was an honest mistake. Why would she do it on purpose?"

"Why would she do *any* of the stuff she does?" I fire back. "From the second I met her, she's been doing everything she possibly can to make my life miserable." I pick up my water bottle and hold the dent in front of his face to emphasize my point. Somewhere deep inside me, past all my petty layers, I know this isn't exactly a fair assessment, but I can't help it. That's how it feels.

"I still think the door thing was a misunderstanding," he says, pushing the bottle away. "She probably just didn't hear you."

"Would you stop taking her side?"

"I'm not taking her side." He fixes his hazel eyes intensely on me. "I'm on your side. That's why I'm trying to mellow you out a little. To show you that it's not worth getting so worked up over."

I shake my head. He just doesn't understand. He's never had to worry about feeling overlooked or brushed aside. When he talks, people listen. That's the way it's been our whole lives. It's probably why Brynn was so taken with him from the start. You just can't help but love Leo.

"And did you *hear* what she said to you? *Hi, Leo.*" I pitch my voice up, trying to imitate her.

He raises his eyebrows, amused. "What's wrong with hi?"

"She ignores you all day, then hits you with a cutesy *Hi, Leo*? Then goes right back to ignoring you! It's like she—"

I stop talking, because suddenly I realize something.

"Like she what?" Leo asks.

Instead of answering him, I maximize my Netzine browser. I go to my profile, where the most recent batch of Talk to Me Tuesday posts are on display. I read the latest submission from New Girl.

Now, though, I'm not sure what I should do. I like him, but I don't want to come on too strong and scare him away. Should I back off a little?

And then I read my advice.

Back off, definitely.

I lean back in my seat, astonished. I'd given up the idea that New Girl could ever be Brynn. It seemed too outrageous—too impossible. And yet, here I am again, watching the advice I gave a stranger on the internet play out in real time.

I look over at Brynn, who is, by definition, a new girl. And I wonder.

Could it be?

"Earth to Jane," Leo says. "Come back from Mars."

I blink at him. "Sorry. What was I saying?"

He laughs a little in disbelief. "You were implying that Brynn had some kind of ulterior motive for saying hi to me."

"Right." I shake my head. "Um. I just think it's interesting."

"Why?"

"Because . . ." I trail off. One thought looms above all the others: *Because I think she might have a crush on you.* I search for something else, *anything else*. "Because it's rude. You know?"

He looks at me skeptically. "Last I checked, it's not rude to say hi to people. It's sort of the opposite."

I take a deep breath. I can't have this conversation anymore. My head is spinning. I need to figure out if New Girl is Brynn. If Brynn likes Leo.

But how?

Chapter 9

"I still can't believe Ethan Gray invited you to his game," Camila says. She's sitting one row behind me on the bleachers, sucking on a cherry lollipop. "I think this is the beginning of a beautiful love story."

"Is it?" I ask, adjusting my hair bow. "He hasn't said a single word to me yet." I turn and point at the back of my head. "Is this straight?"

She puts the lollipop in her mouth. I feel her hands on the bow, wriggling it into position. "He's just preoccupied with the game. But he will. See how he keeps looking over here?"

My eyes drift out to the baseball field, where Ethan stands in shortstop position. His eyes are fixed on the batter.

"Perfect." She leans back, surveying the bow. "You look great. Very Claire Waldorf."

"*Blair*," I correct. "And she wears headbands."

"Really?" Camila cocks her head, letting her glossy dark hair cascade effortlessly over her shoulder in a move that feels very Serena van der Woodsen. Not that she'd know. The only time she ever watches *Gossip Girl* is when I make her. "I could've sworn—"

Her words are interrupted by the batter on the opposing team hitting the ball in Ethan's direction. It skids across the ground; Ethan catches it and throws it to first base just in time.

"Woo!" I sit up straight and clap along with the dozen other people who make up the crowd.

The teams swap places. Ethan jogs to the dugout, and just before he ducks inside, he catches my eye and winks. At least, I *think* it's a wink. Maybe the sun just got in his eye. I turn to Camila to get her opinion on the matter, but she's texting someone, so she didn't see. That's when I notice a familiar face in the distance. More specifically, a familiar camera in front of a familiar face.

"Leo's here."

Camila looks at me, eyebrow raised, then follows my gaze toward the parking lot. "Is that a surprise? Doesn't he usually take pictures at things like this?"

"Yeah, but not today. The other photographer was supposed to be here."

I face forward and slouch in my seat. Leo doesn't know I'm here. If I had told him I was coming to the game, he would've made some snarky comment about me coming to watch Ethan Gray, so I just avoided saying anything altogether.

"Leo!" Camila raises her lollipop and starts waving it around like a flare. I wince.

"What?" Camila looks at me. "Are you fighting, or something?"

"No. It's just . . ." I sigh. "He knows. About Ethan Gray."

Camila's eyebrows shoot up. "You told him?"

"Of course not. The only person who was ever supposed to know was you."

"Aw." She puts her hand over her heart. "That's why you're the butter to my croissant."

I resist the urge to roll my eyes. At least today I'm wearing the stupid necklace.

"How'd he find out?" she asks.

"He guessed."

She snorts. "Well. He always was perceptive."

"Hey." Leo climbs the mostly empty bleachers with his camera on a strap around his neck. He's wearing a Red Hot Chili Peppers T-shirt, and he's got his green baseball cap on backward. "Fancy meeting you guys here."

"*Fancy* yourself," Camila says. "We love baseball. We come to the games all the time."

"Uh-huh." Leo sits down next to me and turns to look at Camila. "What's the position between second and third base called?"

"Uh . . ." Camila glances at me. "Second and a half?"

I cover my face with my hand.

"Right." Leo turns to me. "So how's your boy doing?"

"He's not *my boy*," I grumble. "And he's doing great."

"Hope so," Leo says. "At the away game on Monday, he missed a catch that cost the team two runs."

I frown at him. "Why do you have to be so pessimistic?"

"I'm not being pessimistic," he says. "I'm telling you what

happened. You're the one who's looking at Captain America through rose-colored glasses."

"Captain America?" Camila asks. "What does that mean?"

"You know." He shrugs. "Like, all-American."

"All-American isn't bad," I say, feeling defensive. "He's athletic, classically good-looking—"

"He's cocky," Leo adds. "And he puts the cheese in cheeseburger."

Camila practically guffaws. "Because cheeseburgers are American, and also, he's cheesy." She slaps her knee. "Hilarious!"

I glare at her. She sits up straight, quickly composes herself. "In a cute way."

I turn back to Leo. "You know, you were never this hard on Flynn Rider."

"That Disney prince you used to be obsessed with?" Leo says, cocking an eyebrow. "At least he had a personality."

"You don't know a thing about Ethan's personality."

"And you do?"

We stare at each other, reaching a stalemate. No matter what I say, Leo seems determined to dislike Ethan. It's so frustrating. I wish he'd just support me, the way Camila does.

"Listen," Leo says, standing up again. "As much as I'd love to keep gossiping about boys, I gotta get some good pictures before the game ends."

"What are you even doing here, anyway?" I say, squinting up at him through the sun. "I thought Eddie was taking pictures of the game tonight."

"He was. But his band got a last-minute gig, and he asked me to cover for him."

"Oh. That's nice of you."

Leo waves his hand in a *whatever* motion. "Uh, Jane. Walk with me a sec?"

Camila and I exchange a curious glance.

"Sure." I stand up and smooth my dress. "Lead the way."

I climb down the bleachers and follow Leo to the edge of the field. I want to be annoyed at him, but my irritation dissipates with every step I take. It's hard to stay mad at Leo. I think it's because I know, deep down, that his criticisms are because he cares about me.

We stop walking, and he looks through the viewfinder on his camera, his brow creased in concentration. He pulls back, starts pressing buttons to adjust some setting or other, and then looks through again.

"So what's up?" I ask him. "You want fashion advice or something?"

"If I wanted fashion advice, there are a lot of other people I'd ask first. No offense."

I scoff. "Like who?"

"Well, for starters, any guy."

"Rude. This is a nice dress."

I look down at my blue floral sundress. I bought it with the birthday money I got from Grandma Patty and rush shipped it so it would arrive before today's game.

"I agree," he says. "It looks nice on you. But it might make my hips look big."

I laugh. "Okay, so why am I here?"

He hesitates, focusing instead on photographing the outfield. After what feels like forever he says, "It's about Brynn."

The sky darkens, and there's a sudden chill in the air, as if merely mentioning Brynn's name is enough to scare the sun away.

"What about her?"

He turns his camera toward the infield. "I sort of . . . invited her to the garden party."

The wind picks up, rustling the fabric of the dress and lifting the skirt above my knees. I quickly pinch the sides so I don't pull a Marilyn in front of Leo—or Ethan. I glance toward the dugout, where Ethan leans forward in his seat, his attention fixed on the game.

"To my parents' garden party?"

"Yeah."

He starts walking toward the infield, and I'm so overcome with confusion and surprise that it takes a few seconds for me to realize he's moving. I have to jog a couple of steps in my strappy sandals to catch up to him.

"Why would you do that?"

He adjusts the sun filter on his lens, then takes a slew of pictures of the guy at bat. "Because. She was saying how she's having trouble making friends, and how she was going to spend another weekend watching *Law and Order* with her dad, and I felt bad, so I thought—"

"You thought you'd invite my nemesis over to my house?"

He looks at me like I'm being immature. "Don't be like that.

She feels really bad about the whole food truck article thing."

Despite the sudden drop in temperature, my face feels hot with rage. Yesterday, Leo said he was on my side, but this doesn't seem like it. If he were on my side, he wouldn't be trying so hard to be Brynn's friend. Instead, he'd see what I see: that Brynn is a venomous snake in the grass, slithering just out of sight until she's ready to go in for the kill. I just don't know what I did to her.

"What's going on with the two of you, anyway?" I say. "Why do you care about her weekend plans?"

"Nothing's going on."

"Nothing?"

He takes a picture. "Nothing." Then he puts down the camera, turns toward me. "Why so curious?"

"I'm not *so* curious. I just don't like her."

He holds my gaze like there's more he wants to say. Then the batter hits the ball into the outfield, and Leo's reflexes are instant. He puts his camera up to his eye, kneels, and snaps the outfielder catching the ball.

"Nice," I say, impressed.

Still kneeling on the ground, Leo starts reviewing the photos. I watch him delete about half of them before standing up again.

"Don't you think it's going to be weird for her?" I say, unable to let it go. "It's like, a family thing."

"It is not. There's gonna be like a hundred people there."

"And she won't know any of them."

He sort of laughs. "*You* won't know most of them."

I sigh. He's right—most of them will be Mom's architecture friends, or Dad's office colleagues, or neighbors whose faces I know but names I can never remember. That's why I need Leo. Since Cami's ditching, and Jeremiah will almost certainly hide in his room, he's the only ally I have. If Brynn comes, she'll take him away.

"You gonna invite Captain America?" he says, not quite meeting my eye.

"No." I look toward the dugout for Ethan. He's not there. "Of course not."

Leo looks at me. "Why of course not?"

"You mean, why don't I want to bring Ethan Gray around our parents while there's an open bar?"

He winces. "Right."

"It's not like anything is going on with Ethan anyway," I say, focusing on a chip in my blue nail polish. "He said I should come to his game, that's it."

"Okay." He looks out toward the field. "Well, I already told you nothing's going on between me and Brynn, either."

"Cool," I say, feeling weird for some reason. "Glad we're all up to speed."

He nods, his expression unreadable. Then he gestures to the other side of the field. "I'm going to get some shots from over there."

He walks away, and this time I don't follow. I look back at Cami, who's smiling into her phone, and then through the fence and out at the field, where Ethan Gray is walking up to bat.

Chapter 10

After the game ends, Camila stands up and tucks her phone into the back pocket of her jeans. "Millie's?"

I look over at the dugout, where the coach is standing in front of the team, probably giving them some kind of pep talk. They lost by one run, which might sting even more than losing by two or three. I'm not sure what Ethan's mood will be—whether he'll want to talk to me or go right home.

"Five minutes?"

Camila seems to understand what's going through my head, because she doesn't ask for an explanation. She nods and sits back down.

Thankfully, it doesn't take long for the players to start trickling out of the dugout. I teeter awkwardly between acting like I don't notice and glancing over to see if Ethan will come and find me.

"Incoming," Camila says.

I turn around, and there he is. I scan his face for signs of irritation or frustration, but there are none. He's got an easy aura about him, as if this loss doesn't mean anything at all.

"You came." Ethan smiles. His cheeks and the tip of his nose are a little red from the sun.

"Yeah," I say, one hand moving to my hair bow to make sure it's still straight. "Sorry I couldn't be your good-luck charm."

"We played a good game," he says with a shrug. "Just so happens that today, they played better."

I feel a little flutter in my chest. He's so positive, so *optimistic*.

Camila stands up. "I'm going to say bye to Leo. Meet you in the parking lot?"

"Good seeing you," Ethan says to her. "And thanks for coming."

Bellowing laughter breaks out from a pack of baseball boys by the field. Ethan looks over his shoulder at them for a moment, then back at me.

"So, listen, I don't know if you've got plans after this—"

"E-Gray!" one of the guys calls out, the same guy from the hallway on Tuesday. Ethan glances back and holds up a hand as if to say, *Hang on*. I feel a rush of satisfaction that he's choosing me.

"If you're free, a group of us are going to Millie's. You should come."

I gasp, delighted. "No way! Cami and I are going to Millie's too."

"Really?" he says. "Would you look at that. Must be fate."

Fate.

I press my lips together and nod enthusiastically. I don't trust myself to say anything, lest I reveal how badly I want that to be true.

Millie's is busy for a Thursday. Three booths are taken up by the Brookhill baseball team, and Ethan sits at the one farthest from the door. When he sees me walk in, he smiles and waves us over, and my heart flutters anxiously in my chest.

"Hey, Jane," he says, sliding over in the booth to make room for me. I sit down next to him while Camila sits across from me, next to the boy with the buzz cut who keeps calling Ethan E-Gray.

"Well, *hello*," the boy says to Camila, raising a thick, dark eyebrow. "I'm Chris. And you are?"

"Getting ice cream," she says. She couldn't seem less interested if she tried. She slides out of the booth and walks up to the counter to wait in line.

"Hi." I turn to Ethan, trying not to seem as nervous as I feel. "Um. Did you order already?"

Ethan shakes his head. "I was waiting for you. What do you want?"

"Oh, um," I stammer. "That's okay. You don't have to—"

"I want to." Ethan cuts me off. "So if you don't tell me, I'm just going to guess."

I stifle a smile, feel my cheeks get hot. No boy has ever bought me ice cream before. Not even Jeremiah, and he got discounted sundaes when he worked here.

"Okay. Um, the cannoli sundae? That's what I usually get."

Ethan grins. "Got it."

It takes me a second to realize that I need to stand up too, so I'm not blocking Ethan's way. I hurry to get out of the booth and bang my hip into the corner of the table, causing a loud noise that makes a few people nearby turn to look. I bite my bottom lip to stifle a squeal of pain.

"Oh man." Ethan slides out effortlessly. "You okay?"

"Mm-hmm." I grimace, clutching my side to keep from keeling over. "Told you I'm clumsy."

He chuckles. "Be right back. Try not to slip on any banana peels while I'm gone."

I laugh at his joke, sit back down, and put my head in my hands, finally giving myself over to the pain. When I look up again, I realize the buzz-cut guy—Chris—is still sitting at the table.

"That's gonna leave a nasty bruise," he observes. All I can do is frown at him.

"So," he says, unfazed. "Your friend."

"Camila."

"Cam*ila*," he repeats, drawing out the *i*. "Is she single?"

I don't even flinch. "No."

"Oh." He looks displeased. "Well what am I doing here, then?"

I look at Camila and Ethan in line—there are already two people behind them—and back at the boy. "Aren't you eating any ice cream?"

I can practically see the lightbulb turn on above his head. "Right," he says, then slides out of the booth and walks to the back of the line. I watch him go, really hoping that he's just a teammate and not Ethan's new best friend. Last I was aware, Ethan's best friend was Shane Duncan—tall, nice to everyone, point guard of the JV basketball team. He would've been a much better date for Camila, in my opinion.

That's when I get an idea. With Ethan's help, I could set them up, and then the four of us would be inseparable. We could go on so many double dates! It would be great for Camila and even better for my Netzine. Anastasia, Izzy, and the boys get ice cream, go to the movies, take the train to the city. I put my chin in my hand and smile. The blog posts practically write themselves.

Camila comes back with her ice cream, a soft-serve vanilla cone dipped in chocolate. "I think he's into you," she says, sliding in the booth. "He was going on and on about how smart you are, and how cool it is that you're a writer."

I perk up, the throbbing pain in my hip all but forgotten. "He said that, just now?"

"Yup." Camila bites the tip of her ice cream, cracking open the chocolate casing.

"Did he say anything about my dress?"

Camila cocks an eyebrow. "Like what?"

"I don't know. Like . . ." My thoughts flash back to standing on the sidelines of the baseball game with Leo. "It looks nice on me?"

"No." She nibbles more of the chocolate off her cone. "We were just talking about your article in the school paper."

"But what did he say exactly?"

Camila licks her cone for a moment. I'm clearly testing her patience. "He said, *It's so cool that she's a writer.*" She looks up from her cone. "He must like artsy girls. Wasn't his last girlfriend a lead in the school musical?"

I frown at her. Ethan Gray has only ever had one girlfriend: Alicia Campbell, in eighth grade, who played Mayzie LaBird in *Seussical the Musical*. She looked so pretty in her red leotard with boa feathers that a group of seventh-grade boys had to be physically restrained when she sashayed by their section. For three months, Ethan and Alicia were a couple, until Alicia dumped him for a boy from another school. How *anyone* could dump Ethan is beyond me, but I wasn't complaining. Every time I saw them holding hands in the hallway, a knife cut a little deeper into my heart.

"Thanks for reminding me," I say, just as Ethan returns with two cannoli sundaes.

"You got one too," I observe, brilliantly.

"Yeah." He sits down and puts my ice cream in front of me. "I've never had it before, but I trust your judgment."

Across from me, Camila smirks and wiggles her eyebrows. I try to kick her under the table but miss and kick a pole instead, making the table shake.

"Ow," I mumble. And then, when they both look at me: "Ha. Um, my foot slipped."

I pick up my spoon and shovel a bite of cannoli sundae into my mouth for something to do. When the cold, creamy texture hits my tongue, I realize I'm too nervous to eat, but I force myself to swallow. That's when I notice Chris step out of the line with his ice cream. He looks at our booth, makes a face, and then goes to sit at another table.

"Anyway," Camila says. "Ethan. Tell us about yourself."

If he's taken aback by her abrasiveness, he doesn't show it. He just smiles and says, "What do you want to know?"

"Well." Camila pauses, licks her cone. "We know you're on the baseball team. What else do you like to do?"

He dips his spoon into the cannoli sundae. "Baseball is a big one. From March to May, it's pretty much all I have time for." He takes a bite and raises his eyebrows. "This," he says, turning to me, "is awesome. Can't believe I never tried it before."

"Okay, but that's just three months," Camila says. "What about the rest of the year?"

"Cami," I say, silently urging her to chill with the third degree.

"In the summers, I love to jet-ski," Ethan says. "My family drives out to Blue Marsh Lake most weekends. It's a whole thing."

"That sounds like so much fun," I say, even though I'm not sure it does. I'm not really a water-sports person. Or a sports person, period. "Can you drive a Jet Ski?"

"Oh yeah." Ethan grins. "I have my boating license."

"So you can also drive a *boat*?" I take another bite of my sundae, already picturing the blog posts. Anastasia and Miles: boat parties, sunset cruises, Jet Ski joyrides—

"Yep." He looks at me, and his smile turns suggestive. "Maybe I'll take you for a ride sometime."

I nearly choke on my ice cream. Ethan wants to take me on his Jet Ski—for real. Not Anastasia, but *me*, Jane. This isn't just one of my Netzine daydreams. It's real life, and it feels just as good as I'd always imagined it would.

"I'd like that." I imagine myself on the back of Ethan's Jet Ski, my arms wrapped around his waist. Across from me, Camila hides her smile behind her ice cream cone, now half gone.

The bell over the door rings, and I look up to see Jeremiah and Danny, his best friend, walk inside. My fantasy evaporates.

"Oh *no*," I groan, and sink down into the booth.

Ethan follows my gaze, his smile fading. "What's wrong?"

"My brother," I say. "Stalking me."

Camila turns toward the door. When she spots him, her eyes light up.

"Why do you look so happy to see him?" I say, not bothering to hide my disgust.

Something like guilt crosses her face, but it disappears as quickly as it came. "Because. Now I have someone to talk to while you two have your alone time." She smiles suggestively and slides out of the booth.

"Wait!"

Camila and Ethan both look at me, and that's when it

occurs to me how nervous I really am to be alone with him. With Cami here it was a group date, a kind-of sort-of date. Now, alone, it will be a *date* date, and I've never been on one of those before. What happens when there's an awkward silence, and Cami isn't here to fill it? Ethan will realize the true extent of my perpetual uncoolness and lose any interest he might have had, and I'll have blown my shot with the boy of my dreams forever. It's too much pressure.

Camila holds my gaze. It's like she knows what I'm thinking, because the look she gives me next is exactly what I need. *Stay calm,* her wide brown eyes seem to say. *You've got this.* I take a breath, relax a little. She gives me the tiniest nod of reassurance.

I glance at Ethan, who's still waiting for me to finish my sentence.

"Just . . ." I look at Cami, searching for an excuse that will feel believable. "Keep him over there, please? I don't want him to do anything embarrassing."

"Will do." She touches her croissant pendant, gives me one final, encouraging smile, and walks over to their table. Heads turn as she walks past, but she ignores them all. She puts a hand on Jeremiah's shoulder, and when he realizes it's her, his face brightens.

"Camila and your brother are close?" Ethan says, watching them too.

I shrug, pick up my spoon, and swirl it through the melty edge of the sundae. "We all grew up together."

"Hmm," Ethan says.

I look at him. "What?"

He shakes his head. "Nothing." He scoots a little closer and shifts his body so that he's sort of facing me. Under the table, his knee grazes mine. "So, I'm glad you came."

My heart starts to pound. I keep my eyes fixed on the ice cream, afraid that if I look into his eyes, I, too, will melt. "Really?"

"Yeah. I liked looking out at the bleachers and seeing you there in your pretty blue dress."

I smile, daring a glance. "You like the dress?"

He smiles back. "Absolutely."

He stretches his arm out over the back of the booth, so it's kind of like he's putting his arm around me. I *want* him to put his arm around me, so I lean back until I feel his hand against my upper back, right where my neck meets my shoulder blades. I hold my breath, wait to see if he's going to pull away. He doesn't. I feel his fingertips graze my skin, and instantly I get goose bumps. He must notice, because he smiles. He still doesn't pull away.

"I'm a little nervous," I say suddenly, putting down my spoon. "I've never—this is all . . . new."

"That's okay," he says, fingertips still like fire on my skin. "I'm nervous too."

I snort. "No you're not."

"I am. You're pretty intimidating, Jane Scott."

"Ha!" I finally feel brave enough to look at him directly. "Now I know you're lying."

He doesn't look like he's lying, though. His blue eyes are fixed on me, and he's got a curious crease between his brows.

"Why do you say that?"

"Because, *Ethan Gray*." It feels a little thrilling to say his name out loud. "I'm not intimidating. I'm inexperienced, and klutzy, and like, very *un*-intimidating."

He shakes his head. "You know, after the baseball article came out, I went online and read some more of your stuff."

"You . . . did?" I dig my thumbnail into my thigh to make sure this is really happening, and I'm not dissociating.

"You're really impressive. I mean, you turned an article about soggy lettuce in the cafeteria salad bar into a full-on exposé about school lunch practices."

I smile. "Now the lunch ladies put out fresh lettuce every day."

"Exactly." He laughs a little but then gets serious again. "It's like—I don't know. Like you notice things other people don't care to see."

I blink, surprised. I open my mouth to respond, but I don't know what to say. All of a sudden I feel strangely vulnerable. I look over at Camila. She's talking to Jeremiah, probably telling some dramatic story based on the way she's waving her hands around, and his attention is totally fixed on her. It's like I'm not even here.

"I can't wait to see what you do next," Ethan continues. "Do you think you'll cover another one of our games?"

I look back at Ethan. "Sure, if I can. Freshmen don't exactly get first pick during pitch meetings."

"Well, I think you should," he says, lowering his voice and leaning in. "I'll be sure to give you something to write about."

I want to ask him what he means by that, but then his free hand finds mine under the table and intertwines our fingers together. His touch is so electric, so *romantic*, that I lose my train of thought.

New post from AnaStaysDreaming
Friday, April 11, 4:00 p.m.

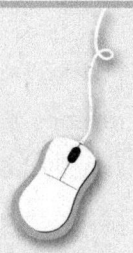

MIA (My Ice cream Affair)

A THOUSAND *I'm sorry*s for not posting at my usual time yesterday. I got caught up on an ice cream date with Miles, and it just might have been the best night of my life?? More deets to come soon.

This weekend is my town's annual Spring Fundraising Gala. If you've been following me for a while, you already know my parents are on the board of directors, which means they get to pick the charity and organize sponsors, while I get to help with the grunt work (thanks, Mom and Dad!). If you don't hear from me in the next twenty-four hours, send a search and rescue party, as there's a good chance I'm still tangled up in this gigantic pile of fairy lights my mom dumped on my bed. Also send macarons. Just because!

One more update regarding everybody's favorite internet boyfriend. Leo is coming to the gala (of course), and he's bringing . . . A DATE.

Dun dun dun!

I know, I know. I tried to talk him out of it, but it was no use. For reasons that have yet to become clear to me, he likes her. Personally, I think she's duller than dishwater. Don't worry, though. Leo is one smart cookie. I'm confident that eventually, he'll figure it out himself.

And if he doesn't . . . well, we'll cross that bridge when we get there.

Stay dreaming,
Anastasia

Chapter 11

On Saturday, I walk into the backyard a few minutes before the garden party begins and look up, wide-eyed. Fairy lights are strewn over the patio and gardens, illuminating the lilacs, the tulips, the hydrangeas. Bistro tables are scattered across the patio next to a long catering table and a bar, both of which appear to be fully stocked. Maggie wags her tail lazily in front of the catering table—she's waiting, in vain, for one of the caterers to give her a scrap of food. The sun is setting, turning the sky orangey pink and casting long shadows over everything. Faint jazz music plays through the outdoor speakers, so it feels like I'm at a café in Paris. It's completely magical.

And yet, unsurprisingly, Mom is still scrambling with the last-minute details.

"No, Marty!" she shouts up at my dad, who's balancing on a ladder, trying to drape a rogue string of fairy lights over a tree branch. They're both dressed to the nines—Mom in her black cocktail dress, Dad in his button-down and slacks. It makes the whole thing funnier somehow. "You need to wrap it *around* the branch to secure it. Or do you want it to fall down again and hit somebody in the head?"

"Behind you."

I turn around to see Jeremiah stepping through the sliding door and onto the patio with a huge tray of sushi in his hands. He's wearing baggy cargo pants and a black T-shirt that says MAKE DO AND MEND.

"No way Mom is going to let you wear that," I say, looking him up and down.

He shrugs and puts the tray of sushi on a bistro table. "I'm not planning on sticking around."

"You can't leave the party," I say, pointing out the obvious. "You'll be in huge trouble."

"They won't even notice I'm gone."

Jeremiah and I have barely talked since Thursday night. When we got home from Millie's, he came to my bedroom and asked me what I was doing there with Ethan.

"I wasn't *with* him," I lied. "Camila and I just ran into him there."

"Be careful with that dude," he said. "He's bad news."

I groaned. "Stay out of it, Jeremiah."

He let out a harsh laugh. "Hey, I'm just looking out for you. But you can do whatever you want; I don't care." And then he shut my bedroom door. For a while I just stared at the spot where he stood, seething. Who did Jeremiah think he was, going all protective big brother on me now, after two years of pretending I didn't exist?

Since then, part of me wondered if he'd bring up Ethan again, asking for more details or checking in to see if I was being careful or *something*. But he didn't say a word. Not to me, or to Mom and Dad. It's almost like it never happened. I guess I should be grateful.

"Janie! Jer!"

Ava walks through the open door and holds her arms out to me. "My god, this looks incredible!" she says, wrapping me in a hug. "Your mom outdoes herself every year."

Roman and Leo are right behind her. Jeremiah, seeing his out, says hi to them and then disappears inside the house, closing the sliding glass door behind him.

"Charli still putting you to work, Marty?" Roman calls out to my dad. "Doesn't she know the party's arrived?"

"I'm on the clock twenty-four seven," Dad replies, fastening the lights around the tree branch with a loose knot. "No overtime pay either."

"Careful," Mom says, joining us on the patio. She kisses Ava on the cheek and turns to Roman. "Or I'll put you to work too. One of the bartenders is a no-show."

"He can still make a mean gimlet," Ava says. "Remember that summer in Saratoga?"

Leo and I make eye contact. We both know when they're about to start waxing poetic over the old days, which is to say, we know when to tune them out.

"Hey," he says, his eyes sweeping over my dress. "You look nice."

I'm wearing a pale pink dress with puffy sleeves, a cinched waist, and a skirt that falls just above my knees. I saw something like it when I was researching West Village boutiques for my Netzine and then found a cheaper dupe at the mall.

"Thanks." I tuck a loose curl behind my ear. "You're not so bad yourself."

Actually, Leo looks great. His hair is tamed by a flex-hold gel, and his pistachio-colored button-down is the perfect shade to compliment his tan skin. The warm light from the sunset brings out the golden flecks in his hazel eyes.

"Where's Brynn?" I say, looking away. I feel a strange, twisty feeling in my stomach when I realize she's the one he's dressing up for. He's never tried this hard for me before.

"She's coming in a little while." He sticks his hands in his pockets. "I thought it would be better if she came late, with more people around."

"Why?"

He shrugs. "Less scrutiny from the parents, and everybody else."

"Ah." I cross my arms. "So it's like, a date?"

"No," he says quickly.

"Well, do you want it to be?"

Leo looks annoyed that I'm even asking this question. He opens his mouth to answer, but my mom's gasp makes us both turn our heads.

"What is this sushi doing here?" Mom picks up the tray

Jeremiah left on one of the little bistro tables. "It's supposed to be covered on the catering table over ice." She looks at me accusingly.

"It wasn't me." I hold up my hands in surrender. I consider throwing Jeremiah under the bus but decide against it. Now we're even.

Just then the garden gate opens, and the first cluster of guests arrives. I can practically see the vein in Mom's forehead start to throb.

"Marty, put that ladder away!" she calls to my dad as he climbs down. "Jane, get this sushi where it's supposed to be and make sure it's stored properly." She watches Maggie run across the yard toward the new arrivals and groans. "Maggie! Hey!" She takes off after her. "Mags!"

I pick up the tray of sushi and thrust it in Leo's face. "Mm. Look at all that raw fish."

"Do you want me to puke?" he says, gently shoving the tray away. "Because I will."

"Oh come on. Broaden your horizons."

"Leo," Ava says. "Go help Marty with the ladder. He's struggling."

I look into the yard, and sure enough, Dad is half carrying, half dragging the ladder through the grass. If it marks up the yard, Mom will have a fit.

"Sorry," Leo says to me, already walking away. "Looks like you'll have to torture somebody else."

"For now," I reply with a sly smile. "But the night is young."

* * *

"What do you mean we're almost out of shrimp?" Mom says to the caterer, her voice high-pitched with panic. "It's not even eight thirty!"

"Mom, chill." I'm slouched over the nearest bistro table, twirling my straw through my glass of raspberry iced tea so the ice cubes clink against the sides. "There's still plenty of food."

"There's so much cocktail sauce left," Mom says, furrowing her brow at the big bowl of it. "How did this happen?" She starts looking around the yard. "Have you seen your dad? Maybe he can run down to the store."

I open my mouth to tell her not to bother—that nobody will care if we run out of shrimp, and anyway, Dad's car is completely blocked in by all the party guests—but as quickly as the idea leaves her mouth, she's off, searching for him in the crowd. And there *is* a crowd—forty or fifty people deep, at least.

I put my chin in my hand and sigh, already bored. This is the first time I've had to endure this party without Leo *or* Cami by my side, and I have to say, I don't love it. I scan the sea of bodies until I spot the back of Leo's head, his hair a little more windswept than it was when he arrived. Next to him, I see auburn waves flowing like silk over a pair of slender shoulders. I scowl.

Why did he have to bring her here? It was supposed to be just the two of us loading up on taquitos from the buffet, or playing the world's worst round of croquet, or sneaking behind the shed to hide from—and laugh at—the overserved adults. With Brynn around, there's no *way* he'll stuff his face with taquitos. He won't do anything fun at all.

I pick up my phone, hoping for a text from Ethan or Cami, but there's nothing. I open my text thread with Ethan, feeling a little tingle of excitement. I *still* can't believe I have Ethan's cell phone number. I look at the last text he sent me, and the tingle shoots all the way down my spine. Good night, gorgeous :)

Good night, gorgeous!!!!!

That was last night. I haven't heard from him today, and it's taken every ounce of willpower I have not to text him first. I'm dying to talk to him, but I don't want to seem desperate.

"Jane!" says a familiar, high-pitched voice.

The tingle fizzles out like a wet rag on a flame. I look up to see Brynn and Leo walking toward me.

"Oh my gosh," she says, a look of amazement on her face. Unfortunately, she sort of resembles a mermaid in her emerald-green maxi dress. "Your backyard is so gorgeous! I can't believe you live here."

I force a smile, start aggressively twirling my straw through my iced tea. "It doesn't always look like this."

"It kinda does," Leo says, pulling out a chair for Brynn. She sits down, and he sits next to her. "Jane's mom is big into landscaping."

Leo's eyes flicker toward the light from my phone screen, still open to my text thread with Ethan. I quickly grab the phone and lock it.

"Well, Leo's mom helped decorate it," I say quickly. "Ava is a designer, did you know?"

"No!" Brynn looks at Leo, impressed. "That's so cool. I bet your house is amazing too."

"It *is*," I say, feeling a sense of satisfaction that I know what his house looks like and she doesn't. "Ava goes to lots of estate sales and vintage markets, and she always finds the coolest stuff. Like, they've got this big hutch in their living room that looks like it came right from Versailles."

"Wow," Brynn says. "I'd love to see it sometime."

I'll bet you would, I want to say.

"Maybe you will," Leo says. I frown at him, surprised, and stir faster.

"Are you mixing a potion?" Leo cocks an eyebrow at my iced tea. I stop twirling my straw. "What's with the aggressive stirring?"

"Yes, actually," I say. "It's a summoning potion. I need some fun to get here, and fast."

"Ah." Leo nods. "*That* explains why my legs walked me over here."

Brynn bursts out laughing. "You're hilarious."

Leo smiles down at the table. I resist the urge to roll my eyes, and take a big swig of my tea.

"Do you want some food?" Leo says to Brynn. "I'm sort of starving."

"Me too," she says. "Let's—"

"Leo!" Roman calls from across the yard, making us all turn

our heads. He and my dad are standing with Mr. Kowalski, an elderly man who lives down the street. "Come here a sec!"

"Quick," I say. "If you start running now, you can make it through the gate before anyone intercepts you."

Leo makes a face. "They're going to ask me to start mowing Mr. Kowalski's lawn again," he explains to Brynn, putting air quotes around "ask."

"Like a summer job?"

"Sort of." Leo stands up. "The kind of summer job that doesn't pay."

"Maybe this'll be the year," I say. "I'll start mixing up a potion for prosperity." I quickly stir my straw through my drink again, making Leo chuckle.

"Be right back." He looks at Brynn. "You can get food—you don't have to wait for me."

"I can make you a plate too, if you want?" she says—a little too eagerly, if you ask me. Like the Evil Queen offering Snow White an apple.

Leo smiles, oblivious. "Thanks."

I watch Brynn watch him walk away, a look of pleasant surprise on her face. She looks at me, realizing she's been caught, and smiles bashfully.

"Do you like him?" I say, cutting to the chase.

"Oh." Her smile falls. "Um, I don't know."

I don't believe her. Call it writer's intuition—or common sense. I want to ask her if she's New Girl, too, but I don't. For *obvious* reasons.

"He's really sweet," she says. "And he *is* cute."

"Uh-huh." I sip the last dregs of iced tea through my straw until it makes a loud slurping noise.

"Well," she says, filling the awkward silence that I refuse to fill. "I should get some food." She sits up. "What's good?"

I shrug. Everything is good. Mom, as usual, went all out with the catering. "The shrimp has been popular. It's almost gone."

"Got it. I'll get some for me and Leo."

I'm about to tell her not to, that Leo hates seafood and he'd much prefer the taquitos or the mac and cheese, but I stop myself. Leo told Brynn to make him a plate. Might as well let her make it.

"Good idea," I say, perking up. "You know, the sushi is also delicious. Oh, and the calamari. *Especially* the pieces where you can see the tentacles."

"I *love* calamari," Brynn says. "Any seafood, really. My dad and I would take special trips into Charleston just for the oysters."

I can't help but notice that her smile falters a little. I don't really want to ask what's wrong, lest she take it as a sign that we're confidants—or worse, *friends*—but curiosity gets the better of me.

"Do you miss it?"

A breeze picks up, blowing a strand of hair in Brynn's face. She tucks it behind her ear and says, "Yes and no. My last school was . . ." She trails off like she's searching for the words. "It wasn't the best. I had sort of a hard time with some girls there."

"What do you mean? Like, you were bullied?"

"Oh, I wouldn't go that far." She tries to sound reassuring, but I can see right through her. "I had this group of friends, but we got into a fight. Then they all turned against me, and they, well—" She smiles warily. "They were mean."

I want to ask her to go on—what was the fight about? Mean *how?*—but I decide against it. The last thing I need is to start feeling bad for Brynn Morgan, article stealer.

"But it was nice being so close to the beach," she says, putting on a positive voice. "Speaking of which—seafood." She puts her hands on the table and stands up. "Be right back."

I push away the feeling of guilt that's rising inside me. It's not like *I'm* being mean to Brynn. Is it my responsibility to tell her about Leo's dietary preferences? I don't think so. And I really *do* think the calamari is delicious. I never told a lie.

Maggie moseys up to my table, tail wagging lazily. At least someone is having a good time at this party. I crouch down and scratch her behind the ears, telling her what a cute little pudge she is. When I sit up again, Leo is walking toward me.

"Your potion didn't work," he says, collapsing into the chair next to me. Maggie moves over to him, and he leans down to pat her on the back. "Apparently, the Leo Amato Lawn Mowing Service is open for business tomorrow, free of charge."

"Sorry," I reply. "You should work on the name, though. How about Leo's Luxurious Lawns?"

"Luxurious?" he says, unsure. "That's a lot of pressure."

I laugh. "By the way, Brynn was practically ogling you over here."

His expression falls somewhere between amused and uncomfortable. "She was not."

"Oh, she was. She said you were cute and sweet."

"Well, I am cute and sweet. It's about time somebody recognized that."

I roll my eyes. "You were cute when you were five and you carried that Spider-Man doll around everywhere."

He smirks. "At least I didn't look like a little hillbilly with one front tooth."

"Hey! My tooth only fell out prematurely because you pushed me up the stairs."

"I didn't push you—I tripped and *fell* into you. There's a difference."

"Uh-huh." I shake my head. "I'm calling sabotage. You wanted me to lose that tooth so you could be the cute one."

He laughs and holds his hands up in surrender. "You got me. Our parents couldn't resist your chubby cheeks, so I had to level the playing field."

He leans forward and tries to pinch my cheek. I laugh and swat his hand away.

"Order up," Brynn says, making us both turn our heads. She's approaching the table with two plates in her hands. "Two *plats de fruits de mer*, as they say in Charleston."

She sets the plate down in front of Leo. His face goes blank.

"Seafood." He does his best to force a smile as she sits beside him. I have to bite the inside of my cheek to keep from laughing. "Thanks." He looks so repulsed that I almost confess I set Brynn up. I could play it up as a joke and all would be well, right?

Brynn eats a piece of calamari and moans a little. "Oh my gosh," she says, covering her mouth with a napkin. "That is *good*. Leo, you've got to try this."

She picks up a piece of calamari—the tentacley bit—dips it in sauce, and holds it out in front of his face. I suck in my breath, waiting for him to refuse. Then we can all have a good laugh about this, and he can make a plate of the food he really wants.

Instead, Leo leans forward, opens his mouth, and Brynn feeds him the calamari. Just like that.

"Hmm." He nods while he chews, and I can tell he hates it, that he wants to spit it out, but he doesn't. He swallows it down and smiles at Brynn.

"You're right," he says. "It's not bad."

My jaw drops. Leo ate fried squid. He ate it! And worse, he pretended to like it! Why would he do that? To protect Brynn's feelings? Why does he *care* what she thinks?

I stand up, mumbling some excuse about needing to go to the bathroom, and walk inside. My mind is spinning. Until today, Leo was the most authentic person I knew. He'd never lie about what he liked to make other people feel more comfortable. It's one of my favorite things about him. I could always count on him to be honest.

I climb the steps to my parents' bedroom in a daze. This is

all Brynn's fault. Brynn, who's been out to get me from day one. She stole my article, and now she's trying to steal my best friend.

I walk into my parents' bedroom and shut the door behind me. Without turning on the light, I cross the room to the window on the side of the house overlooking the garage. I push it all the way open and climb onto the roof. I sit down, the skirt of my dress flaring out around me, and look up.

The full moon glows bright white in the sky, dimming the stars around it. It was a full moon at last year's garden party too. I remember being up here with Camila, lying down with our heads together and making up fake constellations. *Zenus, goddess of math class.* Pray to her for an A on the exam. *Glenfry, god of cute boys.* Pray to him that Ethan Gray will notice me.

It's strange how so much can change, and yet the moon never does. If I look at it for long enough, I can almost pretend everything is exactly the same.

I pick up my phone, click on my text thread with Ethan Gray, and type out a message.

Hey. Hope you're having a good day

I press send. There's no point in holding back. Whether I like it or not, everything already has changed.

I put my phone down and look out toward Camila's house one street over, feeling a pang of longing. She's probably back from her cheer competition by now. Maybe I could text her and beg her to come over, just for a little while. *You don't even have to come to the party,* I'd say. *Just wear your sweats and come on the roof with me.*

I stand up, straining to see if her parents' van is in the driveway.

Instead, I see a familiar teal-and-white truck parked on the street in front of Camila's house. Jeremiah's truck.

The streetlamp makes it easy to see that there are two people sitting in the bed of the truck, facing each other. The person whose back to me is cast in shadow, but the familiar slope of Jeremiah's shoulders gives him away. The person sitting across from him is easier. I can see her face.

Camila.

Camila and Jeremiah.

What are they *doing*?

My phone buzzes in my hand, once, twice. I look at the screen and see Ethan's name. Two new messages.

Hey

I am now ☺

AnaStaysDreaming

Inbox (243)

Anonymous asked: Ana! It's me, New Girl, here to tell you that once again, your advice worked. I backed off, like you said, and a few days later, something surprising happened.
I got invited to a romantic garden party by this really cute boy. It was a perfect night, and I STILL can't stop smiling.
I'm going to ask him to come over to my house on Saturday so we can hang out again. Any ideas what we should do?

Your biggest fan, New Girl
PS: His name is Leo. How funny is that?

Chapter 12

At the end of social studies on Monday, our teacher, Mr. McCarville, tells us to pack up early—he has an announcement.

"Next month," he says, leaning on his desk, "the ninth-grade social studies classes are taking a field trip to . . ." He pauses for dramatic effect and does a little drumroll on his thighs. "The American Museum of Natural History in New York City!"

The room erupts into excited chatter. I gasp and look to my left, exchanging a glance with Camila.

"I know, I know, settle down." Mr. McCarville reaches behind him and picks up a stack of papers. "These are permission forms. Make sure you read them over with your parents, get them signed, and bring them back by April thirtieth."

He splits the stack in two and passes them out. Camila gets hers first, then hands a copy to me. I scan over it ravenously.

"We're taking a bus," Camila says. "Seven a.m. pickup time, *ugh*."

"The earlier we leave, the earlier we get to the city," I remind her, still skimming. "And we get to stay there until seven p.m.! Think of all the things we can do."

"We're probably not going to get to go off on our own." She puts the paper down, already disinterested. Camila isn't really a city person. If she had the choice between moving to Manhattan and moving onto a farm, she'd pick the farm no question. *Cities are too loud,* she said to me once. That was the moment it occurred to me that maybe we wouldn't be neighbors forever. In fact, once we graduated high school, we might never live in the same place ever again. I try not to think about it too much.

"One more thing!" Mr. McCarville calls out over the chit-chat. "There's a section on the permission forms about chaperones. We're looking for parent volunteers. If your parent or guardian is interested in chaperoning, have them fill out the section, cut it out of the packet, and return it to me separately."

"No way is my mom chaperoning," Camila mutters. She looks at me. "You should ask your mom. Then maybe we could actually have fun."

"My mom wouldn't chaperone," I say immediately. "She'll be too busy spoon-feeding Jeremiah his SpaghettiOs."

Camila gives me a chastising look. "I bet she would if Leo's mom volunteered."

I tilt my head, considering. It's not a bad idea. If Ava comes, my mom will be so busy hanging out with her best friend that I could have some real fun with mine. Me, Cami, and Leo in

New York City, just like I always imagined. We could stroll the cobblestone streets in SoHo, get macarons at Ladurée—it will be a Netzine post come to life.

When the bell rings, and Camila and I walk into the hallway, I bring up something I've been avoiding for the past two days.

"By the way." I clutch the straps of my tote bag tighter. "What were you and Jeremiah doing on Saturday night?"

She furrows her brow. "What are you talking about?"

"I saw you in his truck," I say, swerving to avoid running into a sophomore. "During the garden party. I thought you were going to be too tired to hang out after your competition."

"Oh." She doesn't quite meet my eye. "I was. But your mom asked my mom if Jeremiah could park his truck in front of our house during the party. You know, to make more space for guests."

"Yeah." I already knew that. Jeremiah told me on Sunday, when I grilled him about it. "That's not really answering my question, though."

She looks at me with a confused crease between her brows. "What are you implying? That I didn't come to the party so I could hang out with Jeremiah instead?"

I don't say anything. Better to let the silence speak for itself.

She scoffs. "Jane, seriously? I was with him for five minutes. When we got home, he was just sitting in his truck by himself, listening to music."

"He does that."

"I went out to say hi, and we caught up for a little bit. He played me some of the music he was listening to, and then I went back inside and went to bed. That's it."

"Do you have a crush on my brother?"

The question is out of my mouth before I even realize I'm going to ask it.

Camila bursts out laughing. "What? Come on." When she realizes I'm serious, she stops laughing. "Jane, *no*. I would never."

I nod, trying to feel reassured, though my heart is still pounding. If Camila did like Jeremiah, it would basically mean our whole friendship was a lie. Every sleepover, every pool day, every movie night would no longer be about me and Cami—it would be the origins of Cami and Jeremiah's love story. I shudder at the thought.

"We're friends, you know?" she says, shaking my arm. "I'm not just going to ignore him if he's in front of my house."

"Right." I nod some more, convincing myself. "Yeah, of course."

She smiles, already brushing it off. "I *am* sorry I missed the party. I heard it was a rager."

"There was definitely some rage," I say, but don't elaborate. We're almost at the newsroom.

When I walk inside, the first thing I see is Leo and Brynn sitting together at the desks. My heart clenches like a fist.

Brynn is New Girl, and Brynn likes Leo. The realization

is still hard for me to wrap my head around. Sure, I suspected both things, but in my heart, I didn't really believe them. I didn't *want* to believe them. Even after I read Brynn's message, I tried to convince myself it was just a coincidence. Surely there were plenty of other garden parties happening over the weekend. Surely there are plenty of other boys named Leo who befriended the new girl in school. Surely! But combined with the evidence from New Girl's other messages to Anastasia, the truth seemed impossible to ignore. So impossible, it was practically slapping me in the face.

Once the shock wore off, I knew I had to tell Leo. That way, he can get ahead of it—shut it down before Brynn's crush goes any further, and her feelings get hurt. After all, there's no way he'd ever like her back. Not after everything she's done to me.

After Halle goes over assignments, and everybody breaks to do their own thing, I corner Leo at the computers.

"I'm glad you're sitting down, because I've got news. Big news." I pause for dramatic effect and lower my voice. "Brynn likes you."

He looks up from the computer screen, where he's editing photos of the girls' lacrosse team. "She told you that?"

I briefly consider what would happen if I told him the truth. *Actually, she told Anastasia. Oh, who's Anastasia? Just my online alter ego from my blog you don't read. She has no idea it's really me she's spilling her secrets to. Is that ethical, you ask? Well, interesting question . . .*

"Not exactly," I say.

He raises an eyebrow. I can't tell what he's thinking, which drives me crazy. Also, I'm disappointed by his non-reaction. I thought for sure he'd say Brynn is wasting her time, and that he could *never* like her back. I thought we'd be laughing about this by now.

I sit in the empty chair next to him, smooth down the pleats in my skirt to calm my nerves. Halle sent Brynn on an errand to get some kid's class schedule from the front office, so we probably have ten minutes or so to talk without her overhearing.

"What are you thinking?"

Leo's eyes drift back to the computer screen. He starts adjusting the exposure levels on a photo of the goalie. "I guess I'm thinking that I'm not totally surprised."

I snort. "Cocky, much?"

He shoots me a knowing look. "I just mean . . . you know. You told me she said I was cute at the garden party. And she's been texting me a lot since then." A pause. "She sends a lot of winky faces."

"Do you send winky faces back?"

He shrugs. "Sometimes."

I gasp. "Leopold Amato, you're flirting with her!"

He gives me a wary look. "So what if I am?"

I lean forward in my chair, putting my face in front of the computer screen and forcing him to look at me. "You don't like her, do you?"

He doesn't move away. Softly he says, "I don't know. Maybe."

My jaw drops. I lean back, stunned. *Maybe?*

Leo has never had a girlfriend. He's never even confessed a crush to me before.

His hazel eyes are fixed on me, studying me in that thoughtful Leo way of his.

"Does that bother you?"

Yes, I want to say.

"No." I push the feeling away. "Why would it bother me? I like Ethan. We can, like, double-date," I force out, even though the very thought makes me want to vomit into my tote bag.

Leo's mouth becomes a straight line. "Now that's an idea."

I think about New Girl's—*Brynn's*—latest message. She said she's going to invite Leo over to her house this weekend to hang out. I came over here to warn him, thinking he'd need time to come up with a good excuse not to go. Now, though, it kind of seems like he might say yes. What kind of alternate universe am I living in?

Then I remember another message from Brynn: her first Talk to Me Tuesday post. That's when I get an idea.

"Also, she thought that you might like someone else. That you already liked someone before she got here." I raise my eyebrows. "Is that true?"

He looks at me a moment longer, then shifts his eyes back to the screen. "Don't you think you'd know if it was?"

Duh. Of *course* I would. I know Leo better than anyone. Even if he didn't explicitly tell me he liked someone, I'd still feel it deep down.

"Right," I say. "I know, I was just checking." I push off the table and do a 360-degree spin in my chair. When I'm facing him again, I say, "But seriously. You and Brynn?"

"Stop," he says. "There is no me and Brynn."

"Not yet," I retort. "But you like her."

"I didn't say that."

"You said maybe."

He sighs, looks at me again. "What's the big deal? She's fun to talk to. And she's nice."

"To you, maybe. To me, she's a liar and a backstabber. *And* a door non-holder."

He rolls his eyes. "I know you think she stole your article—"

"I don't *think* that," I say, smacking my hand on the table. At a desk nearby, Kat looks up from her sketch pad like I've pulled her from a trance. I lower my voice. "It's what she did! More than once, by the way. Remember the baseball article? She wrote the *entire* thing without talking to me first. Probably so Halle would think she's a go-getter and I'm lazy."

"Halle would never think that," Leo says. "She knows how hard you work."

"For now," I say. "Until Brynn's nice-girl act makes her the new favorite."

"Did you ever think that maybe it's not an act?" Leo points out. "Maybe she's just nice?"

"Leo, she's from the *South*," I say. "Being fake nice is basically her culture."

He laughs, shakes his head. "Whatever you say."

I cross my arms, frustrated. He's not taking me seriously. He's choosing to trust a girl he's known for two *weeks* over his best friend of fifteen years. I'd be offended if I wasn't so worried.

Leo is the nice one. He can't see Brynn for who she really is, but I can, and that's why I can't let this go any further. I have to protect Leo from her. From himself.

I leave Leo and sit down at my usual computer, where I open up an incognito tab and log into Netzine.

New post from AnaStaysDreaming
Monday, April 14, 10:57 a.m.

AnaStaysDreaming: Dear New Girl,

In my opinion, there's nothing more romantic than a scary movie. The lights are off, you're huddled together on the couch, and when the monster jumps out, you can snuggle close to him for comfort. The scarier, the better!

Keep me updated, K? It feels like I've been right there with you from the beginning. I want to see if this love story has what it takes to make it to the happy ending.

Chapter 13

I spend the rest of the week trying to command as much of Leo's attention in the newsroom as I can. I sit with him while he edits photos, ask for his opinions about my story-in-progress, and encourage him to spend class time roaming the halls for photographic inspiration. It's my hope that if I can keep him distracted, he'll forget what I said and lose interest in Brynn. Better yet, if they're never alone together, she won't get the chance to invite him to her house on Saturday.

Naturally, that's just wishful thinking.

On Friday, when I ask Leo if he wants to come over tomorrow for movie night, he tells me he already has plans. With *her*. Apparently, she'd texted him the night before with the invite. My mind starts spiraling with all the other things they could've been texting about this week, memories from the garden party and inside jokes and more flirty winky face emojis. It occurs to me that I'll never know for sure, and the thought makes me feel weirdly, insanely jealous.

"Jane, *hellooo*," Leo says, waving his hand in front of my face.

I blink, snapping out of it. "What?"

"I said I'll come over on Sunday," he says. "Is that cool?"

"Fine." I shrug, trying to push the feeling away. "Whatever."

"I blew it," Leo says with a huff.

On Sunday afternoon, we're sitting at the table on my back patio. The temperature is perfect: high sixties, sunny, with the kind of puffy white clouds that look like they're painted onto the sky. Our backyard has returned to its usual state, with the exception of the fairy lights, which Mom said look too pretty to take down. Really, I think she just doesn't feel like dealing with the hassle of untying them from the trees, but I'm not complaining. They *do* look pretty.

"What are you talking about?" I grab a potato chip from the bag and pop it into my mouth.

"With Brynn." Leo slouches in his chair. "Yesterday was a disaster."

I palm a handful of chips and stuff them all into my mouth to keep from smiling.

"I went over to her house to hang out," he says. "It was good, at first. I met her dad, he made us some waffles—"

I make a face. "Well, isn't that adorable."

He ignores me. "And afterward Brynn and I went into the living room. And she . . ." He trails off, winces at the memory. "She wanted to watch a scary movie."

I drop my jaw, feigning surprise. "No."

"Yeah. And I agreed, because I didn't want her to think I was a baby. But, dude. It was probably, without a doubt, the scariest movie ever."

I raise an eyebrow. "Scarier than *The Ring*?"

"Oh yeah. It was in Japanese."

I bit my lip to try to hide my smile. Leo sees right through it.

"Stop laughing," he says, pulling his hood over his head. "It was humiliating."

"I'm sure it wasn't *that* bad."

He looks at me, deadpan. "I screamed and ran out of the room."

I grimace. Even I wasn't expecting that.

"Ugh." He throws his head back. "What's the matter with me? Why am I such a wimp?"

"You're not a *wimp*," I assure him, pulling my cardigan down over my hands. "Scary movies aren't for everyone. And if she made you feel bad about it, that says more about her than it does about you."

"She didn't make me feel bad, though," he says. "She was super understanding, which made it even worse. She turned the movie off and put on *Talladega Nights*."

I frown. Leo loves that movie.

"But I haven't heard from her today," he says. "And usually she texts me a lot. What if she was just being nice in the moment—you know, to keep it from being even *more* awkward. But really she doesn't want anything to do with me?"

I study the worried crease between his brows. I don't think I've ever seen him so concerned about anything before. Well, except for the time he accidentally cleared his memory card, but even then, he was able to recover most of the photos. This might be a harder fix.

"If that's the case, then so what?" I say, trying not to sound *too* enthusiastic. "She's not that great, Leo. I don't know what you see in her."

The corners of his mouth turn down. "I hate it when you do that."

I look at him. The worried crease is gone, and instead his hazel eyes are narrowed—irritated.

"Do what?"

"Talk about her like that," he says. "She wants to be your friend, you know. If she heard the things you were saying about her—"

"I don't *care*, Leo. Brynn and I aren't friends. I'm only nice to her because of you."

He snorts. "Yeah, okay."

I raise an eyebrow. "What?"

"You aren't nice to her," he says. "You're passive-aggressive."

"I am not."

He pulls down his hood, and his long hair is wild around his face. He runs a hand through to try to tame it, but it only makes it stick up more. It's sort of cute, I think suddenly, and then push the thought away.

"She said she told you about what happened at her old school," he says. "How her friends turned on her."

"She didn't tell me much." I pull my legs up onto the chair and wrap my arms around my knees. "Just that they got into a fight."

He fixes me with an intense stare. "They were bullies. Petty comments about the way she looked, name-calling. At least at first. Then it escalated. One day they made a video making fun of her, and it went viral."

"Oh." My stomach drops. "That's horrible."

"Yeah. She told you her dad's company transferred him, and that's why they moved. What she didn't say is that he asked to be transferred so they could move away."

I shake my head. "I didn't know."

"I know." He takes a breath. "You didn't know, but now you do. So maybe you could be a little bit nicer to her, because she didn't do anything to deserve this . . . *hatred* from you."

I clench my jaw, trying to quell the strange mix of shame and rage that's building up inside me. Of course I feel bad that she was bullied. She didn't deserve that—nobody does. But does what happened to her mean my feelings are suddenly invalid?

"I don't *hate* her," I say. "I—I hate that she's trying to take you away."

He blinks, surprised. "What?"

I immediately regret the words and how pathetic they sound. I should've just let him think what he wanted.

"Never mind." I shrink back in my chair, trying to recede inside myself.

"No." He leans forward, staring at me with his intense hazel eyes. "Jane, come on. She's not taking me away. How can you think that?"

"She took my seat. And you let her."

He groans, frustrated. "You're really upset about that? It's just a desk—it doesn't mean anything."

"Yes it does," I argue. "The seat is a metaphor for our friendship since she's come to town."

"A metaphor?" An amused expression crosses his face, which just irritates me more.

"Yeah, a metaphor. She's taking my seat in your life. Like, at the garden party. We didn't hang out at all. You were with her the whole time."

"That's because you disappeared."

I shake my head. "I was sitting at that table by myself for, like, an hour before you came over."

"Okay, well, sorry," he says. His expression is a mix of frustration and guilt. "There were a lot of people who wanted to talk to me. I came over as soon as I could."

"Exactly! Every other year, that was us together, getting pulled into awkward conversations and hiding out behind the shed. But this year, you didn't need me. You chose Brynn."

"That's because I—"

He stops, glances at me, and then looks away, out toward

Maggie napping in the grass. The sun moves behind a cloud, casting the world in shadow.

"You what?" I ask. My heart, for some reason, is pounding. "You like her?"

"No," he says softly.

But it's a lie.

He looks back at me. I can see how uncomfortable this conversation is making him, but I don't care. I keep my eyes locked on his, and I make him say it.

"Okay, yeah," he says, looking away again. "I guess I like her a little. Do you hate me now?"

Leo likes Brynn. I don't know why the revelation is so earth-shattering. Maybe because, deep down, I knew it would happen all along. From the second I walked into the newsroom and saw them sitting together, I knew she would be the wedge that pushed us apart.

"Jane," he says. "You're on Mars. Come back to Earth and tell me what you're thinking."

I'm thinking that I don't want you to date her, I want to say. *I'm thinking that the idea of you dating anybody makes me feel absolutely rotten.*

My phone buzzes on the table between us. The screen is facing up, so I can clearly see the words "ETHAN GRAY" appear in a text message notification. I quickly pick up my phone and turn the screen over, but it's too late. Leo saw.

"You guys are texting a lot," he says. I don't miss the edge in his voice, and it irritates me. Why does he care? Leo likes Brynn. He has no reason to be anything other than completely happy for me.

"If you must know," I begin, "yes. We've been texting, and he meets me at my locker sometimes, and we even hung out at Millie's a couple weeks ago."

Leo's eyebrows shoot up. There's something unrecognizable on his face. I wonder if he's hurt that I kept this from him.

"Really."

"Yes, *really*. Is it so hard to believe that someone would be into me?"

"Not at all." Leo crosses his arms. "I'm just surprised Ethan is capable of being into someone other than himself."

I let out a harsh laugh. "Now who's being unfair?"

Leo shrugs. "Maybe he'll prove me wrong."

"He will," I insist. "You know what? We really should double-date. You, me, Ethan, Brynn." I pause. "Or—I mean, you, Brynn, me, Ethan. You know, assuming you haven't scared her away with your girly screams."

He cracks a smile. "Sure. Sounds fun."

"Sounds like a *blast*."

"Yep." Leo takes a potato chip from the bag on the table and eats it. "Just say when."

AnaStaysDreaming

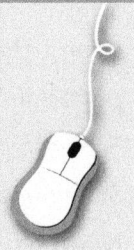

Inbox (333)

Anonymous asked: So it turns out your Leo and mine have something in common. They both hate scary movies!

I picked the scariest one I could find, like you said, and he barely lasted half an hour before running out of the room in terror. He was so embarrassed, bless his heart, but honestly, the whole ordeal only made me like him more. The fact that he agreed to watch the movie at all just proves how sweet he is.

I was busy the rest of the weekend, so I didn't get to talk to him again until Sunday night, and apparently he spent the whole day worrying he'd blown his chances with me. Can you imagine! I felt so bad for making him stress, but it ended up all right. At the end of the night, right before we stopped texting to go to sleep, he told me he liked me!

AHHH!!!!

I can't thank you enough, Ana. This might never have happened if it wasn't for you.

Still your biggest fan,
New Girl

Chapter 14

Monday after school, Ethan is waiting for me by my locker. When our eyes meet, and he smiles at me, all my worries about Leo and Brynn—*and* my thoughts of Leo looking cute on my back patio—melt away. Nobody else exists except for Ethan Gray.

"Hey, gorgeous," he says. It's something he says to me a lot, and admittedly, it's a little cringey, but right now I don't even care. I want to tell him that *he's* the gorgeous one, with his baby-blue T-shirt that brings out the color of his eyes and his perfectly swoopy hair, but all I can do is giggle nervously.

I start on my combination, and he takes a step closer. "How was your day?"

"Fine. You know, same old." I open my locker, start depositing my books. "You?"

"Pretty boring," he says. "Too bad we don't have any classes together. Then at least I'd have something to look forward to."

I dare a glance at him. "Are you flirting with me, Ethan Gray?"

"That depends," he says. "Are you coming to my game today?"

"Do you want me to?"

He takes another step closer, so he's just a few inches away. He smells delicious, like citrus and spice.

"Yes."

I stifle a smile. On the top shelf of my locker, my cherry lip gloss is knocked on its side. I feel a surge of confidence. Now that I know Leo likes Brynn, and has absolutely no right to judge me, I feel extra emboldened to take things with Ethan up a notch. I pick up the lip gloss, unscrew the lid, and then, locking eyes with him, I apply a fresh coat to my lips.

His eyebrows lift a little in surprise, like maybe he's flustered.

"Then I'll be there," I say, dropping the lip gloss into my bag.

We walk together down the hall, toward the boys' locker room. I wonder, at first, if he'll try to hold my hand. It's been eleven days since our last glorious hand-holding moment at Millie's, and aside from flirty texts, he hasn't made a move since.

I'm trying not to get too in my head about it. He was busy last week—he had two away games—and I was distracted too. Between Leo and Brynn, and Camila and Jeremiah, my eye was off the ball. I wasn't as alluring as I could have been. But now that Leo and Brynn are an item—gag—and Camila and Jeremiah are definitely *not*, there are no more distractions. I can shift all my focus toward what's truly important.

Making Ethan Gray fall in love with me.

"So I heard you played a good game against Greenlake last week," I say.

"It was all right."

"A home run to win the game is a little more than *all right*." I nudge him with my elbow, and he smiles.

"Well, yeah, when you put it like that," he says. "But the first few innings were a struggle. Their pitcher throws a tough curveball."

"You don't have to be so modest with me," I say. "You can brag. In fact, I'll brag for you. You are *amazing*."

He laughs a little. "I wish you covered our games all the time. You're way better than the guy who usually writes about them."

"No way," I say. "Max is sports editor. He knows what he's talking about."

"Maybe so," he says. "But you've got something he doesn't."

"Yeah, what's that?"

We get to the end of the hall. Instead of rounding the corner, toward the locker room, Ethan stops. He looks right into my eyes.

"Me."

I shy away from his gaze—it's too intense. I look down at my denim skirt, pull the sleeves of my sweater over my fingertips.

He puts his finger under my chin and tilts my head up. My heart somersaults.

"When can I see you again?" he says, his voice low. "Outside school, I mean."

"Oh." I feel frazzled and take a deep breath. "What—um. How about this weekend? My friends and I were talking about hanging out on Saturday night."

It's a lie—I haven't talked to anyone about hanging out, but the idea of being alone with Ethan still makes me nervous. Better to have a buffer in case things get awkward, right? Plus, a double date will be my chance to prove to Leo how great Ethan is, and how *into* me he is. Once he sees I'm right about that, maybe he'll finally take my advice about Brynn too.

"It's supposed to be nice out," I add. This part is true.

He smiles. "Cool. It's a date."

I feel my cheeks heat up. *A date!* Then I remember.

"By the way," I say innocently. "Are you still friends with Shane Duncan?"

Jane: Millie's on Sat night?

Jane: Us three, plus Brynn, Ethan, and his friend

"Who are you texting?" my mom asks from the driver's seat of our silver Toyota. She just picked me up from Ethan's baseball game.

"Leo and Cami," I say, just as Leo's response comes in.

Leo: Who's Ethan's friend? A mirror?

I scoff.

Jane: If it was, you'd have no room to judge

Jane: Your best friend is a camera, which is basically a mirror in reverse

"What are you talking about?" Mom says.

"Weekend plans."

Leo: My camera isn't my best friend, he's my son

Leo: And he's no mirror. How dare you insult his intelligence like that

I laugh into my phone. Mom, who has just slowed the car to a stop at a red light, leans over to look at my screen.

"Mom!" I angle the screen away from her. "It's called privacy."

"Privacy!" Mom laughs. "Privacy, says my child, while discussing the phone that I pay for."

I roll my eyes, type out a response.

Jane: So are you coming or not?

Leo: Yeah. I'll ask Brynn

"Privacy." Mom shakes her head and chuckles.

"I already told you what we're talking about," I say, irritated. "Why do you have to be such a snoop?"

"Because that's the only way I find out about what's going on in your life." She drives through the intersection. "When you're home, you're shut up in your room."

"I'm surprised you even notice."

"What does that mean?"

She makes a left turn, and the sun shines blindingly bright through the windshield. We both put the visors down.

"You're always so busy worrying about Jeremiah," I say.

"Maybe *that's* why you don't know what's going on in my life. Not because I spend time in my room."

My phone buzzes in my lap.

Camila: Answer Leo's question. Who's Ethan's friend

Jane: It seemed to me like a rhetorical question

Camila: . . .

Camila: Jane

"I do worry about Jeremiah," Mom says. "He's not like you, he—"

"He needs guidance," I say, keeping my eyes on the screen.

Jane: Shane Duncan

Camila: JANE

"He *does*," Mom insists. "But that doesn't mean I don't worry about you, too."

Jane: WHAT

Jane: He's hot! I thought you'd thank me

"You don't need to worry about me," I say. "I'm not Jeremiah. I'm not keeping anything from you."

Camila: I don't want to be set up with Shane Duncan

Jane: Why not

"I never said you were," Mom says with a sigh. "I just want to have a close relationship with my daughter. Is that so wrong?"

Camila: Because I don't like him

Jane: You don't know him

Camila: Neither do you

Jane: Well it's a good thing we're all hanging out on Saturday, so we can get to know him

Leo: Brynn's in

Jane: Swell

"Well?" Mom says. "Is it?"

"Oh. I didn't know you actually expected me to respond to that."

She taps her fingers on the steering wheel, waiting for an answer.

I groan. "It's not *so wrong*. But I'd like to point out that close mother-daughter relationships are built on foundations of trust and understanding. Not snooping through the daughter's texts."

Leo: I can feel your sarcasm through the phone

Leo: You're going to be nice to her, right?

"Fair enough," Mom says, making a right turn so the sun is at our backs. We put the visors up.

Jane: Yes

Jane: I'm offended that you even have to ask

"Well, in the name of *trust* and *understanding*," Mom says. I can't tell if she's making fun of me or not. "Can you please tell me what's new with you? How's school?"

"Fine," I say, preparing to leave it at that just to spite her. Then I remember the permission form in my bag. "Oh, the history classes are taking a field trip to New York City next month."

Mom gasps. "No way! I bet you're psyched."

I make a face. "Yeah, *totally* psyched. It's going to be groovy!"

"Excited, whatever." She waves a hand. "What do the kids say these days? Lit?"

"Stop."

"What! I'm serious."

"Anyway," I say. "They need parent chaperones. And I was thinking, what if you and Ava signed up?"

Mom looks surprised. "You want me to be your chaperone?"

"Well, yeah. You and Ava. It would be fun."

She smiles at me, and I can see the depth of emotion behind it. I didn't realize this would mean so much to her.

"Of course I will. Thank you for asking me, honey."

"Ugh, Mom. Please don't get all sappy."

"I'm not," she says, turning away from me to wipe a tear from her eye.

My phone buzzes again. It's a text from Leo, but it's not in the group chat. It's a text to me privately.

Leo: I need you to like her

Leo: It's important to me

I stare at the screen in disbelief. I already said I'd be nice to her—what more does he want from me? Does he seriously expect me to just forget about everything she's done?

Jane: But why? Who cares what I think?

Leo: Me

Leo: You're my best friend

Leo: If you don't like her, it won't work

I suck in my bottom lip, feeling a wave of conflicting emotions all over again. What does "it" mean? His relationship with Brynn? Or his friendship with me? I'm too afraid to ask. All I know is I don't want to lose him.

Jane: Okay

Jane: I promise I'll try

New post from AnaStaysDreaming
Tuesday, April 22, 10:00 a.m.

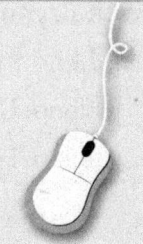

Talk to Me Tuesday

Anonymous asked: My bestie recently started dating this guy, and he's awful. He's a know-it-all, he's rude to servers, and worst of all, he's completely unfunny. I know you're going thru a similar situation with Leo. How do you deal when your amazing BFF has a bad BF?

Signed, Three's a Crowd

AnaStaysDreaming: Dear Three's a Crowd,

I don't think you're going to like what I have to say. I know because I also don't like it.
If your bestie likes him, you've got to try to like him too. Otherwise, she might feel like she has to choose between the two of you, and you probably won't be happy with what she decides.
PS: Tell your bestie to tip the servers extra on his behalf.

Tuesday, April 22, 1:00 p.m.

Anonymous asked: Hi Anastasia,

I miss my brother. We used to be really close. Then he got a girlfriend, a car, and all of a sudden it's like I don't exist. What do I do?

Sincerely, Pushed Aside

AnaStaysDreaming: Dear Pushed Aside,

I'm an only child, so take or leave my advice. It's probably not personal. He's just growing up. You should do the same.

Chapter 15

Millie's is closed for repairs. Camila and I are the first to arrive on Saturday evening, when the sun is setting on the horizon and the sky is a dusky orange. We find the sign taped to the glass on the front door.

"Well, this bites," Camila says, peering into the dark building with her hands cupped around her eyes. "What now?"

I shrug. There aren't many places to hang out in Brookhill after seven p.m. on a Saturday if you're under twenty-one. "We'll just have to get creative."

"Jane."

Down the sidewalk, I see Ethan and Shane walking toward us. The nerves come rushing in.

"Hi!" I wave to Ethan. He looks *so* cute in his navy fleece jacket and jeans. Next to him, Shane Duncan is tall, dark-haired, with sharp features and the lean muscles of a basketball player. He smiles at Camila, and she smiles back, which I take as a positive sign.

"Shane is looking good," I say to her quietly. "Don't you think?"

"Yes," Camila says in a tone that resembles the way I talk to my mom when I'm trying to appease her. "That was never a question."

"Well, what was the question?"

"You know." She tucks a strand of glossy dark hair behind her ear, revealing silver-and-blue butterfly earrings. "Whether there's a vibe."

I don't really know. In my experience, either you like someone, or you don't.

Ethan gives me a hug. His body is warm and strong, and the spicy citrus of his cologne is intoxicating. I wonder if he put it on just for me.

"What's going on?" Shane says, looking through the window. "Why's it so dark inside?"

Camila points at the sign on the door. "Closed for repairs."

"Oh," Shane says. "Bummer."

"No big deal," Ethan says with a good-natured shrug. "We can find something else to do." I smile at him, loving his optimism.

"Hey."

I turn to find Leo and Brynn approaching, and I do a double-take when I see they're holding hands. Despite everything I told myself about keeping an open mind, I feel my chest tighten.

Ethan nods to Leo. "Hey, man." He turns to Brynn and smiles. "What's up?"

"This is Brynn," I say to Ethan. "Leo's . . ." I trail off, unsure how to finish that sentence. Leo's *what*? Friend? Situationship? Girlfriend? None of the words feel good.

"I know," Ethan says. "We have biology together."

Brynn smiles sort of bashfully. She lets go of Leo's hand to give Ethan a little wave.

"Yo, Leo!" Shane says, clearly excited. "What's up, dude?"

Camila looks surprised. "You two are friends?"

"Sports photographer of the century, right here," Shane says, dabbing Leo up in one of those bro handshakes. I scrunch my nose.

"He's the *best*," Brynn gushes, putting a hand on his bicep. "The first time I saw his photography, I was blown away."

"Was it really windy that day?" I mutter under my breath. Leo hears me—oops—and frowns.

"Anyway." I raise my voice. "Since Millie's is closed, what should we do?"

"Let's do *something*," Camila says, jumping up and down. "I'm getting cold just standing here."

"You want my jacket?" Shane says, already starting to take it off. I glance at Ethan, wondering if he might offer me his jacket too, but he doesn't.

"No, no. That's okay. I'll be fine once we start walking." Here, she looks pointedly at me.

"Right." I yank the sleeves of my sweater down to my fingertips and wrap my arms around myself. "Let's walk."

We walk a couple of blocks, past a restaurant (too expensive), a bar (too illegal), a laundromat (does this need an explanation?), and a bookstore that's closed. The cherry blossoms that line the street are in full bloom, draping a silky veil of pink and white petals over everything. It's actually pretty romantic, I notice bitterly. Leo and Brynn are holding hands again, and Ethan still hasn't reached for mine.

"So where are we going?" Brynn asks from behind me.

"Nowhere," I respond. "Everywhere. We're just walking."

"I'd like a destination," Camila says. "And a close one. I didn't exactly wear my walking shoes." She gestures to her platform sandals.

"If your feet start to hurt, I'll carry you," Shane says to Camila. It's clear he's already smitten. She could probably suggest a stroll through an alligator-infested swamp, and he'd go along happily.

"We could go to the movies?" Brynn suggests. "Or the mall?"

"The mall will be packed," Leo says. "On a Saturday night, it's the first place everyone thinks to go."

"So let's find the last place everyone goes," Ethan says. "Someplace that gets overlooked."

I smile at him, charmed by his out-of-the box thinking. Leo, skeptical, raises an eyebrow.

"If it's overlooked, then how are we supposed to find it?"

"Actually," Shane says. "I know a place."

Fifteen minutes later, we're standing in front of a rusty iron gate, lit by a single flickering streetlamp. On the other side of the gate: gravestones, dozens and dozens of them, big and small, old and new, elaborate and simple. They line the hillside and disappear into the tree line. They seem to go on forever.

"A cemetery?" Camila frowns up at the archway. "You've got to be kidding."

"What?" Shane replies. "Ethan said to find the last place everyone goes."

"I don't think he meant literally," I say, crossing my arms.

"Oh. Well, at least we can be by ourselves," Shane says. "This place is always empty."

Camila raises an eyebrow. "Do you come here often?"

"Kinda. My grandma is buried here." He points off to the right. "Right over there, actually."

She responds with a stiff smile that, to Shane, probably looks sympathetic. But I can see the truth behind it. She is *freaked*.

"Not to be rude," Brynn says. She's half hiding behind Leo. "But this place is sort of creepy."

She's right. The sun has set, turning the world blue black, and the surrounding trees engulf the cemetery in darkness. I look up, searching for stars, but all I see is a slim crescent moon that barely emits any light.

I look over at Leo. He hasn't said a word since we arrived.

"Hey," I say, trying to meet his eye. "You okay?"

"Yeah," he replies, his voice clipped. "Why wouldn't I be?"

In a tree above us, a crow lets out two loud caws, making him jump.

"We don't have to stay here," Ethan says to Leo. As he speaks, he drapes an arm over my shoulders. "If you're scared."

I see Leo's jaw clench. He stands up a little straighter. "I'm not scared."

"*I'm* scared," Brynn says. "Y'all can stay. Leo and I can go."

"No," Leo says. He looks at me, and his eyes flicker to Ethan—to Ethan's arm around me. There's something hard in his gaze, almost like a dare. "I want to stay." With that, he reaches for Brynn's hand.

Brynn's forced smile falters. "Okay," she says softly.

"Actually, none of us are staying," Camila says, tugging on the gate. "It's locked."

"Oh, *darn*," Brynn says. "I guess that means we'll have to—"

"They lock it at night," Shane says, smirking. "Luckily, I know a way around it. Come on."

He turns on his phone flashlight, and we follow him twenty yards or so to the left, ducking under trees and avoiding tall weeds while sticking as closely to the fence as possible. Eventually we come upon a gap.

"I can't *believe* you, Shane," Camila whines when we stop. "My shoes are going to be ruined!"

"Hey, did you want to get in, or not?"

"Not," Brynn mumbles. She turns on her phone flashlight and shines it at the gap.

Shane goes first, and then we take turns stepping through. Leo and I are the last ones on the outside.

"We really don't have to do this," I tell him, keeping my

voice low. "We can leave right now and go watch a movie in my basement."

He doesn't reply, just steps through the gap, where Brynn is waiting for him on the other side.

Fine, I think, crossing my arms. If that's how he wants to play, then let the games begin.

"There's a path over here," Shane says, leading the way. "It's lit by streetlamps, but we have to keep an eye out for the groundskeeper. You never know when he's going to make his rounds."

"Wait," Brynn says. "If we get caught, will we get in trouble?"

"Duh," Camila says. "Did you think they locked the front gate just for aesthetics?"

Brynn doesn't reply. I know Camila's attitude has less to do with Brynn and more to do with her ruined shoes, but still. I bite my tongue to stifle a laugh.

As we walk, a heavy silence settles over us. Shane was right. This place is dead—no pun intended. Besides the birds, and the bugs, we're the only ones here. I take in the winding rows of stones, the overgrown grass, the damp, earthy smell, and I shiver.

"You cold?" Ethan says. "Here, take my jacket."

He shrugs it off and hands it to me, and right away, I feel warm. Finally Ethan Gray gave me his jacket! He gave it to me while we're on a date, which turned into a spontaneous adventure with our friends. Anastasia would be so proud.

"What is that?" Ethan says, pointing in the distance.

Under his jacket he's wearing a gray button-down. "A little house?"

On top of a hill, in the middle of a cluster of graves, sits a small concrete building with columns on the front, overgrown with ivy.

"It's a mausoleum," I say. "Haven't you ever seen *The Haunted Mansion?*"

Ethan shakes his head. My jaw drops.

"*What?* Eddie Murphy? The singing busts?"

Ethan snorts. "The singing *what?*"

"*Busts.*" I roll my eyes. "Like, statues."

"Oh."

"I can't believe you haven't seen it," I say.

Ethan grins. "Movie night?"

Leo glances over at us, his expression unreadable in the dark.

My stomach flips. Movie night. With Ethan Gray. What could go wrong?

"Yes," I say, avoiding Leo's gaze. I'm trying to sound confident and not at all terrified. "Definitely."

"Look, this stone is from 1903." Camila shines her phone flashlight on a small rectangular gravestone half-covered in algae and moss. "Alice Fairfax. Wife and mother."

"That's nothing," Shane says. "The oldest graves are on the other side of the hill, under the trees." He looks around playfully. "Any takers?"

"No *way*," Brynn says. "I'll stay on the path."

Shane shrugs. "Want to see my grandma's grave?"

Cami's face scrunches up. "Not really."

We get to the path, where the tall lamps cast circles of light onto the cracked cobblestones. Somewhere in the distance, an owl hoots.

"Let's make this interesting," Ethan says. "Truth or dare."

"A game?" Brynn says warily. She's clutching Leo's hand so tightly, her knuckles are going white. "Isn't that . . . you know, disrespectful?"

"I don't think he was suggesting we desecrate any graves," I say, glancing at Ethan. I *hope* he wasn't suggesting that.

"Definitely not," Ethan says. "No dares about desecrating graves or doing anything else that might get us cursed."

Shane looks confused. "What's 'desecrate' mean?"

"You believe in curses?" Brynn asks Ethan.

"Not really." He shrugs. "But I mean, if curses *were* real, wouldn't this probably be the way they happened?"

"Grammy will protect us," Shane says. "Don't worry."

I look at Leo. All this talk of curses probably isn't doing much to ease his nerves. Then I see his hand, still firmly grasped around Brynn's, and I remember how he ignored me on the other side of the fence. I get irritated all over again. *Why*, exactly, am I worried about Leo's feelings? I tried to give him an out, and he didn't take it. He's got Brynn to worry about him now.

I shift my focus to Ethan, where it should've been all along.

"Truth or dare?" I say to him, trying to sound flirty and mysterious.

Surprise flickers across his face. Then he smirks, pleased. "Dare."

"I dare you to show us an embarrassing picture of yourself from your phone."

Ethan raises his eyebrows. "That's the best you got?"

I give him a smile and a shrug. "I'm just getting started."

Out of the corner of my eye, I see Leo make a disgruntled face. *Good.* I'll show him who the best couple is.

"Okay, give me a sec." Ethan pulls out his phone, starts scrolling through photos. It doesn't take him long to find one. "Here." He turns the screen to face us.

"Oh come *on*," Leo says, already looking away. "That's not embarrassing. It's just a mirror pic of you with your shirt off."

"I mean, it's a *little* embarrassing," Camila says. "I always judge guys who post mirror pics. No offense."

Ethan grins. "None taken. I never posted it."

The photo shows Ethan in front of a mirror with his hair wet and his shirt off, flexing his biceps while taking a selfie. I hate to admit it, but Camila is right. This photo is *cringey*. Not only that he took it, but that he thought it would be a good idea to show it off now. I don't want Leo to know that's what I think, though.

"*Wow,*" I say with a forced smile on my face. "That's a great picture of you."

Ethan pockets his phone. "My turn. Brynn. Truth or dare."

"Truth," she says immediately. Big surprise.

"Okay." He pauses to think. "What's something you hope your dad never finds out about?"

"This," she says. "That was easy."

"Besides this," Ethan says.

Brynn shakes her head. "There were no caveats when you asked the question. Better luck next time."

"Boo," Shane says. "Let's get to the juicy stuff, already."

A breeze picks up, rustling the leaves on the branches. I lean into Ethan. He puts an arm around me and pulls me close, and I can't help it—I shoot a smug glance in Leo's direction. We lock eyes, and he quickly looks away.

"Okay, Shane," Brynn says. "Your turn. Truth or—"

"Dare," he says. "Obviously."

"I dare you," she says, "to call your ex."

Shane's jaw drops. The rest of us erupt into laughter.

"No way!" Shane says. "She's still in love with me."

"Oh please," Camila mutters.

"She is! She sent me a text last week telling me how much she misses me. If I call her, it'll be a huge mess."

"I thought you wanted to get to the juicy stuff?" Brynn says with a smirk, setting off another wave of giggles from the group. Leo looks at her with something like admiration, and I feel a wave of jealousy.

"Please just give me something else," Shane says. "*Anything* else."

"Boo!" Ethan says, mimicking Shane from earlier.

"Fine," Brynn says. "I'm not a monster. Do an interpretive dance for a minute."

"Ha!" Leo belts out. He lets go of Brynn's hand and pulls his phone out of his pocket. "I've gotta get this."

"Your time starts now," Brynn says, and Shane immediately begins jumping around and moving his arms in a way that I think is supposed to look ghostly, but instead just makes him look like a wet noodle. When the minute is up, and the laughter dies down, he turns to Cami with a knowing smile.

"Here we go," she says with an eye roll. "Truth."

"What's your biggest secret?"

She sucks in a breath. Her gaze flickers to me.

"I don't know," she says. "I have to think about it."

"Disagree," Shane says. "Everybody immediately knows their biggest secret. If you have to think about it, it means you're trying to come up with something else."

My mind jumps to my biggest secret: *AnaStaysDreaming*. That's how I know he's right. I'm relieved I didn't get this question.

A strong breeze blows Camila's hair wildly around her face. She struggles to gather it all in her hands. "Fine," she says. "In seventh grade, I broke into Mr. Sheridan's desk during lunch to get the answers to a math test."

"You did?" I say. "I didn't know that."

"I didn't tell anyone," she says, not quite meeting my eye. "I was embarrassed."

"Did you get an A on the test?" Ethan asks. She nods.

"So you're a bad girl," Shane says, nodding his approval. "Nice."

"Shane," Camila says. "Truth or dare."

"But I just went."

"Don't care," she says. "There are no rules against it."

"Fine," he says, unbothered. "Dare."

"I dare you to text your ex."

The group bursts into laughter again. Shane shakes his head, pulls his phone out of his pocket. Camila peers over the screen to make sure he's not cheating.

"He's typing *what was the math homework*," Camila narrates. "He sent it. Oh—now he's typing *sorry, wrong person*."

"There," he says. "Are you all happy?"

"She's typing back!" Camila says, positively giddy. "She said—" She throws her head back and cackles.

"What?" I ask, intrigued.

"She said, *Who's the right person? It's Grace, isn't it?*"

"Told you." Shane pockets his phone. "So thanks a lot."

Camila smiles innocently. "You're welcome."

Shane turns back to me. "All right, Jane. You're up. Truth or dare?"

"But Leo didn't go yet."

"And Leo is perfectly fine with that," Leo says.

I look at Ethan. His arm is still around me, and he wiggles his eyebrows encouragingly.

"Okay," I say, taking a breath for courage. I don't have any exes to text—how bad could it be?

"Dare."

Shane smiles mischievously. "I dare you . . ." He pauses for dramatic effect. "To give E-Gray one big, sloppy kiss."

My stomach drops. Suddenly *what's your biggest secret* doesn't seem so bad.

"Come on, man," Leo says. "That's going too far."

"Why?" Shane says. "They're on a date, aren't they? It's not like I'm daring her to kiss a stranger."

Leo looks at me. His hazel eyes seem to burrow right into my soul. In them, I see the same sentiment I tried to convey on the other side of the fence. *You don't have to do this. We can get out of this together. We can choose each other.*

Except, he didn't choose me. He chose Brynn.

Why shouldn't I choose Ethan? I've been dreaming of kissing him pretty much since I dreamed of kissing. Sure, this isn't exactly the way I imagined it, but so what? A kiss is a kiss, right? It might not be a such a bad idea to get the first one out of the way. Plus, it will probably make Ethan think I'm cool and spontaneous. It might even make him want to kiss me *again*.

I turn away from Leo to look at Ethan. His smile is a little wary, but his gaze is open, inviting. He's waiting to see what I'm going to do next.

Kiss him, says a voice in my head. It sounds a lot like Anastasia.

I lower my gaze to his lips, start to lean in—

"Hey!"

I open my eyes with a jolt. Two headlights in the distance are moving toward us, growing larger with every passing second.

"The groundskeeper!" Shane says. "He's in his golf cart. Run!"

Chapter 16

We scatter in different directions. There's no time to organize, so I pick a row of gravestones and just start running. One set of footsteps keeps a steady pace behind me. I assume it's Ethan, but it's too dark to see, and I'm too scared to call out to him. I need to keep all my focus on my feet so I don't trip.

And then, out of nowhere, an old stone appears. It's hardly sticking out of the ground, so even in daylight I might miss it. My toe collides with the stone and sends me tumbling forward. I land in the dirt on my hands and knees.

"Jane!"

It's Leo. He's crouching down next to me, helping me sit upright. "Are you okay?"

I wince as I assess the damage. My palms are scratched, but not too badly. The worst of it is my knee. It's bloody, and it stings.

"My tights," I say, noticing the runs in both knees. "Aw man."

"You just had a nasty fall, and you're worried about your tights?"

"They're my favorite pair."

We're both quiet, looking around to make sure the groundskeeper isn't on our trail. There's no noise, no light, no sign of him, or anyone. We're all alone.

"Should we try to find the others?" My voice sounds loud, even as a whisper.

"Not yet. The groundskeeper probably went after them. We should wait a few minutes and then get back to the hole in the fence."

I nod. I know he's right. Even though I'm worried about them, it's not going to help things if we all get caught.

He stands up and reaches for my hand. "We shouldn't be so out in the open."

I grab his hand and he pulls me up. When I try to let go, he holds on.

"Stay close to me," he says, his voice low. It sends a shiver down my spine.

Leo pulls me through the dark, toward the mausoleum that Ethan pointed out earlier. His hand is warm and firm, a steadying force against the fear. He doesn't seem scared at all, even though I know he must be. I think he's trying to be brave for me.

My pulse quickens. I suddenly want to intertwine my fingers with his, the way he did with Brynn earlier—the romantic way. The urge is so strong it's almost impossible to ignore.

Then he pulls me around the far side of the mausoleum

and drops my hand. He sits down, leans against the wall. It takes a moment for me to compose myself. When I do, I sit down next to him and stretch out my legs.

The air feels still. The only sound is our heavy breathing, punctuated every now and then by the ominous cawing of a distant crow. Then Leo's voice cuts through the silence.

"I can't believe you were going to kiss him."

I look at him. We're only inches apart, but I can barely see his silhouette.

I smooth down my skirt, feeling weird and vulnerable. That's when I realize I'm still wearing Ethan's jacket.

"It was just a game. If I didn't do it, everybody would've made fun of me."

"I wouldn't have."

He turns to me. Even in the dark, I can feel the intensity in his gaze.

"It's your first kiss, Jane. It shouldn't be a game."

I stare at my exposed, bloody knee. It hurts less than his judgment.

"Why do you care?" My voice sounds defensive and wobbly. "Shouldn't you be worried about kissing Brynn?"

Leo hesitates. He puts his hands in the pocket of his sweatshirt and looks straight ahead.

"Do you ever . . . ," he starts, and then trails off. It's a few long moments of silence before he tries again. "Lately it feels like things are moving really fast. And—I don't know. It's like I can't keep up."

"You mean with Brynn?"

"Sort of," he says. "I mean, she's great, but . . . it's me. I don't know what I'm doing. Like, ever. I feel completely out of my element."

"You just started dating," I say. "It's normal."

He starts nudging a rock with the toe of his sneaker. "I keep thinking about our parents."

I make a face. Not exactly where I thought this conversation was going.

"What?"

"You know the stories they tell about when they first got together," he says. "They always talk about that instant connection, and how right away they felt completely comfortable with each other."

"Yeah, but that's different. They were soulmates."

He looks at me. "So you're saying Brynn isn't my soulmate."

I bite the inside of my cheek, wondering how to respond. I could tell him no and sway him away from her right now. If I did that, I'd get my Leo back—*and* my desk. But then I think about the promise I made to Leo that I would really try to support his relationship with Brynn. I think about Ethan Gray, and his jacket still hugging my body, and his lips that almost touched mine. I think we could probably be happy, the four of us. We could sit together at lunch, and watch movies in my basement, and go on ice cream dates to Millie's. We could find a new normal.

Then my eyes flicker toward Leo's lips, and what comes out of my mouth is all instinct.

"I think a soulmate is someone your heart recognizes instantly," I say. "Someone who feels like home."

He returns his attention to the rock. That isn't Brynn. He knows it, and I know it.

"But that doesn't mean you shouldn't be with her," I say, trying to lighten the mood, to show him that I'm still supportive. "You're just dating to have fun. Who finds their soulmate at fifteen, anyway?"

He nudges the rock with some force so it skids across the grass. When he looks up at me, his gaze is so loaded, it makes the hairs on the back of my neck stand up. It shifts the air around us, making it feel static—alive.

"Did you?" he says, never taking his eyes off me.

"Did—" My mouth feels dry. I try to swallow. "Did I find my soulmate?"

"Yeah," he says. "With Ethan."

The static fizzles out.

"Oh," I say. "Um, I don't know. Maybe."

He keeps watching me, like he's waiting for me to say more.

"We have chemistry," I say with a shrug. "There's definitely something there."

He looks away, breaking whatever spell had been cast upon us. All of a sudden, I feel awkward.

"Should we get back to the fence?" I say, standing up and

dusting off my skirt. There's a damp spot on my butt from the dew in the grass—perfect.

"Do you remember," Leo says, not moving, "in the fourth grade, when Patrick Marks tried to hold your hand at recess? And you said—"

"You better watch it, or my best friend Leo is going to kick your butt," I finish, laughing at the memory. "He was twice your size."

"I would've done it, though," Leo says. "Or tried, anyway. If he did anything to make you feel uncomfortable."

"I know." I smile. "You were always looking out for me."

"I still am," he says. "And I always will. I might not be able to kick Ethan Gray's butt, but I *can* publish a really unflattering picture of him on the front page of the *Grizzly*."

"A psychological butt-kicking," I say, nodding my approval. "Twisted. I like it."

I offer a hand to Leo to help him up, and he takes it. When he stands up, I pull him right into a hug. He smells different from Ethan, like sandalwood and musk. Like Mom's garden after it rains.

We leave the mausoleum behind and start back the way we came. It doesn't take long to spot Camila, running right toward us.

"Where *were* you?" she says, her eyes darting accusatorily between us.

"Back there." I gesture with my hand. "Where's everyone else? Did they get caught?"

"Shane and I didn't, but I don't know about Brynn and Ethan," Camila says. "We lost them. I was hoping they'd be with you."

Leo and I exchange a glance. Brynn and Ethan ran off together?

"This has officially been the worst date of my life," Camila continues. "My shoes are ruined, and even worse, Shane tried to make a move on me in front of his grandma's grave!"

"He *what*?" I say, while Leo bursts out laughing.

"Can we please go, before the ghost of Grandma Duncan decides to start haunting me?"

"You don't have to ask me twice," Leo says. "Let's get out of here."

The three of us swiftly make our way to the hole in the fence. When we get close, I see Shane's familiar, noodley silhouette standing just on the other side, his face dimly lit by the glow of his cell phone. When my eyes adjust, I see two other figures nearby: Brynn and Ethan, standing close together like they're telling secrets. I watch them, my curiosity spiked. What could they possibly have to talk about so intently? How mitochondria are the powerhouse of the cell?

After a moment, Ethan leans down to say something to Brynn, his lips nearly brushing her ear. She responds by laughing and putting a hand on his arm. My jaw drops. That isn't an innocent arm touch. It's a calculated move I've seen from her before, in a transparent attempt to get Leo to notice her at the first baseball game. I *know* it's calculated, because I'm the one who told her to do it.

I look at Leo and Camila to gauge their reactions, but they don't see. They're too busy arguing about how we should flavor the popcorn at our next movie night. I return my gaze to Ethan and Brynn, but in the two seconds I looked away, the moment has passed. They're standing apart from each other, not saying a word. Ethan's eyes lock on mine, and he smiles.

New post from AnaStaysDreaming
Sunday, April 27, 12:00 p.m.

Spring Fever

There's less than six weeks until the end of the school year, and I have to admit, I'm a little restless. Ordinarily I'd round up Izzy and Leo, buy a train ticket, and take an impromptu day trip into the city, but unfortunately, nothing has been ordinary lately. Leo's spending most of his free time with his girlfriend, and Busy Izzy is living up to her name. I'd drag Miles along, but he's not really the spontaneous type—especially during baseball season.

Maybe it's the cherry blossoms, or the first hint of summer in the air, but I always feel a weird sort of pressure this time of year, like I'm not living my life to the fullest. I know I'm lucky. I've got amazing friends, a great boyfriend, and I love where I live, but still: I've got a sneaking suspicion that I'm missing something.

Do any of you ever feel like that—like you're just going through the motions, waiting for something big to happen to you?

Stay dreaming (I definitely will),

Anastasia

Chapter 17

"No, Alec." In the newsroom, Halle is sitting with her legs crossed on top of a desk and frowning over a proof from the *Grizzly*'s arts section. "You can't quote these lyrics. They're not school appropriate."

"But they have to go in," Alec insists, seated at the desk next to me. He's leaning back on his chair's hind legs. "They're representative of the entire album."

"There are five curse words across three lines. Principal Hobson would freak out."

"This is censorship," Alec mutters.

"This is high school," Halle corrects. "If you can't find better lyrics to make metaphors out of, then you're not the writer I thought you were."

Alec rolls his eyes but doesn't argue. Halle smiles, pleased she got her way.

"Looking ahead to the rest of the year," Halle says, consulting her notepad and raising her voice so it projects across the room. "The freshman history classes are going to New

York City in a few weeks, and we need coverage. Any freshmen writers want to volunteer? It can be whatever angle you want, so long as it's interesting."

My hand goes up instantly. Out of the corner of my eye, two desks down, I see that Brynn's does too.

"Jane, Brynn," Halle says. "You guys want to tag-team this one? You did a great job cowriting that baseball story."

"No," I say, at the same time Brynn says, "Sure!"

We look at each other. The surprise on her face only slightly masks the hurt. Next to her, Leo's looking at his camera. His expression is unreadable.

"I, um, just think it's too personal of a story to share with someone," I say, pushing through the discomfort. "New York City means different things to different people, you know? It's not as cut-and-dry as a baseball story."

Halle nods slowly, like she's trying to decide whether or not she agrees with me. "All right," she says after a moment. "Well, you're both great writers. It doesn't seem fair to pick one over the other."

Yes it does, I want to say. *It should be me.* I've been here longer than Brynn—I definitely have more experience. Whatever happened to seniority? Not to mention I write about the city all the time, as Anastasia. Not that anybody knows that, but still—I've spent hours researching the best restaurants, the coolest museums, the strangest subway creatures. I *deserve* this story.

"Wait," Halle says with a smirk. "I've got it. We'll have a competition."

I look at Brynn. She's turned away from me, toward Leo. He seems to be avoiding her gaze.

"Whoever writes the better story in the next issue of the *Grizzly* gets to cover New York."

"What?" I look back at Halle, incredulous. "But she's covering the anime club's art show, and I have to write about replanting the courtyard. Her assignment is way more interesting."

"Anything can be interesting from the right angle," Halle says brightly. I frown.

"And, Leo, you'll take pictures?" she asks him.

I look at Leo. He's staring straight ahead, fiddling absently with his camera strap.

"Leo?" Halle repeats, louder. He turns to her, snapping out of it.

"Yeah?"

"Nice of you to join us. Will you take pictures on the field trip to New York?"

"Oh." Leo glances at Brynn, who gives him an encouraging smile. "Yeah. Of course."

Halle nods once, decisively. She checks something off her notepad.

"Great! Moving on to prom . . ."

I tune Halle out and turn toward Brynn and Leo. She's saying something I can't make out, and his response is clear—*no*. There's a crease in between his eyebrows, like he's frustrated. Are they fighting? Then he turns toward the front of the room, and she looks down at her notebook, and they don't say another word to each other.

I lean forward in my seat, trying to catch his eye without Brynn seeing. It doesn't work. I clear my throat. Kat, seated next to me, looks up from her sketchbook, raises an eyebrow.

"Leo," I whisper. Brynn glances at me, then quickly glances away.

"Leo!" I whisper again. Now he looks at me.

Are you okay? I mouth to him.

He looks away without responding.

"I'm telling you, something is going on with them," I say to Camila at the end of the day. "Maybe they're breaking up."

"No way," Camila says, opening her locker. "They're totally smitten."

"They weren't today. They were arguing."

"Couples argue." Camila puts away her biology textbook. "It happens."

I shake my head. I still haven't told her what Leo and I talked about at the cemetery—or what I saw between Brynn and Ethan. Is it possible Leo saw it too?

"Leo told me he doesn't think Brynn is his soulmate."

She pulls out her math textbook and puts it in her bag. "So? It's his first-ever girlfriend. I'd be more concerned if he said she was."

I cross my arms, let out a frustrated huff. "Why are you so determined to believe that nothing is wrong?"

She closes her locker, gives me the same look she's been giving me since elementary school, when I tried to pretend I didn't care what flavor lollipop I got from the vending machine at the public pool, but we both knew I wanted grape. She ended up trading with me—her grape for my cherry.

"Why are you so determined to believe that something *is*?" Camila says. "Could it be, perhaps, that you want them to break up?"

"No," I say quickly, trying to convince myself that I mean it. "You know I don't think she's right for him, but—"

"Mm-hmm. And *why* is that?" We start walking toward my locker, which is on the other side of the school, about as far away from Camila's as it could possibly be. "Is it because there's someone else who *is* right for him?"

I frown at her. "I know what you're doing."

"Maybe a tall, stunning blond he's known his whole life—"

"Stop."

"Who gets his humor, and has impeccable taste in fashion—"

"I like Ethan Gray," I say, shutting her down. "Have I not made that clear?"

"Oh, you have," Camila says, amused. "Remember last year, when you took a detour to sixth period just so you could walk past him in the hall?"

"No," I lie.

Camila snorts. "You were late to French class almost every day!"

"Okay, *fine*." I roll my eyes. "That just proves my point. I'm all in on Ethan, and I always have been." A strand of hair falls into my face, and I tuck it behind my ear. "Leo is my friend. That's it."

"I'm just saying." Camila glances at me. "People change. *Feelings* change. Someone you've known your whole life can seem like one thing, and then one day, for no real reason, they're everything."

I frown at her. "Tell me more, oh wise one."

"No, I'm done. I'll just keep my very valid observations to myself."

"Thank you." At the word "observations," my thoughts turn back to what I saw at the cemetery.

"There's something else," I say. "Another reason why Leo might be mad at Brynn."

She looks at me, eyebrow raised. "Yeah?"

I tell her what I saw: the whispering, the laughing, the flirtatious hand on the arm. The fact that, when Brynn and Ethan saw us coming, they stepped apart, as if they wanted to pretend that nothing was going on. I see the look of disbelief on Camila's face before I even finish telling the story.

"You're just full of big ideas today, aren't you?"

"I'm not making it up! You would've seen it too, if you and Leo hadn't been so busy arguing about popcorn."

"Whoever heard of white cheddar popcorn at the movies?" Camila says, getting heated all over again. "Cheese doesn't need to go on everything."

"Cami," I say. "Focus."

"Focus on what?" she says, and I don't miss the humor in her voice. "Brynn and Ethan's secret romance?"

"Not a secret romance," I say, offended at the idea. Ethan likes me. Not Brynn. *Me.* "Just Brynn, once again, being a flirty little snake in the grass, thinking she can turn on her Southern charm and get anybody to fall for it." I shake my head. "Well, Ethan *won't* fall for it."

Camila gives me a strange look. "Oh-kay. You are officially reading too much into this."

"But—"

"Jane, you've now gone out with Ethan Gray twice," Camila says in her most mom-like voice. "If you told your thirteen-year-old self that this was happening, she'd probably drop dead from shock, and then be resurrected by happiness."

"Yeah, but—"

"No buts! Stop looking for problems and just enjoy it."

I puff out my bottom lip. I hate it when she's right.

As we round the corner and approach my locker, I see Ethan waiting there, and I picture it again: Brynn touching his arm, Ethan smiling at her playfully, the way he smiles at me.

"Hey, gorgeous," Ethan says now.

I force a smile back and do my best to push the image out of my head.

Chapter 18

On Friday night, the doorbell rings at 8:02, and Maggie lets out a howl.

"Coming!" I run up the basement steps, stumble over one, and almost wipe out, banging my shin. "Ow."

At the top of the steps, Leo's head peeks around the doorframe. I let out a gasp of surprise.

"Did you just fall?" he says.

"No," I grumble, hobbling up the rest of the way. "Did you let yourself in?"

My parents are out with Leo's parents, and Jeremiah and his truck are nowhere to be found. Unless Maggie suddenly grew thumbs, there's no one else here to open the door.

"The door was unlocked. Very irresponsible of you." He looks me up and down. "You look . . . nice."

I make a face. His words say I look nice, but his tone suggests otherwise. "Why do you say it like that?"

"Because it's movie night," he says. "You're usually in sweats for movie night."

I look down at my outfit: maroon flare pants, a cream-colored off-the-shoulder blouse, plus my butter necklace. I was going for a casual-cute look. I straightened my hair and put on makeup too.

"I wanted to do something different," I say with a shrug. That's when I take in Leo's knit button-down, the particular pair of black jeans that fit him just right. His hair looks a little less like a lion's mane than usual. Did he brush it? I feel a wave of strange feelings, but this time their origins are clear. Leo looks cute. Hot, even.

"Where's Cami?" Leo asks, snapping me out of it. He sits down at the kitchen table and angles his chair to face me.

"She's not coming." I walk to the fridge, grab two cans of Coke. "Ashley Gilpin broke her ankle, which I guess screws up the cheer squad's routine, so they had emergency practice all day today to rework it." I offer a Coke to Leo, and he takes it.

"Sucks for Ashley," he says, cracking it open.

"Sucks for us." I sit down across from him. "Now we're really never going to see Cami again."

Leo shakes his head. "I still don't get why she wanted to be a cheerleader."

I remember the day she told us. Last summer, we were lying on the lounge chairs next to her pool when she said it out of the blue. *I'm going to try out for the cheerleading squad.* Leo and I exchanged a confused glance. *As a joke?* Leo asked her. She shook her head. *You have your writing,* she said to me. *And you have your photography,* she said to Leo. *I just want something of my own.*

Camila being a cheerleader wouldn't bother me so much if it was just a casual pastime. But that's not how it's been. Lately, she's been acting like cheerleading is the most important thing in the entire world. I'm happy for her—of course—but it's a little weird, too. I didn't expect her to find her place so quickly, especially not while I'm still floundering.

"You know how she is," I say, feeling snarky. "She craves validation."

Leo looks at me. "Don't we all?"

The simple truth of his words takes me by surprise. I let out an uncomfortable laugh, open up my soda, and take a sip. "I guess."

He nods, looks down at his Coke. "So it's just us, then?"

I furrow my brow. "Isn't Brynn coming?"

"No."

"No?"

"I didn't invite her."

Hmm. I wish Camila were here so I could say *I told you so*.

"I just wanted it to be us tonight," he says, then adds, "or, you know—I just wanted to hang out with friends."

"Oh. Right."

Maggie sits by Leo's feet, looks up at him, and wags her tail. He leans over to scratch behind her ears.

"Leo?"

He glances up at me.

"Is something going on with you and Brynn?"

He returns his attention to Maggie. "Not at all." I can't see his face, so it's hard to tell whether he means it. "It's just what I said before—things have been moving fast, and I wanted a little space."

I hesitate. I still haven't told him what I saw—*might* have seen—between Brynn and Ethan in the cemetery. After Camila's reaction, I didn't want to risk it.

"I saw the two of you fighting in the newsroom," I say finally. "During the pitch meeting."

He sits up. Displeasure darkens his features.

"Yeah."

I blink, surprised he's not even trying to deny it. "So . . . what was that about?"

He doesn't even hesitate. "You."

I scoff. "Me? Why?"

He gives me a skeptical look. "Come on. You know why."

I raise my palms in the air. "I'm not a mind reader."

He sighs. The look on his face can best be described as resigned.

"You won't cowrite the New York story with her."

"So?"

He laughs a little, without any humor, and starts fiddling with the pull tab on the soda can. "*So* she's upset about it. She thought it wasn't nice, the way you handled it, and she wanted me to agree with her. I told her I didn't want to get involved."

I groan. "So what if I want to write it by myself? Why does she have to be so sensitive?"

"She wants to be your friend," he says, unable to hide his disapproval. "She thinks it would be fun to write it together, and she's wondering why you don't feel the same."

"Because I don't like to write with other people," I say. "I'm a lone wolf. I do my best work solo."

"Whatever." He returns his attention to the Coke can. "Is there popcorn? I'm hungry."

"No, not whatever," I insist. "How would you like it if Halle kept forcing you to share your camera with someone? If she made you edit your photos with a partner?"

"I get it," he says. "I do. It's just . . ."

I raise my eyebrows. "Just?"

He fixes me with his intense Leo stare. "I already told you. This won't work if you don't like her."

"But that's not—"

He holds up a hand as if to say, *Save it.* "I was hoping you'd come around, but you clearly haven't, and she's starting to sense it. And so now she's bringing it to me, which means I'm in the middle, and I really don't *want* to be in the middle."

He fiddles with the pull tab so much that it comes off the top of the can. He starts spinning it between his fingers. "The way I see it, the only solution is to separate."

"Separate what? Your laundry?"

"The two of you," he says, ignoring my snark. "In my life. I hang out with you, and I hang out with her, and there's never any overlap."

My mouth falls open. I'm not sure if I want to laugh or yell. "But that's crazy."

He shrugs. "It's either that, or things get even worse, and I have to pick between the two of you."

"But I would never ask you to do that."

"*You* might not," he says, and leaves it at that.

I cross my arms, indignant. "So that's why you didn't invite her tonight. You think I won't behave."

"It's just easier this way." He stands, picks up the Coke can. "Seriously, I'm starved. Let's go make popcorn."

The doorbell rings, and Maggie howls again. Leo looks at the front door and then back at me, his eyes a question.

"Who's that?"

"Well," I say, suddenly a jumble of nerves. "I thought you were bringing Brynn, and I didn't want to be the third wheel, so I—"

Leo's eyes glaze over with understanding. "Oh."

"Sorry." I stand up. "You should've told me you weren't bringing her."

"It's eight seventeen," Leo says, looking at the time on his phone. "He's late."

"I told him to come at eight fifteen," I reply, walking to the door.

"Any particular reason you're staggering your arrival times?"

I shrug. "I wanted you to get here first."

Leo doesn't say anything. I'm tempted to look back at his

face, to see how he might take this bit of news, but I don't. Instead, I open the door. Ethan is standing on the other side with a bouquet of pink flowers.

"This is my favorite part," Leo says, shoving a handful of cheddar popcorn in his mouth.

Leo, Ethan, and I are in the basement watching *The Haunted Mansion*. It's the scene where Eddie Murphy and his kids go into the graveyard looking for the mausoleum.

"This is the part I was telling you about!" I nudge Ethan. He's sitting on the couch to my right.

Ethan nods. "Those are some singing busts, all right."

"They're called the Grim Grinning Ghosts," Leo corrects him. He's seated on my other side, reclining into the corner of the L couch.

Ethan glances over at him, then at me. "You guys watch this movie a lot?"

"Not *a lot*," I say, suddenly self-conscious. I take the bowl of popcorn from Leo, who's been hogging it.

"Only every Halloween," Leo says. "Since we were kids."

Ethan smirks, amused. "Sounds sick, bro."

I shoot Leo a glare—I don't exactly need him reminding Ethan of all the hours we've spent down here, like *losers*, instead of being out in the world, having experiences. Leo ignores me and starts singing along. *"Down by the old mill stream..."*

Ethan bursts out laughing. "Leo, man, don't take this the wrong way, but you're a terrible singer."

Leo stops singing, clears his throat. Even though he obviously wasn't trying to sing well, I can tell Ethan's comment made him self-conscious. For the first time ever, I feel a twinge of irritation toward Ethan.

"Leo actually used to take singing lessons when he was little," I say, trying to diffuse the tension. "He quit when his voice teacher tried to make him sing Beyoncé."

"And it's too bad," Leo says, sarcastic. "Because I was really on my way to becoming the next pop princess."

"Who was the voice teacher?" Ethan says, still laughing. "A raccoon?"

I wince. If Ethan's trying to be funny, he's not exactly succeeding.

"Yes, Ethan," Leo says, taking the popcorn bowl back from me. "You're right. My voice teacher was a raccoon."

We return our attention to the movie. Ethan and I are sitting just a couple of inches apart, his face lit by the glow from the TV and the yellow light of the popcorn machine. All of a sudden, he puts his arm over my shoulders and pulls me toward him, until our thighs are almost touching. I can feel his heart beating through his chest, slow and steady. Calm. Not like mine, which is pounding so fast it's threatening to take flight.

I feel weird about cuddling with Ethan, especially in front of Leo, but I don't want to hurt his feelings by pulling away, so I stay where I am. To my left, I can feel Leo's gaze. I keep my eyes fixed straight ahead, on the decaying skeletons crawling out of their graves. That's less scary than whatever I might find on Leo's face.

We stay like that for the rest of the movie. As soon as the credits start to roll, I slink out from under Ethan's arm to reach for the remote.

"Great movie," I say, cutting through the silence.

"Always is," Leo adds.

I turn to Ethan. "What did you think?"

"Pretty good," he says. "I'll give it a B-plus."

My mouth falls open. "What? Just a B?"

He shrugs. "Some parts were a little too convenient. Like, the ghost just happens to look exactly like the mom?"

"There are singing busts and floating heads," Leo says. "You've gotta suspend your disbelief, man."

Something like annoyance flickers across Ethan's face. Before I have time to read into it, the annoyance is gone, replaced by a playful smile in my direction. "Well, it was hard to pay attention to all that." He reaches for my waist and tries to tickle me. "This one kept distracting me."

I let out a squeal of surprise. I am *very* ticklish. "I did not!" I say, trying to push his hands away.

Leo's phone starts to vibrate in his hand, and I see Brynn's picture on the screen. It's the one he took of her at the baseball game.

Like he can't get out fast enough, Leo puts the phone to his ear and stands. "Hey." Maggie sits up, cocks her head at him. "Yeah, one sec."

He crosses the room, climbs the steps, and takes the call upstairs, leaving the door open so we can still hear his muffled voice drifting down from the kitchen. I turn back to Ethan, and I feel it again: irritation.

"So why is he here?"

I put a piece of popcorn in my mouth and bite down hard on a kernel. Ow.

"What do you mean?" I force myself to swallow. "I invited him."

Ethan smiles a little, like I'm being naive. "You invited Brynn and Cami, too, and they're not here."

"Because they couldn't be." I put the popcorn bowl back on the coffee table. Suddenly I'm no longer in the mood.

"I'm just saying," Ethan continues. "If I went over to Shane's house and he had a girl there, I'd leave. To, you know, give them their space. I'd feel weird staying. Like a third wheel."

All I can do is blink at him. I'm not sure what he's getting at.

"He's into you," Ethan says. "It's obvious."

A sound between a laugh and a gasp escapes my mouth. "He is not."

He leans back and shakes his head, like he doesn't believe a word I say.

"Ethan," I say, trying again. "He doesn't like me. He's dating Brynn. You know, the girl he's upstairs talking to right now?"

"Why isn't he with her, then?" Ethan asks. "He could be, but he's here instead."

I hesitate. Does Ethan have a point? Leo said he wanted space from Brynn to be with his friends, but why? Leo and I see each other all the time. Leo and Brynn, however, have only been going out a couple of weeks. When you like someone, shouldn't you want to be around them as much as possible?

I think back to the cemetery, to the mausoleum, to Leo's golden eyes locked onto mine, cutting through the darkness with their intensity. He was mad I almost kissed Ethan. *Why would he be mad? Is it possible he . . .*

I push the thoughts out of my mind. There's *no way*. Leo and I are best friends. That's all we'll ever be.

"Okay, I get how this looks," I say. "But this is just how Leo and I are. We hang out together, in groups *and* alone, and it isn't a big deal."

"Whatever," Ethan says. "Hey, think you could cover the home game in the *Grizzly* this week? It's going to be a big one."

"Oh." I'm caught off guard by how quickly he drops the subject. "Um, I can try? I know Max is planning on covering it, but maybe I can—"

"Thanks," he says, smiling sincerely. "Max doesn't know what he's talking about half the time, but I know you'll make me look good."

My smile falters. Max definitely knows what he's talking about, but I don't think now is the right time to say that to Ethan.

"Um, yeah." I try to sound reassuring. "Of course."

He leans forward and strokes my cheek with his thumb. Despite the weirdness that just passed between us, I feel a tingle of excitement.

"I like you, Jane," he says. "That's why I want to be alone with you, you know? To show you how much."

My heart does a little leap in my chest. To show me how much? What does that mean? Probably it means he'll try to kiss me. What if I'm not ready? What if I'm bad at it?

The sound of footsteps on the stairs makes us both turn our heads.

"Sorry," Leo says. He sits down next to Maggie, who's wagging her tail at his return. "What did I miss?"

AnaStaysDreaming

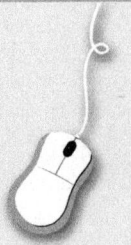

Inbox (415)

Anonymous asked: I need you to tell me if I'm being dramatic. Oh, it's New Girl.

For the past week, Leo has been distant. We haven't had a fight. He doesn't have a test coming up, or a project due, or anything that might explain why. Still, I haven't seen him outside school, and when I text him, sometimes it takes him hours to text back.

One more thing: we had our first kiss last weekend.

Am I overthinking this? Should I confront him, or wait and see if it passes? Does Miles ever get this way? If so, how do you handle it?

Chapter 19

I'm in my room on Sunday evening, working on the courtyard garden story for the next issue of the *Grizzly*, when a cacophony of laughter from the back patio breaks my concentration.

"Oh, Deirdre, you are *bad*." My mom's voice cuts through. I roll my eyes, hoist myself off my bed, and walk over to my open window. It overlooks the front of the house, not the back, but Mom and her book club are so loud that their voices carry.

I'm about to close the window when I notice Jeremiah. He's sitting in his truck, which is parked on the street, and bobbing his head to a steady beat. It's the first time I've seen him all weekend.

"That's what Ava and I used to say about Leo and Jane," Mom says. I go still, my interest piqued.

"It's true," Ava says. "I think we had their wedding planned before either of them could talk."

A wave of fury washes over me. I slam the window shut,

and the loud thunk makes Jeremiah turn his head toward the sound. I storm out of my bedroom and into the kitchen, and slide the patio door open with as much gusto as I can muster.

"Could you *be* any louder?" I say to my mom. She, Ava, and four other women are seated around the patio table. They've all got their monthly book club pick—a novel with a cartoon couple holding hands on the cover—and a glass of white wine in front of them.

"*Jane,*" Mom says, her tone chastising. "We're just having some fun."

"Yeah, well, some of us are trying to work."

A few of the women laugh at this, including my mom, which makes me even more annoyed.

"What?" I snap. "You don't believe me?"

"Of course we believe you," Mom says, though her tone suggests otherwise.

"You're our little working girl," Ava adds, and she and Mom laugh some more, like maybe it's one of their inside jokes.

"Whatever." I turn away, about to go back inside, when Ava calls after me.

"Wait, Janie! Are you so excited for New York?"

The trip is in two Fridays—less than two weeks away. My mom and Ava have both been confirmed as chaperones, which should be great news. In fact, it *was* great news, until this morning, when I read Brynn's latest message to Anastasia and learned that Leo kissed Brynn. Top that off with the fact that Ethan won't be there—the baseball team's biggest game of that season is that night, and it's two hours away—and my big city dreams are quickly diverging into nightmare territory.

"Yep," I say, my voice flat. "Can't wait."

"Convincing," mutters Deirdre. I frown at her.

"Come on! You, me, your mom, Leo," Ava continues. "And Cami, too, right? The whole gang will be there."

"And Brynn," I say, not bothering to hide my disdain.

"Who's Brynn?" Mom asks, taking a sip of her wine.

"Oh, Leo's new friend," Ava says. "Cute little thing. Very polite."

"Not friend," I correct. "They're dating."

Mom gasps, looks at Ava. "I didn't know Leo had a girlfriend!"

"Mom, please. She came with him to the garden party."

"It's nothing serious," Ava says. "Just puppy love. I doubt they'll last the summer."

"It's a *little* serious," I say under my breath. But they both hear me.

"What do you mean?" Mom says.

I shake my head. "Nothing."

"Don't worry, Charli," Ava says. "It'll run its course, like all first boyfriends and girlfriends do. We won't lose the deposit on the venue."

My mouth falls open. "*What?*"

Mom and Ava burst out laughing.

"It's a joke, Jane," Mom says. "Jeez, lighten up!"

"Although it would be sweet," Ava says. "The two of you, together."

I think back to the cemetery, to Leo's hand in mine, to the soft, supple slope of his lips, inches from mine in the dark, and for a split second, I imagine it. But then I remember that Leo's lips touched Brynn's, and the image is quickly replaced with a knot in my stomach.

"I'm going inside now," I say, as they giggle some more.

"Check on your brother," Mom calls out. "Make sure he's doing his homework."

"He's not," I say. "He's in his truck."

Mom sits up. "He's what?"

"Listening to music," I add. "At least that's what I think he's doing."

Mom puts down her wine glass, runs a hand through her hair.

"Charli—" Ava starts, her voice immediately consoling.

"Why must he *always* push me?" she says. "I don't know what to do with him anymore, I really don't."

I hover in the doorway. "What's going on?"

"He's grounded," Ava explains. "No truck for a week, except to and from school."

I scoff. Typical Sunday.

"What did he do this time?"

"He broke curfew," Mom says. "Snuck in through the window, as if Maggie wouldn't hear him."

"Little fool," Deirdre says, shaking her head disapprovingly.

Last night, after midnight, I woke up to the sound of Maggie's howling barks coming from my parents' room. I heard their door open, followed by my dad's voice, then Jeremiah's, then silence. I figured she just saw a squirrel out the window or something.

"Go tell him to get out of his truck and bring me his keys," Mom says. "He lost the privilege of hanging on to them."

"Why do I have to—"

Ava gives me a look that's equal parts pleading and stern. *Do it*, the look seems to say. *If not for your mom, then for me.*

"Fine," I grumble.

Inside, I walk past the living room, where Dad is reclining on the couch, watching some History Channel documentary with Maggie at his feet. I slip on my sandals by the front door and go back outside.

Fireflies flicker across the front yard. Behind them, the sky is a gorgeous gradient of pinks, purples, and navy. Jeremiah is still in his truck. He sees me coming and turns down the music.

"Let me guess," he says after he rolls down his window. "I'm in trouble."

"You're not supposed to be out here," I say. "Apparently."

He leans back in his seat, showing no urgency to go anywhere. "I'm still home. Technically, I didn't break any rules."

"You want to tell Mom that?"

"Nah, I'm good."

We're both quiet for a moment. I hover awkwardly outside his truck, listening to the chirping of the crickets, the distant, muffled laughter of Mom's book club. A new song starts playing through the speakers. It's one I recognize.

"'Jamie All Over'?" I say, pointing to the speakers.

Jeremiah nods. "Wanna get in?"

I hear the click of the door unlocking. I hesitate only a moment before opening it up and climbing in.

The inside of Jeremiah's truck smells like leather and allspice. It's messy, lived in. Empty Gatorade bottles litter the floor. A tree-shaped air freshener that lost its smell a long time ago hangs from the rearview mirror. He's got a gym bag in the back seat, though he doesn't play sports, so who knows what's inside.

He's eating from a bag of Flamin' Hot Cheetos. He holds it out to me, and I take one.

"So you broke curfew."

He shrugs, eats another Cheeto.

"Where were you?"

"Out." He chews, swallows. "With Danny."

"Where?"

He doesn't respond. I can't help but laugh a little.

"Right, I forgot. It's top secret."

He glances at me. "Nowhere special, just around."

"Nowhere special," I repeat, reaching for another Cheeto. "Sure. That definitely seems worth being grounded for a week."

"It was," he says simply.

The conversation tapers off. We're both quiet, listening to the song. *Please don't tell me that I'm dreaming...*

"So. What's new?" he asks me. "You still dating that guy?"

"We're not *dating*," I correct, feeling immediately defensive. "We're . . . hanging out."

"So, yes."

"He's nice," I say. *To me,* I add silently. Ethan definitely wasn't nice to Leo at movie night. I've been trying to forget, but I still feel a little weird about it.

"Mm," he replies. It's one syllable, but it's practically drenched in sarcasm. "Sure."

"Why do you care, anyway?" I say. "Aren't you too busy committing misdemeanors all over town?"

"I don't care," he replies. "I just think you could do better."

I blink, surprised. "What?"

He eats another Cheeto, keeps his eyes straight ahead. "He's a player," Jeremiah says. "And he's so preppy. It's cheesy."

"Ugh." I roll my eyes. "Have you been talking to Leo?"

Jeremiah smiles. "No."

"I'm happy," I insist. "Actually, I've never been happier."

"Okay."

"Ethan is nice."

"You already said that."

"He likes me."

Jeremiah laughs. "That's your criteria? He's nice, and he likes you? Maybe you should date Camila, then. At least she's cute."

I roll my eyes.

"Or Leo. He's got nice hair."

How stupid was I to think that Jeremiah and I could have a normal bonding moment? He doesn't care about me or my love life—he just wants to make fun of me. All he cares about is his music, and his truck, and himself.

"Mom said to go give her your keys," I say, opening the door and stepping onto the curb.

Jeremiah makes a disgruntled face. "Now?"

"Unless you'd rather wait until they open their fourth bottle of wine."

Jeremiah groans and turns off the ignition. I slam the door and cut across the yard without waiting for him to follow.

Back in my room, I open my laptop and try to refocus on the courtyard story. I skim my notes, glancing over budgetary restrictions and the significance of the milkweed plant for butterflies, hoping an interesting angle will jump out at me. It doesn't. I'm even boring myself.

I minimize the document and open Netzine.

My following has grown steadily over the past month, thanks in part to Brynn. People are *loving* her and Leo's love story. I get dozens of comments a day asking for updates, and even more messages in my inbox from people wanting me to help them the same way. I've tried my best to keep up, but admittedly, it's been a little overwhelming. Between schoolwork, assignments for the paper, and Ethan Gray, I've hardly had any time for Anastasia.

I click over to my profile, scroll through the recent posts. There's yesterday's entry about movie night, a photo of coffee and a croissant, a quote from a novel about the inevitability of change. I scroll down a little more to find last week's post about Anastasia's triple date. The location was changed from a cemetery to a museum, and truth or dare was changed to a scavenger hunt. Find a piece of art where the subject is reading a book. Find another where you'd ask the subject out on a date.

As I scroll, something strange occurs to me. For the first time ever, my life and Anastasia's are starting to blend together. Sure, her outings are more glamorous, her dates more debonair, but the foundation is the same. I don't have to completely make up scenarios anymore, because I have my own experiences to pull from.

My life is becoming more like Anastasia's, but it still doesn't feel right. It feels like something is missing. But what? I've got the friends, the adventures, the guy—what *is* it that I'm not seeing?

Just wait until New York, I remind myself. When I get to New York, I bet I'll finally feel like I'm where I'm supposed to be.

I move to my inbox, scroll until I find Brynn's message, and stare at it. I still haven't responded. I don't know how. Jealousy courses through my entire body. I keep picturing it: Leo's lips on hers. Leo's hand on her neck. His *lips* on *hers*.

He didn't tell me about the kiss. That fact alone feels like a slap in the face. Leo had his first kiss, and he kept it from me. There are so many things I want to ask him—when did it happen? How did it happen? What about what you said in the cemetery, about things moving too fast?—but I can't. If I told him I knew, he'd want to know how I found out. I can't tell him the truth—not without putting the blog at risk.

My only option is to pretend I don't know anything about the kiss. To pretend that everything is normal, and Leo isn't lying to me, and the lurching feeling I got in my stomach when I read the words *we had our first kiss last weekend* was just from bad sushi.

I repeat it to myself like a mantra: Leo kissed Brynn, and it doesn't bother me.

Not at all.

AnaStaysDreaming

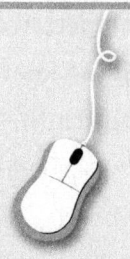

Inbox (382)

Anonymous asked: Hi Anastasia,

It's New Girl. Did you get my last message? Leo and I KISSED for the first time last weekend, and since then, he's been acting weird. I could really use your advice if you've got the time? I don't have any friends I can talk to about this.

Chapter 20

On Wednesday, Halle pulls me and Brynn aside in the newsroom to tell us who won the contest.

"You both did a good job on your articles," Halle says. "They were well written, thoroughly researched, and each got over a thousand clicks on the website yesterday. However..." She turns to look at Brynn. "The art show piece had three thousand clicks, nearly triple as many as the courtyard garden piece."

Brynn's eyes light up with surprise. "Really?"

"Yep." Halle smiles. "So that settles it. Congrats, Brynn. You're covering New York."

Brynn claps her hands together and squeals with delight. My jaw drops.

"You're judging by clicks?" I say. "That's not fair."

"No?" Halle says. "Clicks are objective. It seems like the most fair way to judge, in my opinion."

"But of *course* her piece is going to get more clicks," I argue. "It's a student-interest story. Nobody under the age of fifty cares that the courtyard has milkweed now."

Halle frowns at me. Brynn smiles sympathetically.

"I'm still happy to cowrite the story with you, Jane," Brynn says. "I think it would be fun."

"No thanks," I say quickly, and turn back to Halle. "I just think the fair thing to do is judge the stories based on merit."

"Merit," Halle repeats.

"Yeah. You know, which story you, as the editor in chief, think is better."

"And you think I haven't done that?"

I blink, processing her words, then dare a glance at Brynn, who suddenly looks very uncomfortable.

"Your story was good, Jane, but it wasn't great," Halle continues. "Frankly, it seemed to me like you phoned it in a little."

I open my mouth to respond, but no words come out. I want to tell her that she's wrong, that I worked hard on that story, that I had to work three *times* as hard as Brynn to make it something worth reading. But Halle keeps going.

"Brynn's story went the extra mile. It wasn't just a feature on the art show. It was a think piece about anime as a form of storytelling and escapism. I was really impressed."

Brynn smiles bashfully down at the floor. I curl my hands into fists, wishing I could sink into it.

Halle dismisses us. Immediately Brynn goes to the cafeteria for an interview, while I make a beeline toward my usual computer in the back corner of the room, where I can sulk in peace. Inside, I'm a dangerous mix of devastation and rage. New York was supposed to be my story. Really, it's the story

I've been working toward all year. Now it's just another thing Brynn has taken from me.

I open an internet browser, find my article on the school website, and start to read. I want to prove to Halle, and to myself, that she was wrong, but it only takes a couple of paragraphs for my eyes to glaze over. That's when a sinking feeling starts to form in my gut. Was Halle right? *Did* I phone it in? It's true I was distracted while I wrote it—thanks, *again*, to Brynn, and her first-kiss revelation—but I thought I still made good use of my interviews. I thought my conservation angle was interesting enough. Maybe not. Maybe *I* was wrong.

I close out of the web page and put my head in my hands, utterly defeated. I'm mad at Halle for making this contest, furious at Brynn for winning it, and outraged at myself for not being good enough. I have so much anger swirling around inside me, and I don't know where to put it. All I can do is close my eyes, stay as still as a statue, and focus all my energy on crumpling the anger into a little ball, making it smaller and smaller until—

"Hey."

I open my eyes.

It's Leo. Leo the liar. He's standing over me with a concerned look on his face.

"I just heard," he says. "You okay?"

I stare at him, deadpan. Is he really asking me that?

"I know how much covering this trip meant to you," he says, sitting in the vacant chair next to me. "You sure you don't want to cowrite it with Brynn? I know she'd still do it."

More staring. More silence.

"Who knows?" he continues, annoyingly optimistic. "Maybe it would be even more interesting this way. You'd find an angle you wouldn't normally—"

"Leo," I cut him off. "Go away."

He raises his eyebrows. I've caught him off guard.

"What?"

"You heard me." I spin away from him, face my computer screen. "Go back to your girlfriend. She's better than me, anyway. Even Halle thinks so."

He sighs. Wheels his chair a little closer. "Jane. C'mon."

"There's nothing you can say to make me feel better," I tell him. "You already chose her side."

"There aren't any sides."

"Yes there are. You said so yourself, at my house last weekend."

"No, I—"

"You said, if things get worse, you'll have to pick sides. Well, things have gotten worse. So go. Be on her side."

He doesn't say anything for a moment. His mouth becomes a straight line.

"Why do you have to be like this?" His voice is quiet, pained. "You agreed to the contest, and you lost, fair and square."

"Not fair and square," I snap. "I was set up to lose."

He scoffs. "Oh, yeah. But if Brynn lost, that would be fair, right?"

I shrug my shoulders a fraction of an inch. It would be a small bit of justice in the world, at least.

"This is ridiculous." He shakes his head. "You're so selfish."

I turn to face him, stunned.

"You can't just let her have this. Even if she deserves it, and even if it would make things easier for me. You hate her that much."

"I already told you, I don't—"

"Right. You don't hate her, you just hate that she's taking me away. But that's the funny part—she isn't doing anything. She wants us all to be friends. You're the one that's *pushing* me away."

I'm too shocked to speak. Leo never talks to me like this. His voice is cold as ice, and it chills me to my core.

"You promised that you'd try," he continues. "You said you'd do it for me, but I guess that was a lie. I guess you don't care about me as much as I thought."

I rear back like I've been hit. How can he say that? Of course I care. I care about him more than anything; that's why I don't want him to be with Brynn. He deserves the best, and she is *not* the best.

And yet . . . he chose her. He *kissed* her. And he didn't even tell me. Can't he see how much that hurts? Can't he see that he's the one who's ruining everything?

"Well," I say, when I finally find my voice again. "It seems like lies are going around."

A crease appears between his brows. "What does that mean?"

I look away from him, into the black of the computer screen. My reflection stares back at me. Her expression is desperate, a little crazed. I hardly recognize her.

"Please, Jane," he begs. "Why do you have to make it so hard?"

Because you kissed her, I want to say. *When all along, it was supposed to be me.*

The thought comes without warning, as shocking as if I were hit by lightning in the middle of a sunny day. But it feels true. And it unleashes the frustration I've been trying so hard to crumple up inside me. It unfolds and then expands into its final form: cruelty.

"You're right," I say. "I don't care. I don't care about you, or Brynn, or your stupid relationship, and I'm counting down the days until summer break when I don't have to see either one of your faces for a long, long time."

He doesn't react, just sits there and stares, almost like he's under a spell. If I were talking quietly, I might wonder if he'd even heard me. But I wasn't talking quietly. I know because Kat, at a desk nearby, is looking up from her sketch pad, openly gaping at me. Next to her, Daria and Alec exchange an uneasy glance. Finally, standing in the doorway, there's Brynn. She's back from her interview, and judging by the wide-eyed Bambi look on her face, she heard every word I said.

New post from AnaStaysDreaming

Wednesday, May 7, 9:00 p.m.

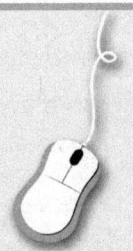

Everything Is Great

Sorry, does that sound braggy? I can't help it—life is pretty much perfect. Miles and I are coming up on our one-year anniversary, and to celebrate, we're going into the city to see the ballet. He surprised me with the tickets (I know, so romantic!) and booked a reservation at a fancy Italian restaurant nearby. It's going to be a fairy-tale night! Actually, even better, since my carriage won't turn into a pumpkin at the end of it.

In another pinch-me moment, I get to write about my NYC adventure in my local paper, as part of a travel series they're doing. I'd love to post it here for you all to read, however, that would give away where I live, so my lips are sealed :) But don't worry—you'll still get all the juicy details.

Now, for the news you've all been waiting for: Leo has FINALLY dumped the dud. He realized that I was right, and she was a sneaky snake in the grass. I was so happy he finally came to his senses that I didn't even say I told you so. Mainly, I'm just happy to have my best friend back. As Jane Austen said:

"Friendship is certainly the finest balm for the pangs of disappointed love."

Stay dreaming (it just might come true!),
Anastasia

Chapter 21

"I'm sure it's not as bad as it seems."

Camila and I are in her backyard, sitting on two lounge chairs by her pool. It's a nice evening, the temperature hovering in the low seventies, but the pool is still covered for the winter. It will stay that way for two more weeks, until Memorial Day weekend, when her parents celebrate the uncovering with a backyard barbeque. This, to me, has always been the unofficial start of summer.

"You're right," I tell her, taking a sip of my iced tea. "It's way worse. Leo is going to hate me forever."

We haven't spoken since yesterday's awful fight. I walked into the newsroom today prepared to apologize for the things I said—the things I definitely didn't mean—but I didn't get the chance. As soon as the pitch meeting was over, Leo booked it out of the room with his camera and didn't come back until right before the bell rang.

"No he's not," Cami says. "You guys have had fights before. You've always been able to work through them."

"Not like this." The only thing that even comes close is the time he broke his mom's favorite baby Jesus figurine, and I ratted him out. He didn't speak to me for three days, and it was excruciating. That was seven or eight years ago. "He was so hurt, and I don't blame him. What I said was horrible."

Camila runs a hand through her wet hair. I texted her and told her I needed to talk, and I was coming over after cheerleading practice whether she wanted me to or not. I barely gave her time to change out of her sweaty clothes and shower before I showed up like a feral animal freaking out on her doorstep.

"Okay," Camila says. "Well, you obviously didn't mean it, and he knows that. Maybe he just needs some time to process."

"Yeah," I say, though I'm not holding my breath. "Maybe."

Camila sips her iced tea and looks at me thoughtfully. "Why *did* you say it?"

A firefly lights up right in front of my face. I watch it fly upward, into the pale blue sky, and then disappear.

"Because I was mad," I say, like it's obvious. "I was mad Brynn got the story, and I was taking it out on him."

"And that's the only reason?"

I don't respond, just swirl the ice cubes around and around in my glass so they make a pleasing clinking sound. *No*, I want to say. It's not the only reason. It's not even the *main* reason. The main reason is that Leo kissed Brynn, and it turns out I'm upset about that because I wanted Leo to kiss me. But I can't tell Camila that without telling her how I know about the kiss in the first place.

"Jane." Camila puts her iced tea down on the concrete,

pulls her sweatshirt sleeves over her fingers. "We're at my pool. And what is the pool?"

I laugh a little, roll my eyes. "The rectangle of trust."

"Exactly. The rectangle of trust. What we say here does not leave this rectangle. If it does, may the person who breaks the trust die a painful, chlorinated death."

"Do those rules still apply if we aren't technically inside the rectangle?"

"Yes," she says without hesitation. "So tell me the truth. What's the real reason you freaked out?"

I sigh, long and loud, and give her a measured look.

"I like him."

A small smile slides across her face.

"Well, I wish I could say I was surprised."

My mouth falls open in disbelief. "You're not surprised?"

She shakes her head. "I've had my suspicions. I mean, you and Leo have always had crazy chemistry."

"No we haven't," I argue. "We just . . . we know each other really well. It's comfortable with him."

"Exactly." She smiles wider. "See? It was always going to happen. It's just taken you until now to realize it."

"Saying it like that implies I've been harboring a secret crush this whole time."

Camila cocks an eyebrow. "Like you haven't been?"

"No!" I say, but I'm not sure if it's true.

Suddenly Camila's dad slides open the patio door. "Camila!" he calls out. "The computer is acting up."

"Coming!" She looks back at me. "Last time the computer *acted up*, he couldn't figure out how to exit out of print preview." She laughs a little. "Be right back."

While she's gone, I consider her question. *Like you haven't been?* I only realized my deeper feelings for Leo yesterday, when it was officially too late to do anything about them. But how long had they actually been there, lurking just beneath the surface? Only the weekend? Since the cemetery, when one meaningful look from him sent chills down my spine? Or longer?

I think back to the first day after spring break, when I walked into the newsroom and saw Brynn and Leo laughing together, like there was already something between them. That's when I realize it. I wasn't mad that Brynn took my seat. I was scared that Leo might one day develop feelings for someone who wasn't me. But I didn't know it at the time. I was so focused on the fantasy of Ethan Gray that I ignored reality. I couldn't see what—or who—was right in front of me.

Camila comes back outside. "He was trying to type on a PDF," she says, sitting down in her chair. "I swear, my dad is the least technologically literate person on the earth." She fixes her gaze on me, suddenly serious. "Anyway. When are you going to tell him?"

"Leo?" I say, taking a sip of my drink to stall. She's got to be kidding. "Never."

"Oh come *on*."

"There's no point. He's with Brynn."

Camila makes a *psh* noise. "Barely. Aren't they already on the rocks?"

I shake my head, thinking of the kiss. "I was wrong about that. Like you said."

I prepare myself for the *I told you so* moment I definitely deserve, but it doesn't come. Instead Camila smiles, small and sympathetic. "I still think you should tell him. You never know what could happen."

"No," I say, meaning it. "I'm done getting in between Leo and Brynn. If he wants to be with her, then I'm going to respect that."

She gives me a look like she doesn't believe me.

"Seriously," I say. "I want him to be happy."

"But *you* would make him happy." She leans back in the lounge chair and picks up her iced tea. "Or are you still in denial about that?"

I rest my head against the back of the chair and look up at the sky. It's dusty blue now, the color of faded jeans, with orange-gold light peeking out over the horizon. This has always been my favorite time of day.

"I'm not in denial," I say to the sky. I *know* I'm not good enough for Leo. I'm just Plain Jane—self-conscious, awkward, clumsy, moody. How could he ever love someone like that?

"And what about Ethan?" Camila asks. "That's over, right?"

Ethan. Things have been weird between us ever since movie night. I didn't like the way he talked to Leo, and I still feel strange about the way he asked me to cover the baseball game for the *Grizzly. I know you'll make me look good,* he said, as if that was the most important thing. Since then I've had this nagging feeling that something isn't right.

"I don't know. He invited me over to his house on Saturday."

Camila's jaw drops. "No way. Your mom's okay with that?"

"She doesn't care what I do. With Jeremiah around, I'm practically invisible."

"That's not true. She just doesn't worry as much, because she trusts you."

We both go quiet. The sky is already shifting from gray blue to a deep navy. Soon it will be black. I wonder if we'll be able to see any stars.

"Are you sure you want to go?" Camila says after a while. "Ethan Gray's house, just the two of you . . ." She trails off.

The truth is, I'm not sure of anything. I might have realized my true feelings for Leo, but does that mean what I've felt for Ethan all these years just goes away? And what *did* I feel, anyway? My crush on Ethan was based on a fantasy. Now that I'm getting to know him, I have to admit he's not like I thought he'd be.

But of course he isn't, says a nagging voice in my head. I should know better than anyone how impossible it is to live up to a fantasy. Nobody's perfect, not even Ethan Gray, and it's unfair of me to expect him to be. Doesn't he deserve a chance for me to fall for the real him, without any preconceived notions of how he should be?

"I want to go." I tell her, as much as I tell myself. "Maybe we'll have a great time, and I'll forget all about Leo."

"Maybe," Camila says. "Or maybe you'll have a horrible time, and you'll realize that I'm right, and you're meant to be *with* Leo."

I crack a smile. "At least then you could tell me *I told you so*."

"I would never," Camila says. "Even though I'd really, *really* want to."

We both laugh at that. Then a gust of wind blows my hair out of my face, makes Camila shiver and wrap her sweatshirt more tightly around her.

"I'm sick of the cold," she says. "When's it going to feel like summer?"

"Probably when your parents take the pool cover off," I say. "That usually does it for me."

Camila nods in agreement. Then she gasps. "I forgot to tell you! I got an A on my math test, which means the last-day-of-school pool party is officially a go."

I sit up, delighted. Last year, it rained on the day of Camila's end-of-year pool party. She's spent the last eleven months waiting for the chance to redeem herself.

"Yes! I knew you could do it."

She smiles sheepishly. "I didn't. Polynomials will be the death of me."

I wave away her concern with my hand. "You won't need to use them in real life."

Camila laughs. "Well, please begin your nightly prayers to Mother Nature asking for nice weather. If it rains again, then actually, *that* will be the death of me."

"Got it." I hold up my hand and start to count on my fingers. "No polynomials, no rainy weather, and absolutely no breaching the rectangle of trust. Did I miss anything?"

"Artichokes."

I make a face. "Artichokes?"

"I just don't like them."

We look at each other and burst out laughing—the kind of deep, bellowing laughter that goes on longer than it should and makes my stomach ache. We start to compose ourselves, then lock eyes and fall into another fit of giggles. It's not even that artichokes are particularly funny. It's that all of a sudden, my problems don't seem so bad anymore. That's how good it feels to laugh over nothing with my best friend.

AnaStaysDreaming

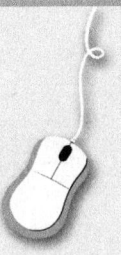

Inbox (299)

Anonymous asked: Dear Anastasia,

New Girl again. I wanted to let you know that you can disregard my last two messages. Things are all fixed between me and Leo.

I'm not sure if you've just been busy, or if I'm bothering you with all my messages. If the latter, I'm sorry. This is the last time I'll write you without a response.

Chapter 22

I'm standing in front of the mirror that hangs over my bedroom door, trying to pick out an outfit for my date with Ethan. I pull a pink shift dress out of my closet, hold it up to my body. Cute, but too formal on its own. Maybe over a white baby tee?

"Jeremiah, come back here right now!"

I put the baby tee on the hanger, put the dress on top. Better. But is a dress trying too hard for a casual hangout—especially considering I still don't know how I feel?

In the hallway, a door slams. I hear thunderous footsteps approach.

"Jeremiah." It's my mom's voice. "Open the door."

I put the outfit on the bed, next to where Maggie is curled up like a big cinnamon roll. It's an option. I return to my closet, pull out a blue blouse that Leo once said looked nice on me.

A shudder rolls through my body. *Don't think about Leo.*

I put the blouse back.

"Jeremiah, if you don't open this door—"

I open my bedroom door. Mom is standing on the other side with a hand on her hip and her back to me.

"Mom," I say, and she turns around. She looks tired. Her dark blond hair is poking out of her messy bun at odd angles. "Can you drive me to a friend's house in half an hour?"

"What friend?"

"A new friend."

She raises her eyebrows. "Does she not have a name?"

I twist the doorknob, stalling. I was hoping it wouldn't come to this.

"It's a he."

Jeremiah's door flies open. He's got headphones hanging around his neck. The music coming from them is so loud I can hear it across the hall. "What?" he says to Mom with attitude.

But she's not paying attention to him anymore. She's looking at me, her face slack with surprise. "A *he*? Do you have a boyfriend?"

"No. He's just a friend."

"And I don't know him?"

"No," I say. "Well, you might know of him. I wrote about him in the *Grizzly*."

She doesn't respond, just waits for me to fill in the blanks. Behind her, Jeremiah watches me with a blank expression on his face.

"Ethan Gray."

Jeremiah laughs a little and rolls his eyes. Mom glances back at him.

"What?"

I stare at him, my eyes like daggers. *Say nothing.*

"*What?*" Mom says again, harsher this time.

"Nothing," he says. His voice is light—mocking. "Nothing at all."

"Jeremiah," Mom warns. "What do you know about this boy? Is he bad news?"

"*No,*" I answer for him.

"He's not exactly good news," Jeremiah sort of mumbles.

"Shut *up*, Jeremiah."

"Why do you say that?" Mom asks him, like I'm not even here.

"Well for one, he was all over Jane at Millie's a few weeks ago."

Mom's mouth falls open. She looks at me, accusatory.

"He was not! He had his arm over the back of the booth, that's it!"

"Jane," Mom says, aghast. "You went to Millie's with this boy?"

"No, I went with Camila. He just happened to be there."

"Sure," Jeremiah says.

"Butt out! You don't know anything."

"I know guys," Jeremiah says. A look passes over Mom's face like maybe he has a point.

"Well, you don't know Ethan. He had one girlfriend last year, and *she* broke up with him."

"She broke up with him because he was talking to Kelsey Welles, from my year, behind her back."

"That's not true!" I say, and Jeremiah laughs a little, like I'm naive. "It was because—"

"Okay, okay," Mom says, raising her voice. "That's enough. Knock it off, both of you."

"But—"

"Jane," Mom says, giving me her warning voice. "I don't like you going over to some strange boy's house."

"He's not strange," I tell her. It comes out like a plea. "He's my friend. We're just going to hang out for a couple hours. You let me hang out with Leo all the time."

She gives me a knowing look. "Leo is different."

"He's a boy who's my friend."

"Was," Jeremiah mumbles.

I look at him, shooting daggers out of my eyes. "What?"

"Nothing."

"Did you say *was*?" Mom says to Jeremiah. She turns back to me. "Did something happen between you and Leo?"

"No."

Jeremiah raises his eyebrows. I want to scream at him, to ask him how he knows about my fight with Leo, and how *dare* he bring it up in front of Mom, but before I get the chance, he slinks back into his room and shuts the door.

"Are you and Leo fighting?" Mom says, worried now.

I groan, loud enough that Jeremiah, and probably the

neighbors, can hear. "We just had one little fight. It'll be fine."

But inside, I don't know if that's true. He ignored me at school again today, choosing to stay close to Brynn, and effectively create a barrier, the whole time we were in the newsroom. That's the juicy cherry on top of this argument sundae—Leo and Brynn seem stronger than ever. So much for moving too fast. They probably even kissed again, right after bonding over their mutual hatred for me.

"Of course it will," Mom says. "You two are soulmates."

"*Mom.*"

"Well, you *are*!" she says. "Soulmates don't have to be romantic. They can be platonic, too."

I remember what I said to Leo by the mausoleum. *A soulmate is someone your heart recognizes instantly. Someone who feels like home.*

"I have to finish getting ready," I say, swallowing the lump in my throat.

Mom sighs. I can tell she wants to press me for more information, but she doesn't. I'm grateful.

"Do you promise you'll behave?"

I resist the urge to roll my eyes. "Of course."

"And his parents will be there?"

I'm already nodding when it occurs to me that I don't know if that's true.

"Yes," I force out, *hoping* it's true. Parents are a buffer. They keep things from moving too fast.

"All right," she says. "I'll take you. But it'll be a couple of hours before I can pick you up. I'm running over to Ava's for a while."

"Okay," I say. "Thanks."

She looks past me, into my room, where the pink dress is draped over the edge of the bed. Maggie has shifted in her sleep and is using the skirt as a pillow.

"That's a pretty dress," she says, her voice casual. "For a friend."

I bite my lip and look down at the floor, trying to hide the evidence of what we both already know to be true. She turns to walk away.

"Um. Mom?"

She looks back at me. "Hmm?"

"Don't tell Ava," I say. "About me and Leo."

She gives me an innocent smile. "Tell her what?"

Chapter 23

Ethan's house is across town, in one of those wealthy McMansion neighborhoods I've never had a reason to visit before today. Mom and I are mostly silent on the drive over, and I can practically hear my heartbeat thumping faster with every passing minute.

"Somebody will be back to get you at nine," Mom tells me when we pull up in front of the house. "Either me or Dad, or—"

"Please don't send Jeremiah," I say. "I'd rather walk."

"Don't walk," she tells me, her voice firm, as if I actually would.

I unbuckle my seat belt, pick up my purse, and open the door. "Have fun with Ava."

"I'll stay here until you're inside."

I slam the car door and look up at Ethan's house. It's way bigger than mine—bigger than Leo's and Cami's, too. Most of the lights are off, except one shining through a small window at the side of the house and the chandelier visible through the huge window above the front door. It occurs to me, as I walk up the stone pathway, that this is the kind of place Anastasia might live.

There's a large brass knocker on the front door. I debate whether to use it or ring the doorbell, but it turns out I don't need to do either. The door swings open, and Ethan appears on the other side.

"Hey," he says with a grin. He's wearing a hoodie and joggers, and I feel horribly overdressed.

"Hi." I glance down at my dress self-consciously. "Did you see me coming?"

He shakes his head. "The camera told me someone was at the front door. Come on in."

I glance behind me one last time. Mom's car is still idling. I have the sudden urge to run back to her, dive headfirst into the passenger seat, and tell her to floor it. Instead, I step into the foyer, and he shuts the door behind me.

I follow him down a dark hallway, into the kitchen. A chunky yellow lab is chewing on a bone under the kitchen table, not paying us any attention.

"This is Arnold," he says, adjusting the dimmer lights from low to medium brightness. "He's all about his bone right now, but he'll be social later."

"Hello, Arnold," I say to the dog. I take a look around, listening for other signs of life, but there's nothing. The house is quiet. "Um, are your parents upstairs?"

"They're out," he says, walking to the fridge. He opens the

door, pulls out two little plastic water bottles, like the kind they give you on an airplane.

"Out?"

"Yeah, with friends."

He hands me one of the water bottles and I force a smile. We're alone—*really* alone. The realization makes me feel queasy.

"Oh. Um. Do they know I'm here?"

He replies with a smirk that makes my heart start to pound. I unscrew the cap on the water bottle, take two big sips.

"Living room's this way," he says.

I follow him through a doorway into a wide, dark room, the whole time hearing his voice in my head: *I like you, Jane. That's why I want to be alone with you.* He turns on the light—another dimmer, what *is* it with the dimmers?—but keeps it as low as it can possibly go. I sit on the couch, but I don't get too comfortable. It's white and spotless, and I'm afraid if I breathe wrong, I'll mess it up somehow.

"I'm really glad you're here," he says, sitting down next to me. "I was hoping I'd see you at the game the other day."

"Yeah." I laugh uncomfortably. "Sorry I couldn't cover it. I asked Max, but he said no."

It's a lie. I never asked Max. I didn't want to cover the game.

"No big deal," he says, and it seems like he means it. "There's always the next one."

I nod. "Right."

I take another big sip of water. My mind is racing. *Always the next one?* What if there isn't going to be a next one, and Max covers the games for the rest of the year? Will Ethan still like me then?

The answer comes to me instantly. No. I don't think he would.

"Should we watch TV?" Ethan says, reaching for the remote on the coffee table.

"Sure," I say, relieved. "I like TV."

I wince. I *like* TV? Why didn't I just say the sky is blue?

He turns it on and starts scrolling through the movie channels. I wonder if he's going to ask me what I want to watch, but he settles on a rom-com I've seen a million times and don't particularly like.

"I love this movie," he says. "It's hilarious."

"Yeah," I agree, because I don't know what else to say.

He puts his arm around me and pulls me close. I try to get comfortable, but his couch is too stiff, and my shoulder is jammed under his arm awkwardly. I adjust my position by leaning down, hoping that will fix the jamming issue, but that just puts my cheek into his shoulder.

"You comfortable?" he asks, rubbing my arm.

"Um. Yep."

I stay like that for as long as I can manage, which is only a minute or two, and then reach for my water bottle as an excuse to sit up again.

"You want another one?" he asks, gesturing to the bottle,

which is how I realize I've almost drunk it all. I do want another one—drinking water gives me something to do with my hands—but I don't want to have to pee, so I shake my head.

"That's okay."

I lean back but stay upright, letting Ethan's arm hang over the back of the sofa. In the movie, the main character slips and falls on a wet floor, and Ethan bursts out laughing.

I take a deep breath. *Relax,* I tell myself. *You've watched a movie with Ethan before. This isn't a big deal. It's just two friends, one boy and one girl, hanging out on a Saturday night, the same way you've done with Leo a thousand times.*

Leo. Like the opening of a floodgate, thoughts of him come rushing back. If I were here with Leo, it wouldn't be this awkward. Right away he'd point out the stiffness of the couch, how bad this movie is, how impractical these little waters are, and we'd laugh about all of it together. I'd get the second water bottle, because I wouldn't be worried about having to pee, because I'm not afraid of doing the wrong thing in front of him. With Leo, I've never had to pretend. I've only ever been completely myself.

That's when I realize it. I don't like Ethan *at all*. I never did. To be fair, I don't think he really liked me, either. We only liked the idea of each other. He pursued me so I'd keep writing nice things about him in the *Grizzly*. I pursued him so I'd have material for *AnaStaysDreaming*. It was mutually beneficial while it lasted.

There's one thing I know for certain: Anastasia and Miles might be soulmates, but Ethan and Jane definitely are not.

"Hey," Ethan says, snapping me out of my thoughts. He's watching me, smiling softly. "Did I tell you how pretty you look tonight?"

"Thanks." I force a smile. I want to go home.

"You know I like it when you wear your hair back."

"I know." I touch my ponytail. I left a few strands loose around the front of my face, and he lifts his arm off the couch to brush them back with his fingertips. My pulse quickens. I know this move—I've dreamed about this move. Now this move is my nightmare.

"Jane," Ethan whispers, his hand still cradling my cheek. He's leaning forward, his eyes focused on my lips. "Come here."

I stay where I am, knowing I have approximately two seconds to figure a way out of this.

He's so close I can feel his breath on my lips, warm and a little minty. He must have chewed gum right before I got here. In preparation maybe?

He closes his eyes....

"I, um..."

I slip out from Ethan's grasp and stand up. He opens his eyes.

"Where's the bathroom?"

He blinks at me. "Uh. It's around the corner to the left."

I pick up my purse and move as fast as I can without actually running. When I'm inside, I turn on the light and lock the door behind me. Hands shaking, I unzip my purse, pull my cell phone out of my bag, and dial my mom. It rings four times and then goes to voicemail. I hang up, call again. Same thing.

Next, I try Ava. Her phone doesn't even ring, it just goes right to voicemail. I feel my eyes start to burn. I don't want to call my dad, because then he'll know I've been at a boy's house. I don't want to call Jeremiah, either. But I need to call someone. I need to get out of here. Right. Now.

I take two deep breaths, click on Leo's name, and press call.

It rings twice and then goes to voicemail. He ignored me.

I call again.

This time he picks up on the third ring.

"What?"

It's the angriest "what" I've ever heard, but I don't care. The sound of his voice makes me want to cry with relief.

"I know you hate me," I say, keeping my voice low. "And you have every right to. I was a jerk, and I'm so sorry. But right now, I need your help. My mom is at your house, and if you're home, I need you to go find her and tell her that she needs to come and get me immediately."

"What?" he says again, but this time it isn't laced with venom. There's only concern. "Are you okay? Where are you?"

I hesitate. He's not going to like it.

"Ethan Gray's house."

For a second, silence. And then:

"Hang on. I'll get her."

Chapter 24

When I walk into the newsroom on Monday, I'm nervous to see Leo. I thought maybe he'd text me on Sunday to see how I was doing, or at least to get more information about what went down at Ethan's, but he didn't. I haven't heard from him since he passed the phone to my mom on Saturday night.

Leo is sitting in his usual spot, with Brynn next to him in *my* usual spot. His eyes flicker toward me as I sit down at a desk but then quickly refocus on Brynn. I bite the inside of my cheek, hard, to keep from getting too upset. He hates me.

I love him, and he hates me.

After the pitch meeting—the last one of the year—I don't feel like sticking around to see Leo and Brynn rub their happy, kissy relationship in my face. I decide to get a jump start on my feature story—also the last one of the year—by roaming the halls, looking for people to interview. Halle assigned me to a roundup of students' favorite memories from the year, a feel-good fluff piece that will require approximately zero creativity or critical thinking skills. Whatever. At least it gets me out of the newsroom.

I'm not in the hallway for thirty seconds before Leo follows after me with his camera.

"Wait up," he calls out. As I turn and spot him jogging to catch up to me, my heart flutters with something like hope.

"I thought you weren't talking to me," I say when he catches up. He's wearing this old band T-shirt that's faded and tattered at the hem. I've tried to get him to throw it away so many times, but he won't do it. He loves that shirt. Now, strangely enough, I find that I love it too. I love everything about him—his lion's mane hair, long and a little windswept from running in the hall; the sort of silly way he runs, with his long stride and his arms held close to his chest; his hazel eyes that look like sunshine over a meadow speckled with daisies; the way those eyes are fixed on me now, so thoughtful, so intense. Ethan has never looked at me the way Leo does. Nobody has.

I avert my gaze. It all hurts too much.

"Halle said I should come with you to get some pictures," he says, and my heart sinks a little. Of course he's not here because of me.

We walk in awkward silence for a minute. The whole time, there's not a single other person in the hallway. Typical.

"So," Leo says finally, his eyes fixed on his camera. "Are you doing okay?"

And there it is. *No*, I want to say. *I ended things with Ethan because I want to be with you, even though I know it's pointless because you want to be with Brynn. Also, we're not speaking, which is even more horrible than if you yelled at me. I miss the sound of your voice.*

Instead, I shrug.

"What happened at Ethan's?" he asks. "You sounded pretty freaked out on the phone."

"You mean you actually care?"

I see the muscles in his jaw tighten. I struck a nerve.

"Whether *I* care about *you* was never the question," he says.

"You know I care about you."

"I do?" He shoots me an irritated glance. "You said you didn't."

"Well, I lied, obviously. I was just mad."

He shakes his head, runs a frustrated hand through his hair. It's so cute when he does that. I want to reach out and fix the pieces he messes up.

"You can't just say whatever you want and expect it not to hurt."

He's right, of course. He's always right. "I know. I'm sorry."

"I'm not over it," he says. "But I just want to know that you're okay."

I smile a little. He still cares.

"I'm okay."

Leo nods. "Did . . ." He hesitates, clearly uncomfortable. "Did anything happen?"

"No." I pause, debating whether to tell him the whole

truth. The last time I almost kissed Ethan, he was *not* happy about it—and that was when we were still speaking. But I don't want to lie to him.

"I mean—he tried to, um. He tried to kiss me, but I didn't . . ." I sigh. "It wasn't right."

He looks at me, his hazel eyes wary.

"It wasn't right," he repeats.

"Yeah. I didn't go through with it."

Suddenly a girl turns the corner. Gabrielle Micco, a sophomore.

"Excuse me, Gabrielle?" I call out, grateful for the interruption. "Can I ask you a question for the *Grizzly*?"

I do the short interview—*what's your favorite memory from this school year and why? What are you looking forward to most next year*—and jot down her answers in my notepad. After Leo takes her picture, she walks off, and I wait until she's a safe distance away before daring to look Leo in the eye.

"So you and Ethan . . . ," he says when we start walking again.

I wince. I've tried to mentally block out the minutes after I emerged from Ethan's bathroom on Saturday night, but unfortunately, I think they'll haunt me forever. The confused, slightly offended look on his face, still reeling from the fact that I ran away. The moment the offense turned to irritation when I said I wasn't feeling well and needed to go home. He knew I was lying, but he didn't bother to call me out on it. There was no point. We both knew it was already over.

"I don't think he'll be waiting by my locker any time soon, if that's what you mean."

I had hoped this news might excite him—after all, he hasn't exactly been on board the Ethan train—but the expression on his face gives nothing away. It's like he doesn't feel anything at all.

"Sorry," he says after a while. It doesn't really sound like he means it.

"I'm not," I reply. "It's for the best. He never really felt like home."

Leo nods. This, at least, he understands.

New post from AnaStaysDreaming

Tuesday, May 13, 9:00 a.m.

Talk to Me Tuesday

Anonymous asked: Lately everything feels terrible. My parents are getting a divorce, the guy I like doesn't like me back, and I'm finishing the school year with a C average. Plus all my friends are going on great summer vacations, while I'm stuck at home (or should I say at homes, plural). I just feel like there's nothing to look forward to, and I'm going to be stuck in this bad feeling forever. Please help!

Rainy Days and Tuesdays

AnaStaysDreaming: Dear Rainy Days and Tuesdays,

I know I've been bragging about how great my life is, but believe me, it hasn't always been that way. If there's one thing I've learned on the side where the grass isn't greener, it's that everything is temporary—especially feelings. Right now it seems like the end of the world, but one day, you'll be laughing with your bestie about something completely arbitrary. It will be the kind of laughter that knocks you over, the kind that comes out in gasps and squeaks because you're laughing so hard you can't breathe. And then, suddenly, life will feel like living again. Wait for that day. I promise it will be worth it.

Tuesday, May 13, 10:00 a.m.

Anonymous asked: Hi Anastasia,

How do you know that Miles is the one?

Becca

AnaStaysDreaming: Dear Becca,

You're not supposed to sign your real name! Kinda ruins the whole "anonymous" thing.

To answer your question, I don't know that he's the one. I just know that for now, he makes me happy, and that's enough.

Tuesday, May 13, 11:00 a.m.

Anonymous asked: I've gotta know, how is Leo doing post-breakup? Is he ready for a new lady in his life?? If yes, maybe you could pass on my phone number?

Yours truly, Leo's Lady

AnaStaysDreaming: Dear Leo's Lady,

I've received approximately 876,437,820 questions like this. Get in line!

He's doing well. We're closer than ever. I'm so happy to have my friend back.

Chapter 25

I'm at the top of the Empire State Building, watching the sun set over the Hudson River. It reflects off the skyscrapers, sends sparkling ripples over the water. Everything is cast in golden light. A warm breeze blows my hair into my face. When I brush it away, I see Leo walking toward me.

You're here, I say, amazed.

He smiles. His long brown hair is held back by his green baseball cap, his hazel eyes like sunlight through amber. He reaches for my face, tucks a strand of hair behind my ear.

Hello, gorgeous.

My smile fades. It's Leo's mouth that's moving, but the voice that comes out isn't his. It's Ethan's.

Leo's hand cradles the back of my neck. He's looking at me like he wants to kiss me, and a tingle of excitement rushes down my spine.

This is so romantic, I say. *But what about Brynn?*

There is no Brynn, he says in Ethan's voice. He leans forward, closing the gap between us. *There's only you.*

Only me. I close my eyes, bask in the glory of the golden sun and being Leo's chosen one. *Finally.* I raise my lips, expecting to feel the soft warmth of his mouth on mine, but there's nothing. Only air.

Anastasia, Ethan's voice says.

I open my eyes. Leo's mouth is inches from mine.

I'm Jane, I tell him, feeling desperate all of a sudden.

Anastasia, Leo whispers again. *Kiss me.*

I open my eyes, jerked awake by the bus going over a pothole.

"Ow." I put my hand on the side of my head where it smacked against the window.

"Good morning, sunshine!" Camila says in the seat next to me. She points out the window. "Look!"

I follow her finger. There, in the distance, is the Manhattan skyline. It's a cloudy day, casting the whole thing in an eerie sort of fog. My eyes land on the Empire State Building, and my stomach flips.

I tear my eyes from the city and look behind me, across the aisle. Leo is sitting by the window, scrolling his phone. Brynn's in the seat next to him, her head on his shoulder, her eyes closed.

"The mandrill monkey's nose is red," I say, reading the answer off my phone and scribbling it on the worksheet. "And that's the last question! Now we can go."

"But we didn't actually see it," Camila argues in front of a dinosaur fossil. "What if the one they have in the museum has a different color nose?"

"They all have red noses," I say, looking at my phone. "According to the internet."

Before we got off the bus, Mr. McCarville gave us all a worksheet with a scavenger hunt for the American Museum of Natural History. "To make learning fun!" he said when someone asked why, although I suspect the real reason is to ensure we actually spend some time in the museum. Some of the questions require you to physically be there—*what is the allosaurus eating? List five insects on display in the Extinct and Endangered exhibit*—but the rest can easily be looked up on the internet. By the time I write the answer to the last question, it's not even noon.

"Nice work. Should we go get some lunch?" Mom says. "I'd love a New York slice."

"*Mom.* Try not to sound like such a tourist."

She raises her eyebrows at me. "But I am a tourist."

"Yeah, Charli," Ava says. "Don't be so *uncool*."

My mom and Ava exchange a glance and then burst out laughing. I roll my eyes.

"Do we have to leave so soon?" Brynn says, her eyes scanning the map. "I kind of wanted to see the Hall of Ocean Life. Oh! And the Hall of North American Birds."

"I'm fine skipping the birds," Leo says.

Brynn looks at him curiously. "Why? Do you have something against birds?"

I can't help but laugh. "Seriously? Leo is terrified of birds."

Leo frowns at me. "'Terrified' is a strong word."

"You are?" Brynn says. "Since when?"

"Since always," I say, without thinking. "Where have you been?"

Something like annoyance flickers across Brynn's face. Leo must recognize it too, because he reaches for her hand and gives it a squeeze of reassurance. I look away.

It's still unclear where Leo and I stand. Since our conversation in the hallway on Monday, he hasn't been quite as hostile. He doesn't actively avoid me in the newsroom anymore, and once, he even asked me a question about grammar. But that's as far as it goes. I wish he would just yell at me and get it over with, because at least then we could talk it out and move forward. Instead, we're stuck in friendship limbo.

"Maybe we could all go get some lunch and then come back?" Ava says. "Is that allowed?"

"I think so," Camila says. "As long as we hang onto our tickets."

"Okay," Brynn says, still holding Leo's hand. "Sounds great to me."

I do my best to hide my scowl, but Camila catches it.

"Deep breaths," she says, low enough that only I can hear. She knows how much this hurts.

The six of us leave the museum and regroup on the sidewalk out front. The clouds have finally cleared, revealing a blue sky and a bright, beautiful sun. I pull out my phone, take a picture of a taxi driving by, and smile. *This* is the New York I've been waiting for.

People start googling places to eat—the search bar on my mom's phone reads *NY slice near me*—but I don't need to search. I already know where I want to go.

"There's this really cute French place that's known for its macarons," I say. "But they also serve lunch, and I've been dying to go."

"This one, in SoHo?" Brynn says, turning her phone toward me.

"That's it." I grin. "Apparently the pastries are amazing."

"Works for me," Camila says. "I'm starving."

"SoHo is pretty far from here," Ava says. She comes to New York sometimes for work and is more acquainted with the city than any of us. "I'm not sure it's smart for us to go all the way down there."

"Please, Ava?" I beg. "It will be worth it, I promise."

"According to Maps, there's another location," Brynn says. "At Columbus Circle. That's closer, right?"

Ava agrees, and I'm so relieved, I could hug Brynn. So relieved, in fact, that I don't even bother to question why she's trying to help me. All I can think of are the photos I'll be able to take for *AnaStaysDreaming*: the pretty pastel decor, fancy food with French names, and, of course, the macaron tower the place is famous for. They'll perfectly match the aesthetic of my page—the aesthetic of my dreams. A post like this could be just the boost the blog needs.

Just the boost *I* need.

My excitement dims. Admittedly, since everything that

happened with Ethan, Anastasia's life seems a little less dreamy than it used to. All week I've had writer's block. Every time I sit down to write, I just stare at the blinking cursor until my mind inevitably drifts toward Leo, and then I exit out of the draft and post a stock photo of flowers or the city skyline instead. I didn't even post *anything* yesterday, which is the first time I've done that since . . . well, since I started the blog two years ago.

I know I need to make a change—but what kind of change? Maybe Anastasia and Miles should break up. Then again, I'm not even sure that would fix the problem. I don't know what would.

"Great. Let's go!" I take a few steps down the sidewalk and then stop, look back at the rest of the group. "Uh. Does anyone know how to use the subway?"

Half an hour later, we're in a mall on the second floor, standing in front of what appears to be a pistachio-colored cart kiosk. A janitor in uniform is mopping the white floor tile in front of it.

"I thought it was a restaurant?" Mom says.

"It is," I say. "It's *supposed* to be. The SoHo location has a dining room."

"Hey, they've still got macarons." Camila points at the signature macaron tower displayed on the counter. "And croissants."

I turn to Brynn, my tone accusatory. "Did you not notice this was just a kiosk when you looked it up?"

"It didn't say." Brynn pulls out her phone again. "It just

says the name and—oh." She grimaces. "I guess I should've looked at the pictures."

I put a hand on my hip. "Ya think?"

"It's not her fault," Leo says. "It's an honest mistake."

I roll my eyes. How many times has Leo used that line to defend Brynn's shady actions? Next to me, Mom's stomach growls loudly. "Whoops," she says with a giggle.

"This actually works out," Ava says. "Jane can get her macarons, and then we can go find some pizza for Charli. We could even eat in Central Park, wouldn't that be fun?"

Mom gasps. "Like they do in *When Harry Met Sally!*"

"It's not just about the macarons," I argue. "It's about the experience. The *ambiance*."

"The park has plenty of ambiance," Ava says. "Tree-lined paths, a boathouse, a lake—"

I groan. I know a lost cause when I see one. "Fine."

Mom gives me her credit card, and Camila and I walk up to the kiosk, careful to avoid the WET FLOOR sign and the area around it. I smile at the woman behind the counter and examine the macarons behind the glass.

"Oh my gosh, this is so exciting," I say to Camila. "Okay. Should I pick out specific flavors, or go with the variety pack?"

She doesn't reply. I turn around. She's texting on her phone, not paying me any attention.

"Hellooo," I say, and she looks up. "Which ones should I get?"

"Sorry." She pockets her phone and joins me by the glass. "Umm, the pink ones are pretty. I like the blue ones too."

"I think I'll just do the variety pack," I say to the woman behind the counter. "Cami, are you getting anything?"

She shakes her head. "Nothing for me."

"Really? I thought you were starving."

"I am, but I'm going to save my appetite for lunch."

"It's just pizza," I say, watching the woman place a pastel rainbow of macarons in a pretty green box. Would it be rude to take a picture? "It's not going to be anything special."

"Actually . . ." Camila gives me a guilty look. "Some girls from the squad invited me to go to Bubba Gump's in Times Square."

I snap out of macaron heaven to stare at her, dumbstruck.

"But you're not going, right? We have a whole day planned."

"It's just lunch," she says quickly. "I'd go with them for a couple hours, and then I'll meet back up with you guys at the museum."

My mouth hangs open. I can't believe what I'm hearing. "Cami, come *on*. When's the last time we spent the whole day together without cheerleading getting in the way?"

A crease appears between her perfectly arched eyebrows. "Getting in the way? They're my friends too, Jane."

"Clearly," I mutter. "You're always with them. You're *never* around anymore."

She crosses her arms. "That's not true."

"It is true. Even Leo thinks so."

She looks taken aback. "You've talked about this with Leo?"

"Cami, every time the three of us hang out, you're either

late, or you cancel last minute. It would be impossible *not* to talk about it."

She presses her lips together. "Wow. Okay. I didn't know you felt this way."

"How could you know?" I sort of snap. "You're never around!"

"I'm *sorry*," she says, her voice firm. "It's really hard to juggle school, and the squad, and still hang out every single weekend like nothing has changed. I'm doing the best I can."

"Well it doesn't feel like it." I grab the butter charm around my neck and hang on like a lifeline. "It feels like our friendship isn't a priority anymore."

Camila's dark eyes quickly go glossy. "How can you say that?"

Out of the corner of my eye, I see that the woman has finished boxing up the macarons and is waiting, awkwardly, for me to acknowledge her. I smile apologetically and give her Mom's credit card.

"Of course I care about our friendship," Cami says, clearly trying not to cry. "But I have other responsibilities too. We're not ten years old anymore."

"Oh really? It's your *responsibility* to go to Bubba Gump's and get some coconut shrimp?"

A single tear falls down her cheek. She quickly wipes it away. "You know what? You say I'm not making our friendship a priority, but I could say the same thing about you."

"*How?*"

Another tear falls. This time, she doesn't bother to wipe

it away. "I feel overwhelmed a lot of the time, spread so thin trying to make everyone happy, but you have no idea. Nothing I do is ever good enough."

I open my mouth to reply, but no words come out. *You're right*, I'm tempted to say. *It's not.*

"You never want to make the best of the time we *do* spend together. You're always in your head, absorbed by your own problems." She holds up a hand and starts counting on her fingers. "It's your love triangle with Ethan and Leo, or how annoying Jeremiah is, or how you wish Brynn never moved here, or *your* macarons. You never ask how I'm doing, or what's going on with me."

I glance over at the others, worried they're listening, but they aren't paying us any attention. Mom is leaning over Ava's shoulder, both of them engrossed in something on her phone, while Leo takes Brynn's picture as she poses in front of a clothing store's window display. The only one who notices something is up is the janitor. He's paused his mopping to watch us.

"Friendship is a give-and-take, but all you do is *take*. You take everything I have to give, and it's still not enough." Camila pauses, steeling herself. "And I'm tired of it. I'm tired of feeling like I'm not enough for my best friend."

My face feels hot with anger and shame. I can't believe she's saying these things to me now, when *she's* the one who wants to leave. Doesn't she know you can't give *or* take in a friendship when one of you is never around?

"Same here," I say.

The woman behind the kiosk clears her throat loudly. I turn to her, suddenly remembering that she's there.

"I'm so sorry." I take the box of macarons. "Thanks."

"Receipt?"

"No thanks."

She doesn't say anything, she simply frowns at me and then goes back to reading her magazine.

"You know what I think?" Camila says, wiping her cheeks. "I think you're jealous. I've got new friends, and I'm finding my place, and you can't stand it, because it's separate from you."

"You're *so* right, Cami," I say, my voice dripping with sarcasm. "I'm so jealous that I don't get to wave pom-poms around and yell 'rah rah rah' while everybody objectifies me."

She laughs coldly. "You can mock cheerleading all you want, but I know the truth. You're against anything that doesn't fit in with your plan of how you think my life should be. Because everything always, *always* has to be about you!"

"God, just *go!*" I tell her, gesturing wildly with the box. "Go to Bubba Gump's with your new best friends and their PTA moms, since that's where you really want to be."

"Fine," she says. "I will."

She reaches into her bag for a tissue. She wipes under her eyes, then her nose. When she's composed herself, she says, "They're meeting me here. I'm going to tell your mom."

She turns and walks off. It's only then that my guard falls down, my eyes well up. This isn't how this was supposed to go. We were supposed to eat macarons, stroll cobblestone streets, wander into bookstores and record shops. Leo, Cami, and me, together again, and *happy*, like old times. Instead, they're both mad at me. How did this happen? It's uncharted territory.

I start to follow her when the woman behind the kiosk calls out to me.

"Miss? Your credit card."

I spin around and take a step, but the floor here is wet and slippery. It doesn't help that the ballet flats I chose to wear today have basically no grip on the bottom. Instead of my foot landing firmly on the floor, it slides forward, hurtling me toward the kiosk. I hold out my arms to steady myself, but the force rocks my body forward, sending me face-first into the tower of macarons. They come crashing down all over the kiosk, skid across the freshly mopped floor. The woman behind the counter shouts something in French and jumps out of the way.

When I regain my balance, I look up. Everybody in this section of the mall is silent, staring at me.

That's when a flash goes off to my right. I follow the source of the light to find Leo's camera pointed right at me.

The flash goes off again. When he pulls the camera away from his face, I can tell he's laughing. It's a shocking sight that sends ripples of relief through my whole body. I don't even care that he's laughing *at* me. It's the first time in weeks I've made him smile, and I missed this feeling terribly. Before I know it, I've forgotten all about feeling sad or mad or embarrassed. With tears still in my eyes, I look at Leo, and I start to laugh.

Chapter 26

"This is the best pizza I've ever tasted!"

Mom practically moans when she takes a bite, much to my dismay. The five of us are seated at a picnic table in Central Park, gathered around an extra-large box of pepperoni pizza. The slices are thin but massive—when Mom holds hers up for Ava to take a picture, it's almost the same size as her head.

"Have you ever had deep dish?" Leo asks her. Roman is from Chicago, so deep dish is practically part of his ancestry.

"Once," Mom says. "But it's not the same. It feels more like you're eating lasagna than pizza."

He raises his eyebrows. "That's a hot take."

"Not in New York City," I add. Leo doesn't reply, just folds his slice in half and takes a big bite. I look down at my paper plate, feeling uneasy. The moment we shared in the mall already feels like a thousand miles away.

A chirping bird in the tree above us catches my attention. The cloudy morning gave way to a gorgeous and sunny afternoon, and the park is so serene, it almost seems fake. All around us people lie on blankets, reading books or bathing in the sun. Tulips bloom brightly in bushels of reds, pinks, and yellows; the trees are lush and green; and behind them, skyscrapers loom above the leaves like a majestic movie backdrop. If I wasn't so busy being miserable about Camila and Leo, this would be a dream-come-true moment. I pull out my phone and take a few pictures anyway. If the picture is perfect, it's easier to pretend everything else is too.

"It's too bad Cami isn't here to see this," Mom says. "She'd love it."

"I can't believe she wanted to go to Times Square," Ava adds. "Doesn't she get nervous in big crowds?"

"Yeah," Leo says. "But it's a team bonding thing. She probably felt like she had to go or else she'd get FOMO."

"FOMO?" Mom says.

"Fear of missing out," Brynn explains.

"God forbid Busy Izzy misses one team bonding activity," I mutter into my pizza.

"What did you say?" Brynn asks.

My chest tightens as I realize my mistake.

"Oh." I keep my voice casual, try to play it cool despite my colossal slip of the tongue. "Nothing."

I glance at Brynn, my heart racing, and try to gauge how much she really heard, but she just keeps chewing her pizza. Her face gives nothing away.

"I understand that," Mom says. "So where to after this? We have a little time before we have to get back to the museum."

I relax a little. Mom is right next to me and she didn't hear me—or she's choosing to ignore me.

"We could go to Levain Bakery for something sweet," I say, grateful for the change of subject. "It's not far from the museum."

"Why don't we walk to the water?" Leo says, not quite looking at me. "I'd like to take some pictures of the boathouse."

"Yeah, that'll be great for the article," Brynn says.

"Oh, what article?" Mom looks at me. "Are you girls working on something together again?"

"No," I say.

Brynn smiles at her. "It's just me. I told Jane we could write it together, but she didn't want to."

Mom looks at me with surprise. "Why not? You love New York."

I look up at the bird again, telepathically begging it to swoop down, snatch me up, and carry me away.

"Because she has too much pride," Leo says.

I tear my eyes from the bird to look at him.

"They had a contest to see who would write it, and she lost," he continues. "And instead of being mature and taking Brynn up on her offer, she said no. So now she's stuck writing some fluff piece that's way beneath her."

"Leo," Ava chastises. "That's not very nice."

"It has nothing to do with maturity," I say to him. "I wanted to earn it. I didn't *want* her charity."

"She was being nice," Leo said. "And you were being immature."

"*She's* right here," Brynn says quietly.

"God, how long are you going to punish me?" I say to Leo. "I told you I'm sorry about what I said."

"What did you say?" Mom asks.

"I'm not punishing you," he replies. "I'm just telling it like it is."

Out of the corner of my eye, I see Mom and Ava exchange a glance.

"Right," I say, thinking of the kiss he shared with Brynn. "Because you're *so* honest."

Leo makes a face. "What does that mean?"

"Okay, you two," Ava says. "That's enough."

"Leo," Brynn says. "Do you want my crust?"

He shakes his head, his eyes still locked on me.

"You tell me what I mean," I say. "Mr. *Tell It Like It Is*."

"Jane, knock it off," Mom says. "Now, this is ridiculous. You two love each other. Whatever's going on between you, just let it go."

Brynn gets up from the table with her crust in her hand. She walks over to where a pair of pigeons are pecking at the grass, rips the end of her crust into a few tiny pieces, and tosses it to them.

"I'm trying to let it go," I say. "He's the one with the problem."

"Yeah, you're clearly not holding on to anything."

Two more pigeons land by Brynn's feet. She tosses more crust.

"You're the one holding on to something!" I remind him.

"*What?* Jeez, just say it."

I raise an eyebrow. Game on. "Fine. Play any tonsil hockey lately?"

His expression goes slack with surprise.

"Jane Elizabeth Scott!" Mom says. "Don't say that."

"I was just wondering," I continue. "Since you didn't tell me that you kissed Brynn."

Ava's eyes widen. "You did?"

Leo glances at his mom, mortified, and I immediately regret spilling the secret in front of her. If Leo was mad at me before, there's no telling how furious he'll be now.

"Why would I tell you?" he says. "It's none of your business."

"You certainly made it your business when I almost kissed Ethan."

Mom's jaw drops. "You almost kissed that boy?"

"That's different," Leo says, but his voice falters a little. "I didn't want you to make a mistake."

"Well maybe I didn't want *you* to make a mistake—ever think of that?"

Brynn walks back to the table, a tense smile on her face. She doesn't have any more crust—she must have fed it all to the birds.

"Let's go for a walk," Ava says, her voice forcefully bright. "The boathouse isn't far, we can—"

She's interrupted by Leo's bloodcurdling scream. Two pigeons have landed on the table in front of him, next to his half-eaten slice of pizza. A third bird, a tiny sparrow, perches on his arm. He thrusts himself back, falling off the bench and onto the grass and sending the sparrow flying.

The walk to the lake feels long. Leo and Brynn are in front, and as far as I can tell—I'm about twenty paces behind—they aren't saying much. I, on the other hand, am walking with Ava and my mom, who won't stop yapping. They spend most of the trip grilling me for details about what's going on with me and Leo. *How long have you two been fighting? What did you say that made him mad? When did he kiss Brynn?* They don't seem mad so much as concerned, and if I'm being honest, a little intrigued by the drama of it all. It makes me feel bad all over again for bringing up the kiss. Then again, he started it by calling me immature.

And no, that doesn't prove his point. It's just a fact.

"You're going to have to talk about this again," Ava says. "There's still too much tension."

"And sooner is better," Mom adds. "The longer you put it off, the more it will fester, and the worse it will be. We've got the beach trip next month, remember?"

"Leo is sensitive," Ava says. "He latches onto things and lets them turn into this giant storm cloud above his head—"

"I know," I grumble.

"It's because he really cares," Mom finishes. "That's obviously why he's so upset now."

"Did you hear him? *I didn't want you to make a mistake.*" Ava gives my mom a knowing look.

"Oh, I heard him." They share a conspiratorial smirk.

I let out a groan. "Can you guys *please* stay out of it?"

"We are staying out of it," Mom says. "We're just giving you a little perspective."

"And reminding you that your friendship is stronger than some silly feud," Ava adds.

I resist the urge to roll my eyes. Ava and my mom are biased—they have a vested interest in us working things out, after all—but it doesn't mean they're wrong. Leo and I have been through so much together. If one little fight can break us, what does that say about our friendship as a whole?

We take a left down a winding path and, finally, come upon the lake. It's bigger than I thought it would be, though I guess I shouldn't be surprised. Central Park, in general, is much larger than I ever realized. There's a bridge up ahead, and Leo and Brynn are already making their way toward it. I quicken my pace to catch up to them.

"Right in the center." Leo is calling out to Brynn, who's posing a few yards away. He's got his camera in one hand and is directing her with the other. "Yeah. No—a little to the left. Put your hand on the railing."

"Hey."

He doesn't look at me. He puts his camera to his eye, takes a couple test shots.

"I shouldn't have said that in front of our moms. I'm sorry."

"Lift your chin a little," he calls out to Brynn. Then he lowers his voice and says, "I'm getting really tired of your apologies."

"Me too. I'm no good at them."

He crouches down, turns the camera so the shot is vertical. "Look out at the water!" he says. Brynn does as she's told.

"I was hurt that you didn't tell me," I say. "I mean, I get it. It's none of my business. But a kiss is such a big thing."

"I sort of started to tell you." He pulls the camera away from his eye to check the photos. "At the cemetery."

I think back to that night—how tense he was, how uncertain. *Lately it feels like things are moving really fast. It's like I can't keep up.* I thought he was just nervous about being in his first relationship, but it was more than that. It was *earth-shattering*. And I told him it wasn't a big deal. *You're just dating to have fun. Who finds their soulmate at fifteen, anyway?*

I want to smack myself.

"But then . . . I don't know." He puts the camera in front of his face again. "It just felt weird. We don't really talk about that stuff."

"I know what you mean."

I shuffle my feet uncomfortably. For a second, I want to tell him everything. *I like you. I have this whole time. Don't be with Brynn. Be with me.* Out of the corner of my eye, I see my mom and Ava. They stop a safe distance away, as if they can sense the conversation we're having and want to give us some space, but it's enough to break the spell.

"We're going to have to start," I say instead. "I mean, what's the alternative? You find out I'm married when I change my last name on social media?"

He cracks a smile. "At least I wouldn't have to get all dressed up."

"I wouldn't make you wear a tie. I know you hate them."

He stands up. Brynn, still posing in the middle of the bridge, relaxes her chin.

"I've gotta get some close-ups," he says. For a second, it seems like he wants to say something else but then decides against it. He walks away.

I sigh, then glance at my mom and Ava. They give little smiles and waves of encouragement.

I follow Leo and Brynn to the center of the bridge. There are a few other people here, and none of them seem to care about the photo shoot happening nearby. If this were Brookhill, every passerby would stop and stare. A few might even ask what the photo shoot was for. That's just the magic of New York City, I guess. You can disappear in plain sight.

"That's good," Leo says into his camera. Brynn is smiling in front of the lake, her hair flowing in the breeze. "Now relax your face and look past me."

She makes the change effortlessly, and it occurs to me that she's good at this. Suddenly I understand why Leo likes photographing her so much.

Leo smiles. "Got it." He turns the camera and shows her.

"Wow." She grabs the camera and pulls it closer. "That's great."

"Not great," he says. "Beautiful."

The sincerity in his voice tears my heart in half. Any doubts he might have had about his feelings for Brynn are gone now, left by the mausoleum alongside whatever spark I thought I felt between us. Leo is happy with Brynn, that much is obvious. He's happier with her than he could ever be with me.

Brynn grins. "Let me take one of you."

"Me?" Leo blinks, surprised. "No, that's okay, I—"

"Yes." She pulls the camera out of his hands. I let out a little gasp. Leo never lets *anyone* hold his camera. It's his cardinal rule.

"Wow, it's heavy," she says, sounding surprised.

Leo's confliction is plain on his face. He runs a hand through his hair, ruffling it up.

"Okay," he says, relenting. He reaches forward and turns the knob on top. "It's on automatic now. Just point and shoot."

She backs up to the railing and puts the camera to her eye. "Take a couple steps back."

He does as she says. He puts his hands in the pockets of his denim jacket and looks at the camera without smiling.

"Hot," she says, snapping a few. I scrunch up my nose, even though she's right. With his stoic confidence and long hair blowing wild in the wind, Leo *is* hot.

Brynn checks the photos she took and smiles, pleased with herself. She holds the camera out to him.

"Come look."

Leo walks over to Brynn. He reaches for the camera at the same time it slips from her hand.

When terrible things happen, people sometimes say they

experience the events in slow motion. This isn't like that. It happens so fast that, for a moment, I wonder if it even happens at all.

Leo tries to catch the camera, but he ends up sort of smacking it instead. The force sends the camera over the railing and into the lake about ten feet below. When it hits the water, it barely makes a sound.

All the color drains from Leo's face. He leans over the railing to stare at the place where the camera disappeared.

Brynn puts her hands over her mouth. "Oh my gosh. Oh no."

Leo is silent. I watch him in horror, too afraid to move. I feel like if I move, it will make the moment real.

"What do we do?" Brynn says, her voice high pitched with panic. She looks over the railing. "Do you think we can get it out?"

Leo doesn't answer her. I think he's in shock.

"How?" I answer for him. "Unless you see a guy with a pool net."

Brynn looks frantically at me, then back down at the lake. Her eyes well with tears. "Oh, Leo," she says, and her voice cracks. "Oh no."

Finally, he looks at her.

"You're crying."

Brynn sniffles and wipes at her cheeks. As Leo watches her cry, he starts to come back to life. His expression goes from shock, to surprise, to disbelief, to the big one: rage.

"You're crying," he repeats, harsher this time. "I'm the one who just lost my camera and memory card *forever*, but you're crying."

"Well." Another sniffle. "I feel bad."

"You should feel bad!"

My eyes widen. I've known Leo for fifteen years, one month, and sixteen days, and I have *never* heard him yell. Leo yelling is like Mister Rogers yelling. It just doesn't happen.

"This is why I don't let people touch my camera," he continues, furious. "For situations *exactly* like this. You should never have taken it!"

Brynn's sniffles turn to sobs.

"Okay," I say, cautious. "She gets it."

"I'm sorry," she cries. "I'll help you buy a new one!"

"That camera goes for six hundred dollars. And that lens took me months to find on eBay." He runs a hand through his hair, frustrated. "And all those pictures . . ." He shakes his head in disbelief. Finally, he looks at me. I see past the anger immediately.

He's heartbroken.

"What's going on?" Ava comes rushing over. Mom is right beside her, looking at me.

I open my mouth, trying to find the words to explain. But before I get the chance, Brynn lets out another sob and runs off the bridge.

AnaStaysDreaming

Inbox (461)

Anonymous asked: Leo and I are done.

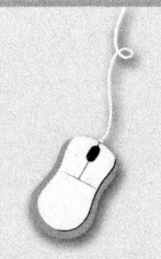

Chapter 27

A week goes by before I work up the courage to press reply on Brynn's message. I see it right away—Saturday, the day after the field trip. But for a while, I don't know what to say. The Central Park Bridge Incident, as Mom and I have taken to calling it, ends up being so catastrophic for everyone involved. No words are a strong enough salve.

Brynn and Leo break up on the bus back to school. I don't know the specifics, except that she breaks up with him. Apparently, she didn't like his reaction on the bridge. This is the explanation Leo offered to Ava, who told my mom, who told me. I didn't like his reaction either, but the difference is I understand it. That camera is—was—everything to Leo. It was as vital as an organ. Now that it's gone, he can't function properly.

They spend the next week avoiding each other in the newsroom. Brynn stays in my seat, but Leo moves to an empty desk on the other side of the room. That is, when he's even there at all. Most of the time he's doing damage control, out reshooting the photos he lost using one of the school's cameras, or in the back of the room, editing on a computer. No matter what, he's completely locked in, as if giving himself over completely to the task might lessen the blow of his loss.

The only silver lining of this whole mess is that Leo starts speaking to me again. "You know the worst part about losing my camera?" Leo says on Tuesday when we're both on the computers. It's so out of the blue that I look around first, to make sure it's me he's talking to.

"What?"

He keeps his eyes on the monitor. With a completely straight face, he says, "I lost those pictures of you falling into the macaron tower."

I laugh a little. "You could always take a picture of Mom's credit card bill. The proof is in the debt pudding."

"They're too epic to replace," he says with a small smile. "Even better than the shrimp hitting your eye, or the time you fell into Cami's pool with all your clothes on."

"Are you sure it was Brynn who dropped your camera, and not karmic justice?"

He glances toward Brynn, who's hunched over her desk, writing in a notebook, and his smile falls.

"Sorry," I say quickly. "Too soon."

"It's fine." He looks at me. "Gotta laugh about it sometime, I guess."

"I guess."

Neither of us actually laughs, but at least the air doesn't feel so heavy anymore.

Jane Stays Dreaming 269

My reconciliation with Leo comes at the perfect time, since Camila and I still aren't speaking. It's been radio silence since New York. I think we're both waiting for the other to be the first to cave.

Still, I keep hearing her voice in my head: *Friendship is a give-and-take, but all you do is take.* My initial reaction is indignance. Whenever I asked about her love life, or school, she always replied with vague indifference. It was only when I asked about cheerleading that she opened up, rambling on about choreography and stunts, which I never understood, and a dozen teammates whose names I could never remember. She thinks I don't care about her, but I *do*. I just don't care about cheerleading.

I say as much to Mom in the car, when she picks me up from school on Friday afternoon. I had to stay late to finish my assignment for the paper—a full-page spread featuring cutouts of students, mostly photographed by Leo, and their favorite memories quoted in speech bubbles above their heads. Despite being a puff piece, it was actually a ton of work.

"Did you ever consider that not caring about cheerleading might come off, to Cami, like not caring about her?"

"No," I say, switching through the radio stations. "Cami isn't cheerleading."

Mom makes a face like she disagrees. "Cheerleading is a huge part of her life. How would you like it if she checked out every time you started talking about the paper?"

"I wouldn't care," I say, though I'm not sure if that's true. I don't exactly have a point of reference. Cami has always been a good listener. When I want to vent about an annoying source, she's sympathetic. When there's tension among the staff because, say, Alec and Daria disagree about a music review, she's appropriately intrigued.

"But I've always been a writer," I argue, landing on the alternative rock station. "I wrote my first story in kindergarten."

"The one about the superhero basset hound," Mom recalls, a smile on her face.

"You remember?" I look at her, surprised.

"Of course. She used her big ears to fly, and her loud bark to scare away bad guys."

I sigh. "Cami never cared about cheerleading until this year. Now all of a sudden I'm supposed to act like it's the biggest deal in the world?"

"That's friendship," Mom says. "Learning how to grow together when things change."

I look out the window, letting her words sink in.

The next day, Saturday, I know Camila has a cheerleading competition in Cherry, a couple of hours away. I send her a text in the evening.

Jane: How was the competition?

I watch the dots appear, then disappear. When they don't come back, I lock my phone and return my attention to Netzine. A minute later, my phone vibrates with a new text message.

Camila: Fine. We came in third

I let out a breath. Progress.

Jane: Did you land the back handspring?

Camila: Yep

Jane: Awesome

Jane: I can't wait to hear more!

I watch the screen, waiting for more dots, but they don't come. Twenty minutes later, she sends me the invitation to her pool party on the last day of school. An olive branch. All hope isn't lost.

Meanwhile, Anastasia's inbox is overflowing. Between all the drama with Leo and Camila, working on the *Grizzly*'s end-of-year issue, and my ongoing battle with writer's block, I've been majorly slacking. I managed to write a detailed entry about Ana's New York City date with Miles, pictures included, but I missed this week's Talk to Me Tuesday. I just don't have the energy to take on anybody else's problems.

It doesn't help that every time I open my inbox I see Brynn's message. I've tried to answer a few times—to tell her that it's not such a big deal, they were only together for like a month, just move *on*—and every time, I picture Brynn's devastated, tearstained face on the bridge, and I second-guess myself.

Since the first day I met her, I've been blaming Brynn for all my problems. Sure, some of that blame was deserved—she purposely didn't hold the door for me, and that's a hill I'll die on—but most of it was projection. My feelings were never really about Brynn at all. Hating her was just easier than admitting the truth to myself—that I love Leo. And now that I *have* admitted it, there doesn't seem to be much of a reason to hate her anymore.

Lying on the bed next to me, Maggie lets out a heavy sigh.

"I know," I say, scratching her behind the ears. I told myself I needed to protect Leo from Brynn, but I was wrong. Actually, I was lying. The only person I ever cared about protecting was me.

I *am* selfish.

I roll my shoulders back and look at my laptop screen, a new sense of determination settling inside me. Just because things are broken doesn't mean they can't be put back together again. I haven't done right by Brynn in the past, but I can still redeem myself. It's not too late.

All I have to do is follow my instincts, put my feelings for Leo aside, and finally write the truth.

New post from AnaStaysDreaming

Saturday, May 24, 8:49 p.m.

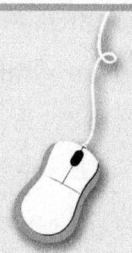

AnaStaysDreaming: Dear New Girl,

You didn't sign your name, but I know it's you. Maybe it's because I feel connected to you, or maybe it's because there's nobody else in my inbox writing about their (ex) boyfriend named Leo. Either way, I feel your pain, and I'm very sorry I left you in the lurch for so long. I hope you aren't too angry at me.

I've been waiting to respond until I felt like I had something insightful to say, but as it turns out, sometimes there are no words. Breakups happen, and they hurt. Nothing I can say will make that less true.

You didn't share the specifics of your breakup with me, so I'm guessing you don't want to talk about it. Or maybe you just don't want to talk about it with me. If that's the case, I understand. I haven't been a good friend to you. I indulged your questions when they benefitted me and my readers, and then abandoned you when you needed me most. In short: I was selfish. If it makes you feel any better (it might not), my silence wasn't about you. It was about me.

I know it might seem like I have it all together, but I don't. There's a lot going on in my life that nobody knows. That's the beauty and terror of the internet. It's too easy to hide behind, sometimes.

If you *are* looking for some words of wisdom, you might want to take a look at <u>this post</u> from April 8, from a reader looking for advice on how to heal a broken heart. Maybe you'll find it helpful.

xo,
Anastasia

Chapter 28

On Monday, the final issue of the Grizzly is almost ready to go to print.

"These margins don't look right," Halle says, standing over me at the computer, where I've got the center spread open in InDesign. "Are you sure they're half an inch?"

I click into the margins to double-check. "Yep. Half an inch all around."

"Hmm." She cocks her head. "Something is off. But what?"

"It could be the font," I say. "We went half a point smaller than usual to get all the speech bubbles to fit."

She nods, never taking her eyes off the screen. "Yeah. I think you're right."

"Daria said it was fine," I tell her. "But I can try to rework the spacing if you think it's hard to read."

"No, no," Halle says. "Making the font bigger will just crowd everything else. We'll leave it as is."

"Got it."

"Everybody," Halle raises her voice. "Double-check your

margins. This issue is our swan song, people! We don't want to look like amateurs."

I look at Leo, seated at a computer across from me. He meets my gaze with a smile.

Halle has been freaking out all day. I learned recently that she's a finalist for the Pennsylvania Leadership Award in Student Journalism. First place gets a cash prize, along with a summer internship at a major newspaper. If all goes well with this issue, she could win.

"Alec," Halle says, locking in on his entertainment spread two screens down. "That does not look like an eleven-point starting line."

I make sure she's fully occupied before I minimize InDesign and open up my incognito tab. I'm logged into Netzine, scheduling tomorrow's posts for Talk to Me Tuesday. I still don't feel like doing it, but I can't miss two weeks in a row without facing the wrath of my followers. I tried to make it easy on myself: I decided to do a theme, so all the questions I'm answering are related to the end of the school year. We've got graduation anxiety, someone whose boyfriend is going abroad for the summer, a girl who's moving schools, someone searching for the perfect bikini—

"Jane."

I minimize the tab, look up. Brynn is standing there with a proof page in her hand.

She gestures to the empty chair behind me. Leo was sitting there earlier, helping me fine-tune the edges on the cutout student photos. "Can I sit?"

"Yeah," I say. "You don't have to ask."

She smiles a little uncomfortably and sits down. I glance at Leo—or, where Leo was. All of a sudden, he's nowhere to be found.

"I was kind of hoping you'd look this over for me?" She holds out the proof page. "Since, you know. You were there."

I take the proof. It's one of the opinion pages. At the top of the page, the headline of Brynn's New York City article: *I Heart(break) New York: How my dreamy NYC day ended in disaster.*

I look up, stunned. "You're writing about the breakup?"

"Well." She shrugs. "It was a defining part of my trip."

"Yeah . . . but aren't you supposed to write about, like, the history museum?"

"That's in there." She points to a paragraph about halfway through.

I hesitate. Just a brief glance at this article tells me it will be completely humiliating for Leo. There's no way Halle will let it go to print. How did Brynn even get it this far?

I put the proof page down on the table and spin in my chair to look at her directly.

"I'm not sure this is a good idea."

If Brynn is surprised by my reaction, she doesn't show it. Her expression is distant—devoid of any real emotion. I didn't realize it until now, but she's angry.

Really angry.

"It's just . . ." I smile to show her that I'm not trying to be judgmental. It probably comes out more like a grimace. "It's kind of mean."

She raises an eyebrow. "You don't think he was mean to me? When he *yelled* at me?"

"No, I mean, he definitely shouldn't have done that," I say. "But he didn't *mean* it. He was upset, you know? He wasn't thinking. But this—" I gesture to the article. "This required a lot of thought."

"The assignment was to write about my trip from an interesting angle," she says. "Don't you think this is an interesting angle?"

I frown. An article like this would definitely generate clicks on the website. But at what cost?

"Brynn."

"Jane."

"Don't you think this is going a little far?" I say. "This article would destroy him."

She leans back, crosses her arms. There's something hardened about her, like this whole ordeal wore away her sweet-as-pie exterior to its rotten core. While most of me feels bad for her, the tiniest part feels justified, like I knew it all along.

"I wrote the truth."

"You wrote your opinion," I correct. "He'd probably tell it differently."

"Yeah," she says, like it's obvious. "Good thing I'm writing the article and not him."

I stare at her in disbelief.

"Well . . . did you even run it past Halle?"

She purses her lips, looks away. "Most of it."

I nod. That's what I thought. "You know she's not going to approve this."

For a while, her gaze stays fixed on the proof page. When she looks back at me, her eyes are watery.

I sigh, softening. "Listen. I know you're mad at him. And I know you're really hurt. But publishing this isn't going to make you feel better." My mind flashes to *AnaStaysDreaming*. I'm hit with a wave of guilt. "Trust me."

Halle appears, seemingly out of nowhere. She looks frazzled. "Brynn, what's the status of your op-ed?"

Brynn looks at me, panicked.

"It needs more work," I answer for her. "It'll be ready soon."

"What?" She reaches over me to pick up the proof page. "But I approved it."

Her eyes start skimming the article. They narrow, then widen. She looks at Brynn.

"What is this?"

Brynn's mouth opens and closes a couple times, like a fish. "It's my—"

"This is *not* your article." She tosses the proof down on the table. "Put it back the way it was. Now." At first, it seems like she's going to walk away. But then she sighs, shakes her head. "Why did you do this? You *know* the paper is due at the printer today, and this is a really irresponsible—"

The bell rings, seeming to surprise all three of us. Around

the room, everybody starts packing up. I spot Leo, standing at his new desk across the room.

"*Ugh.*" Halle puts her hands on her cheeks. "Okay. Brynn, come back at the end of the day. Expect to stay late."

"But—"

"No." Halle cuts her off. "We *have* to send all the pages in by four. There is nothing more important than this."

Brynn presses her lips together, nods. As she does, a single tear falls down her cheek. She wipes it away.

I quickly save my center spread into its correct file on the computer and exit out of InDesign. I pack up my tote bag, stand up. Brynn is still sitting down.

"You okay?" I ask her.

Brynn tries to smile, but the effort is weak. "Sure."

I glance around the room. Besides Halle and a couple of other stragglers, all the staff is gone.

"Are you coming?" I say. "We could walk together."

She shakes her head. "I have lunch next period. I'm just going to stay and fix this now."

"Okay." I start to walk away.

"Hey, Jane?"

I look back. This time, her smile is a bit more convincing.

"Thanks. For talking to me."

I nod, smile back. "Any time."

The last thing I see before I walk out the door is Brynn taking my seat at the computer.

Chapter 29

Jeremiah is running late.

"Hurry up!" I say as he walks out the front door. I've been leaning against the passenger side of his truck for ten minutes, scrolling my phone and waiting for him to grace me with his presence. "It's seven thirty-five!"

He cuts across the front yard, making no effort to quicken his pace. He points the key at the truck, unlocks it.

"Finally," I mutter, picking up my tote bag. I swing open the door and climb inside.

"Dude, chill," Jeremiah says when he gets in the driver's seat. "It's the last week of school. Who cares if you're a couple minutes late?"

"It's distribution day for the *Grizzly*. I wanted to get there a little early so I could see how it's going."

He puts the key in the ignition and starts the engine. "Fine. I'll speed."

"Don't," I say, my voice firm. "There's no point. I won't have time."

He backs the truck out of the driveway, and we're off.

By the time he pulls into his parking spot seven minutes later, the student parking lot is mostly empty. I have three minutes to get to homeroom before the bell.

"Great," I say, barely waiting for him to put the truck in park before I open the door. "I have to run. Literally."

"Exercise is good for you."

I roll my eyes and get out of the car.

The halls, like the parking lot, are mostly empty. I pass a few people standing at their lockers and lingering in doorways, the new issue of the *Grizzly* already in their hands. Every time, they look up from their papers and watch me as I hurry past them.

I get to homeroom just in time—ten seconds before the bell. When I walk in the door, I'm breathing hard. Everybody turns to look at me. I ignore their eyes as I cross the room and sit down at my desk, where there's already an issue of the *Grizzly* waiting for me.

The bell rings. I put down my bag, pull out my day planner. I double-check my Tuesday tasks, just to make sure there's nothing I missed. When I look up from the planner, the girls at the desks across from me are glancing in my direction and whispering.

I smooth down my hair, run my tongue over my teeth. I touch my eyelashes to make sure I put mascara on both eyes. Nothing seems to be amiss. What are they looking at?

One of the girls leans forward. "Is it true?"

I furrow my brow. "What?"

In response, she reaches onto my desk and taps the *Grizzly*. I pick up the paper, look at the front page—

My heart stops.

Somewhere in the distance, a phone rings. A few seconds later, my teacher calls my name. It's all muffled. I can't focus on anything except the paper in front of me, but even there, the words blur together. Only one thing remains clear: the headline. The headline that was delivered to every single student at Brookhill High. The headline that will be burned into my brain forever.

ANASTAYSDREAMING IS JUST PLAIN JANE

"Jane," my teacher calls again, louder. I tear my eyes from the paper to look at her.

"Principal Hobson wants to see you in her office."

Some of the shock wears off while I'm waiting outside the principal's office. Only then do I pick up the paper and start to read.

AnaStaysDreaming is Just Plain Jane
By Brynn Morgan

I've been following *AnaStaysDreaming* on Netzine for about a year. From the beginning, it's been one of my favorite accounts. Anastasia's life was full of spontaneity and romance. She was fun, witty, and insightful: all the things I've always wanted to be. I looked up to her. When I moved to this school, and I had no friends, Anastasia was there for me. Every train ride into the city, every party, every movie night with her friends, it felt like I was right there with her. I wasn't alone.

And then something amazing happened. I wrote in to her advice column, and she wrote back. I'd written a few times before, but it was this post, about a crush at my new school, that got her attention. We started writing back and forth, and thanks to her advice, my life offline started getting better too. I had a boyfriend, I was writing for the school paper, and finally, I was making friends. Or so I thought.

The truth is, all of it was a lie. Anastasia wasn't this cool, jet-setting city girl, wise beyond her years. She was—is—Brookhill High's very own Jane Scott. Not only did she manipulate me into doing what she wanted, but she's been manipulating all of you for years.

Jane uses Anastasia's voice to write exaggerated stories about people in her own life. Most of the names and locations are different, but the details remain the same. What follows are excerpts from her Netzine account, *AnaStaysDreaming*. I've included a key listing the pseudonyms Jane uses along with their real-life counterparts.

Interestingly enough, the only name that she didn't change was Leo's. Looking back, that should've been my first clue.

Jane writes the things she's too cowardly to say in real life. I hope her so-called friends read this and see her for who she truly is.

I flip through the rest of the paper, and there they are: dozens of excerpts of blog posts written over the last year. The formatting looks rushed, the excerpts roughly copy-pasted onto the pages seemingly at random. There are posts obsessing over Miles (Ethan), criticizing Izzy (Camila), hating on Leo's girlfriend, and of course, the messages with Brynn. She even included a post where I talk about how much I love being an only child. My blog takes up half the paper, until center spread. After that, everything looks the way it's supposed to.

"I don't understand," I say out loud, to no one. How did she do this?

How *could* she do this?

Just then, Brynn walks around the corner. She stops walking when she sees me.

I open my mouth, but no words come out. I have so many questions, and yet, absolutely no idea what to say. All I can think is that everyone is going to see this. Cami, Leo, Ethan, the newspaper staff, the baseball team, the girl in sixth period who sits in the back corner and never says a word—*everyone*. They'll know who I am, and what I've done. This will follow me forever.

Principal Hobson's door opens. Halle walks out. Her face is red and her eyes are glassy, like she's been crying.

"I'm out as editor," she says, and then locks eyes with Brynn. Her gaze is like a blade. "You. You're *done*."

"That's enough, Halle," Principal Hobson calls out from behind her desk. "You can go. Brynn Morgan, Jane Scott, come in."

Principal Hobson is tall, blond, and fierce. Nobody wants to mess with her. I've had to interview her a few times for the paper, and she's always been nice to me, but that's because I've been on her good side. I've heard horror stories about kids who've gotten in trouble and had to face her wrath. They were probably sitting exactly where I'm sitting now.

"I'm not sure where to start," she says, peering at us from behind her glasses. "This is extremely serious business, girls. Printing a private blog that says defamatory things about other students in a school newspaper?" She shakes her head in disbelief. "What do you have to say for yourselves?"

I glance at Brynn, sitting in the chair next to me. She's silent, staring at the floor.

"I didn't have anything to do with it," I say. "The blog was anonymous. Nobody here was ever meant to read it. And if they did, they definitely weren't supposed to know who wrote it."

Brynn lets out a harsh cackle. "You knew I was reading it."

"Not at first," I say. "You followed me way before we ever met. Once I realized it was you, I didn't know what to do."

"You didn't know what to do," she repeats, her voice flat.

"So you pretended to be someone else to give me bad advice about dating your friend?"

"No, I—"

"You wanted me to mess things up with Leo," she says. "You never liked me."

"Okay." Principal Hobson raises her hands. "Okay. I understand there are hurt feelings on both sides. But what we need to get to the bottom of is how *this* blog ended up *here*." She holds up the *Grizzly*. "Now, Halle said she was blindsided. She said she finalized the issue, copied the files onto a hard drive, and then sent them to the printer. When she checked this morning, the files on the hard drive were correct, but the ones the printer received were wrong." She looks at Brynn. "Fill in the blanks, please."

At first, Brynn is silent. Principal Hobson lets the silence linger, never breaking her gaze. Finally, Brynn sighs. "I told Halle I was staying after school to edit an article, but really I was doing this."

"Making these pages, you mean."

Brynn nods.

"And how did the printer get them?"

Brynn hesitates. "I replaced the real pages with the ones I made after Halle finalized the issue. I made sure the file names were the same so she wouldn't know the difference."

Principal Hobson doesn't even flinch. "How did you have access to files that belonged to the editor in chief?"

"All the computers in the newsroom use the same file share," she says. "Everyone has access."

Principal Hobson nods slowly. She leans back in her chair, seeming to consider her next words carefully.

"Why did you do it?" she asks. "You had to know this would get you into trouble. It doesn't seem worth it to me."

For the first time since we walked into the principal's office, Brynn turns to me. Her eyes are hard, unforgiving. She looks almost unrecognizable.

"I felt betrayed."

I don't reply. She has a right to feel betrayed. I did use the blog to try to sabotage her relationship with Leo. But the thing is, it didn't work. I gave it my best shot, but he liked her anyway. Then I decided to back off, and they still broke up. Anastasia had nothing to do with Leo's camera falling into the lake. Brynn is just looking for someone else to blame.

Principal Hobson moves on to the punishment portion of the meeting. The paper has swept through the school like wildfire, she says. She thinks it would be best if we both went home for the day so as not to fan the flames. She called our parents to come pick us up. Brynn's dad is already on his way, and she left a voicemail on both of my parents' cell phones. I have to wait in the office until one of them can be reached.

While Principal Hobson tells Brynn how dangerous her actions were, and how disappointed she is, my mind flits from Cami, to Ethan, to Jeremiah, to my parents, and finally lands on Leo. Things just started getting better between us. What's he going to think of me now that he knows I was behind so many of his relationship's missteps? Will he feel just as betrayed as Brynn?

"... and that's why," Principal Hobson continues, her eyes still on Brynn, "I'm taking you off the paper, effective immediately. You'll be moved to a study hall for the rest of the week, and you won't be able to participate next year."

Brynn bites the inside of her cheek and looks down at the floor. She was probably expecting this—how could she not?—but still. That doesn't make the blow any less crushing. I'd feel bad if she hadn't just blown up my entire life.

Principal Hobson turns to me.

"Jane," she says. "Technically, you didn't break any school rules, so I'm not going to punish you further. But I do want to caution you. Posting on the internet is like throwing a boomerang into the void. You never know when, or how, it might come back around."

I nod. "Yes, Principal Hobson."

She clasps her hands together and leans forward. The look on her face is almost sympathetic. "Next time, you might want to try a diary."

Chapter 30

Brynn and I return to the chairs outside Principal Hobson's office. We're not allowed to go back to class, or even to our lockers. All we can do is sit and wait. Together.

"How did you find out?" I ask once the silence becomes unbearable.

Brynn, with her arms crossed and her head leaning back against the wall, answers with her eyes closed.

"You left the tab open on the computer yesterday."

I blink, stunned. *That's impossible,* I want to say. I always log in using incognito mode and then make sure to log out and erase all the evidence when I'm done. But then I think back—to Brynn sitting next to me, to her article bashing Leo, to Halle standing over my shoulder, to the bell ringing—and let out a little gasp.

Brynn is right. I didn't close out. She was with me the whole time, so I never got the chance. When she sat down at my computer and opened the internet, Anastasia's inbox was the first thing she saw.

"I heard you call Cami Busy Izzy in New York." She looks

at me. "I thought that was weird, but after everything that happened with Leo, I forgot about it. Then yesterday, I put the pieces together."

I nod. So it was all my fault. That figures.

"I had no idea you hated me so much," she says. "I just wanted to be your friend."

"Did you?" I ask, skeptical. "Because it seems like you only started being nice to me after you found out I was friends with Leo."

The corners of her mouth turn down. "What are you talking about? Leo introduced you to me as his friend. I didn't know you before that."

I fix her with a hard, knowing stare. "The door?"

Her face softens with surprise. "Oh." Then she actually has the audacity to *giggle*. "Yeah, well. My bag was heavy, and you were too far away."

"Ha!" I slap my leg, vindicated. "I *knew* it. And you stole my food truck article on purpose too, didn't you?"

She purses her lips, shrugs. "It was way more interesting than the piece about new dress code regulations that Halle assigned me."

I shake my head. If only I were recording this conversation so Leo could hear it. When I tell him later, he'll never believe me.

That is, if he ever speaks to me again.

"But it still doesn't excuse what you did," she continues.

"You wrote to all your followers and called me duller than dishwater, a snake in the grass, a dud—"

"I know," I say. "It was mean, and I'm sorry."

She scoffs. "No you're not."

"I am. It was never about you." I take a breath. She's being honest. I might as well be too. "It was about Leo."

She raises an eyebrow.

"I didn't realize it at first." I grab a strand of my hair, start anxiously twirling the end around my finger. "I just thought you were wrong for him. But honestly, anybody would've been wrong for him. Anybody—you know, other than me."

Down the hall, the vice principal's door opens. A goth girl with swoopy bangs and combat boots steps out, looking irritated. I wait until she walks by and turns the corner before speaking again.

"When I saw you guys together at the baseball game, being all flirty, it was like—I don't know. All these confusing jealous feelings started happening, but I didn't know where they were coming from. It took me a really long time to figure it out. An embarrassingly long time, actually."

Brynn looks straight ahead. I study her face, trying to gauge her reaction. I wonder if she's surprised, or if deep down, some part of her already knew. She wouldn't be the first person to realize my true feelings before I did.

My thoughts flicker to Camila. The blog posts in the *Grizzly* were especially tough on her.

The only reason Izzy invited Emily to the concert instead of me is because she's desperate for attention.

Sometimes it feels like Busy Izzy cares more about being a cheerleader than being a friend.

And, worst of all:

Izzy got me the weirdest gift for my birthday. I don't know why she thought I'd like it. Does she even know me at all?

"Baseball game?"

I snap out of it.

"What?"

"You said baseball game." She shifts in her chair, crosses her legs. "But Leo and I didn't really start talking until the garden party at your house."

"Right . . . ," I say slowly. "Not officially, I know. But you liked him at the baseball game."

She furrows her brow, tilts her head.

"I saw you guys flirting there," I say. "And then after, when you wrote in asking for advice, and I told you to back off. It seemed like you did."

Something shifts on her face.

"Yeah. I did." She hesitates. "But I wasn't talking about Leo."

It takes me a second to understand. Wasn't talking about Leo?

I try to remember some of the things she wrote to Anastasia.

I just started a new school and am kinda crushing on a boy in my class.

We've been talking a lot at school, and I think he might be into me.

I backed off, like you said, and a few days later, something surprising happened. I got invited to a romantic garden party by this really cute boy.

"I always thought Leo was sweet," she says. "But he wasn't the main guy I was interested in. At least, not until he asked me to the party."

"But if you weren't talking about Leo," I say, trying to wrap my head around this new information, "then who were you talking about?"

The look she gives me next—a little guilty, a little mischievous—tells me all I need to know. It's a look I've seen before. Directed at Leo, yes, but directed at someone else, too.

"Ethan," I say immediately, knowing I'm right.

Brynn and Ethan have biology together. He was at that baseball game, obviously, but I was so fixated on the idea that Brynn might have liked Leo that I didn't think anything of it when she spoke to Ethan after. I thought she was just getting some extra quotes for the article. And then, of course, I told her to back off. That must have been when Ethan shifted his attention toward me. It also gave Leo room to swoop in and ask Brynn out—which he only did *because* of me. I'm the one who told him Brynn liked him, after all. I'm the one who planted the idea in his head.

"It was just a little crush," Brynn says, almost apologetic. "Just some flirty texts here and there. It wasn't anything like what I ended up feeling for Leo. And it was before you and Ethan started going out."

"Was it?" I say, remembering what I saw between them in the cemetery. "You and Ethan looked pretty friendly that night we all hung out."

"So what? We're friendly."

"Were you still texting him?" I press. "Even after you started dating Leo?"

She purses her lips, like she's debating whether to tell me the truth.

"It was innocent," she admits. "Well, on my part, anyway. He's kind of a big flirt."

I raise my eyebrows, waiting for her to say more.

"He told me it wasn't serious with you," she says matter-of-factly, like she's simply relaying the weather or last night's homework. "That he was just using you for coverage in the paper."

My jaw drops. It takes me a few seconds to regain my composure.

"I don't believe you."

But it's true, isn't it? Deep down, I suspected as much. I just can't believe he would actually admit it. To *Brynn*, of all people.

She pulls out her cell phone, presses a few buttons, and starts scrolling up. Finally, she shows me the screen. It's her text thread with Ethan. The texts are from late April, a couple of days before the cemetery date.

Ethan: Hey, gorgeous ☺

Ethan: Heard we're all hanging on Saturday

Brynn: Yep

Brynn: You and Jane? That's a surprise

Ethan: Nah. It's not like that

Brynn: Really. What's it like?

Ethan: Ha

Ethan: I mean, yea, she's into me, but I don't like her like that. I just want her to keep writing about me in the paper

Ethan: Gotta play nice til the season ends

Brynn: You know, I could write about you in the paper

Ethan: Yea but you won't. Too worried about what your bf would think

Brynn: He's not my boyfriend

Brynn: I just want to keep a low profile right now, that's all

Ethan: Uh huh

Ethan: You can try to hide behind the scenes all you want Morgan, but it's not gonna work. I see you

Ethan: And you look good to me 😉

I stare at the last message. It's exactly what he said to me that first day in the hallway.

I hand the phone back to her, feeling equal parts disgusted and humiliated. Ethan Gray was just using me. He *is* a player—and not only on the baseball field. Leo, Jeremiah, the rumor mill—everybody was right.

"You could've told me," I say, not looking at her.

She lets out a harsh laugh. "Yeah. Just like you could've told me you were Anastasia."

I sigh and sink down in my chair. Everything is such a mess.

Such a mess, and all because of me! If I hadn't wrongly assumed Brynn wanted Leo, she probably would've gone out with Ethan instead. He would've remained a perfect idea in my head, and Leo and I wouldn't have fought, and he wouldn't have lost his camera, and maybe Brynn and I could've even been friends.

I can practically hear Leo's *I told you so* voice.

"For what it's worth," Brynn says. "I think Leo feels the same way about you."

I finally look at her. "What?"

"He's never said anything." She looks down at her hands, starts picking at her chipped purple polish. "But something about the way he looked at you . . ." She shrugs. "I could just tell. And I always felt a little insecure about it."

Despite everything, her words send a rush of warmth through me. *Leo feels the same way about you.* Just thinking about it makes my heart flutter a little in my chest.

And then, just as quickly, the fluttering stops, and my heart sinks.

Because whatever Leo might have felt for me before, surely he doesn't feel that way now. Between what I said to him in the newsroom and what I wrote about his relationship, I can forget about Leo ever being my boyfriend. I'll be lucky if he even speaks to me again.

"So what now?" I ask.

Brynn looks at me out of the corner of her eye. "What do you mean? You got what you wanted. I'm off the paper. Leo and I broke up. I'm out of your hair for good."

"That's not what I wanted," I say. "I mean, okay, sure, I guess I wanted you guys to break up. But you deserve to be on the paper. You're a good writer."

She doesn't say anything.

"Seriously," I continue. "I just don't get it. I mean, I know you hate me, but there were other ways you could've gotten back at me. Publishing *AnaStaysDreaming* in the *Grizzly* hurts you just as much as it hurts me. It seems like a waste."

She's quiet for so long that I don't think she's ever going to reply. Then, finally, she takes a deep breath.

"I told you what happened at my last school. There were these girls who I thought were my friends, and then they turned on me. They made this video making fun of me, and it went viral."

"Leo told me."

"It was awful." She's staring straight ahead with a haunted look on her face, like she's peering into the past. "I became the laughingstock of my entire school. It's why we had to move."

I nod. Leo told me that, too.

"So when I found out that you were behind Anastasia's account, and everything you told me was a lie, I just—I don't know. I *snapped*. Here was someone who I wanted to be friends with, making fun of me online to thousands of people." She pauses, her voice wobbly with emotion. "Last time, I just took it, and then I ran away like a coward. But not this time." She looks at me, seeming to snap out of her trance. "This time, I wanted to make you feel exactly what I felt."

Suddenly Principal Hobson's door opens.

"Jane," she says, stepping into the doorway. "Your mother is on her way."

"Great," I mutter.

"And Brynn, your father is in the lobby. You can head out now."

She steps back into her office and shuts the door. Brynn stands up.

"The last message I sent to you as Anastasia," I say. She turns to look at me. "I meant every word of it. I abandoned you when you needed me, and I really am sorry."

She hesitates, and for a second, I think we might be able to call a truce. After all, we both hurt each other. Don't we both deserve forgiveness too?

"Seriously, Jane," she says finally. "Save your sorrys for someone who cares."

And then she walks away.

Chapter 31

It takes half an hour for my mom to come and get me from the principal's office. When she arrives, her hair is in a messy bun, and she's wearing her gardening sweats.

"You look like you got in a fight with a bear," I tell her when we walk out of the office.

She gives me a stern look. "I wouldn't be cracking jokes right now, if I were you."

"Why? I didn't *do* anything."

"We'll talk about it in the car."

The bell rings, and all at once students flood the halls. I feel their eyes on me as I walk past, even people I don't know. I look down at my feet, getting the sudden urge to transform into a roly-poly, so that I could curl into an impenetrable ball for the next four minutes, until the late bell—until it's safe.

I bump into someone's shoulder and look up. Down the hall, I spot a familiar, handsome face walking right toward me. Ethan Gray.

The urge to hide grows stronger.

"Mom," I say, my heart pounding. "Can you give me a second? I need to talk to—"

"No," Mom says. "Your principal said to take you right home."

Ethan is getting closer. A few more seconds and he'll walk past me, and I'll miss my window.

"Please?" I can practically feel the desperation oozing from my pores. "Ethan is right there, and I need to talk to him. It's important. Please."

Mom hesitates. She looks from me to Ethan Gray, and then back to me. "All right, fine. Make it quick. I'll be right over here."

"Ethan," I say when he gets close enough. "Can I talk to you?"

Ethan stops walking. The look he gives me next makes me wonder if I actually *have* transformed into a roly-poly—like I'm a disgusting bug he wants to flick away.

"What for?" he says, stepping out of the flow of foot traffic. "So you can stalk me some more?"

"I—I know how this looks," I stammer. "But just let me explain—"

"Explain what?" His blue eyes are as cold and hard as ice. "It was all pretty clear in the paper. You're, like, obsessed with me."

The cruelty in his voice is shocking. I feel hot all of a sudden, and a little dizzy, like I could faint. "No, I—"

"You know, I thought you were cool," he says. "But you're a fake. You sit in your room and you write these creepy stories, and you use me to make your life seem more interesting. But there's nothing interesting about you at all, is there?"

His words hit me right in the gut. The pain is so acute, so *real*, that it feels like I've actually been punched. *Do not fall apart*, I tell myself. *Do not let him see how much his words hurt.*

"Are we done here?" he says, impatient. "I've got to get to math."

I'm tempted to let him walk away. This conversation has been so humiliating that all I want to do is sink into the floor and disappear. But I can't do it. Because even though Ethan Gray might be right about me, he's dead wrong about my writing.

"I hate to burst your bubble of self-righteousness," I say, fighting through the wobble in my voice. "But the person I was writing about wasn't you."

He snorts. "Sure, okay."

"Really. Miles might have looked like you, and played baseball like you, but he was his own person. I mean, how could he have been you? I didn't *know* you. The Ethan I had a crush on—the one Miles was based on—was just an idea. He was honest, and selfless, and generous, and *kind*." I look him up and down. "As it turns out, that's nothing like you at all."

Around us, the hallway starts to clear out and quiet down. Ethan doesn't move. His arrogance is slipping like a mask, revealing the insecurity that has probably always been hiding underneath.

"I know about you and Brynn," I say. "Just like I know about you and Kelsey Welles while you were dating Alicia."

"Kelsey?" he sneers. "God, you *were* stalking me."

"No! My brother told me," I say. "Your reputation as a liar precedes you."

"Whatever, Jane. We were never together, so why does it matter?" He puts his hands in his pockets, shakes his head. "And by the way, everybody's a liar, not just me. Why don't you ask Cami who picks her up from cheer practice?"

The late bell starts to ring. *Ding*.

"What?"

Ding.

Ethan looks positively smug. "You know him pretty well. The whole school knows his truck. That's the wildest part, honestly. She's not even trying to be subtle."

Ding.

My heart is pounding. "What are you *talking* about?"

"Cheer and baseball finish at the same time," he replies.

Ding.

"Every day, we all walk to the parking lot together, and every day, Jeremiah is there, in his ugly truck, waiting to pick her up. Sometimes they leave right away. Other times . . ."

Ding.

Ding.

Chapter 32

"Did you know?" I say to my mom once we're in the car. "About Jeremiah and Cami?"

Mom grips the steering wheel with both hands. She keeps her eyes on the road.

"Yes."

My eyes start to burn. A second later, they're filled with tears.

"How could you?" I shout, letting them fall. "How could you keep it from me?"

"Honey," she says, her voice soothing. "This is the reason, right here. I knew you'd be upset."

"When did you find out?"

Mom puts on her blinker. "Last month." She makes a left turn. "I was walking Maggie, and I saw them in his truck. It was parked in front of her house."

"What were they doing?"

Mom looks uncomfortable. It's pretty clear she wishes she didn't know either. "They were kissing."

I let out a sob. The thought of Cami and Jeremiah touching mouths—touching *tongues*—is too much to bear.

"It's not the end of the world," Mom says. "In fact, I think it could be good for him. Cami is a good girl."

"She was my best friend! *Mine*, not his."

"She still is," Mom replies. "Being with Jeremiah doesn't change that."

"Yes it does." I sniffle. "It changes everything."

I look out the window and dry my cheeks with my sleeve. My mind flashes back to the night of the garden party, when I saw the two of them in the bed of his truck. I couldn't see his face, but I could see hers. She looked happy, at ease. Maybe even in love.

I feel tears threaten to spill over again. Not because they're together, but because I didn't know. My best friend and I don't seem to know each other at all.

"Jane." Mom sounds tired. "We need to talk about what you did."

"I already told you," I say, frustrated. "I didn't do anything. Brynn is the one who put my blog in the paper."

"Yes, but the things you wrote. Hurtful things about people you love—"

"No," I insist. "People who don't exist. Characters I created."

"Who are based on people you love," Mom says. "I didn't get a chance to read it yet, so I don't—"

"What a surprise," I mutter.

She gives me a stern look. "What?"

"I said I'm not surprised you haven't read it, because you never read anything I write. You or Dad."

"That's not true."

"What's the last article I wrote that you read?" I ask. My tone is mocking, but I am genuinely curious. I wait for her to respond. Several seconds go by, the low hum of the car engine the only sound between us.

"See? You can't even remember! Dad's always working, and all you do is worry about Jeremiah, and it's like you forget sometimes that you have another kid."

"Oh, Jane." Her voice cracks. "I'm sorry, honey. I really am."

I start tugging on my seat belt, suddenly uncomfortable. "Well, don't *cry*."

"I'm not," she lies. "I just—I don't want you to think that we don't care, because we do. The reason I worry about Jeremiah is because I have to. He has no focus, or discipline, and if I wasn't on top of him, he'd probably have flunked out a long time ago."

I don't reply. That's probably true.

"But you're different. You're smart, and driven, and *special*. I don't have to worry about you, and I'm so, so grateful for that."

Ethan's words echo in my head. *There's nothing interesting about you at all.*

"I never want you to feel overlooked," she says. "Your dad and I are so proud of you."

A tear falls down my cheek. I quickly brush it away.

"It would be nice to hear that a little more," I admit.

Mom's phone rings. Dad's name pops up on the dashboard. She answers the call through the car.

"I just got out of a meeting and saw the school called," he says. "What did Jeremiah do?"

"Not Jeremiah," Mom says. "Jane."

"Jane?"

"Hi, Dad."

A pause. "Hey, Janie." Another pause. "Shouldn't you be in school?"

I take a deep breath, and I start to explain.

At home, Mom asks to see my Netzine. We go into the den, where the family computer lives, and I open up the internet and type my profile URL into the browser. She sits down and starts to read.

I hover behind her awkwardly for a while, until the silence is too much, at which point I retreat to the living room, where Maggie is sleeping on the couch. I turn on the TV but don't watch it. I'm too busy checking my phone every thirty seconds, looking for a text from Leo or Camila or anyone. But nothing comes.

My stomach is in knots as I wait for Mom. It's not that I'm worried about *what* she's going to read—it is fiction, after all. I'm more worried about how she'll interpret it. I don't write about Anastasia's parents much. They're distant figures in her life, which, now that I think about it, might offend Mom even more than if I'd written something nasty.

After what feels like an eternity, she joins me in the living room.

"I don't know what to say." She sits with me on the couch, on Maggie's other side. "It feels like you've got this whole other life I know nothing about."

"You always knew about it," I remind her. "You just didn't care."

Mom pets Maggie in long strokes down her back. "I didn't understand it. I still don't, really."

"It's not real," I tell her. "It's just a story I made up."

"Sort of," she says. "But there are things I recognize. Izzy is a cheerleader, Leo is a photographer, Anastasia loves New York—"

"Yeah, I pull from my own life," I say. "But doesn't every writer do that?"

Mom makes a face like she hadn't considered that. "I suppose."

We're both quiet for a minute. Our eyes are on the sitcom playing on TV, but neither of us really watches it. Every now and then, the laugh track punctuates the silence.

"Am I in trouble?" I ask finally.

Mom hesitates. "I'm not sure. This is new territory for me."

"I know I shouldn't have written those things about Brynn," I say. "I know it crossed a line, and I already apologized."

"You've written a lot of things to a lot of people," Mom says. "How many followers do you have, exactly?"

"A hundred and twenty thousand."

Mom gasps, causing Maggie to lift her head. "That many, really?"

I nod. "A lot of people like my writing."

"Well, of course," she says. "You're a wonderful writer."

I smile. I can't help it. She has no idea how long I've waited to hear her say that.

Mom decides to take away my laptop for the week. I think she feels like she needs to draw a line under this whole mess somehow, even though I don't think she really knows what she's punishing me for. She doesn't even seem all that mad. She keeps interrupting the show to ask me about Talk to Me Tuesday. How many questions do I get a week? What kinds of topics do I get most often? Are there ever questions that I don't know how to respond to? Every time I give her an answer, she nods thoughtfully, and it makes me feel like she's really listening. I think she's impressed that so many people care about what I have to say. Maybe she's even proud.

"Do you think you'll keep it going?" Mom says when the show is over. "The blog."

Her question takes me by surprise. *Of course,* I almost say. Anastasia is a huge part of my life. Who would I be without her? But then reality comes crashing down.

Everyone at school knows Anastasia isn't who she pretends to be. In a matter of days—or maybe even hours—the truth will find its way to the internet, and my followers will know too. Nobody will want to read about Anastasia's life once they learn it's all made up—by *me*, no less. Anastasia exists to inspire and entertain, and there's nothing inspiring *or* entertaining about me.

Nothing interesting at all, like Ethan said.

"I don't know if I can," I admit.

The simple truth of it breaks my heart.

Chapter 33

It's just after eight that night when I ring Camila's doorbell. The sun is setting, the crickets in her bushes are chirping, and in the distance, a sparrow sings. It's so peaceful, you'd never know the day started with a colossal explosion.

Camila's dad opens the door. He's small, tan, and black haired, like Cami. Unlike Cami, he's almost always frowning.

"Hi, Mr. Mendoza." I force a smile. "Is Cami home?"

He nods but doesn't make any moves to welcome me inside. "She's in her room studying."

"I won't be long," I say. "I just really need to talk to her. It's important."

He considers me for a long moment. Finally, he opens the door wider. "Not too long."

I nod. Understood.

I climb the stairs and walk to the end of the hall, stopping in front of Cami's door. I take a deep breath and recall, again, the Talk to Me Tuesday post from a while ago, from someone who felt like she was growing apart from her best friend. What advice did I give her?

It seems like maybe all you two need is a chance to reconnect.
If things still feel off after that, address it head-on.
Communication is key in any relationship.

I knock on the door. From the other side comes a faint "Yeah?"

I open the door. Camila is sitting at her desk with her history textbook open in front of her. Her hair is pulled back in a ponytail, and she's wearing her reading glasses. She could've been wearing sunglasses; they still wouldn't conceal her scowl.

"We need to talk," I say, hovering in the doorway.

"Go away."

"No." I step inside, close the door. "I know you're mad at me, and I get it. Some of the stuff that got printed in the *Grizzly* was awful."

Camila turns away from me, returns her attention to her book.

"Brynn only pulled the worst things that I wrote." I walk over to her bed and sit down on the edge. "She wanted to make me look bad. If you read my Netzine, you'd know—"

"I did read it," she says with her back still toward me. "I read as much as I could until my eyes started to hurt from all that squinting at my phone screen." She glances over her shoulder at me. "*Really* helpful of you to add an Izzy tag, by the way."

I wince. "Izzy isn't you. She's based on you, sure. And yeah, sometimes, when I'm mad at you, I take it out on her character. It's just, like, a coping mechanism." I grab one of her throw pillows, the blue fuzzy one, and hug it to my chest. "But nobody was *ever* supposed to know it was you. And you were never meant to see it."

She abandons the book and spins around in her chair. "That doesn't make me feel better, Jane. I'm not upset because people know the character is based on me." Her eyes go glossy. "I'm upset because you feel those things."

"But I *don't*," I say. "At least, not most of them. Most of them are just things I said in the heat of the moment, because I was mad, or hurt."

"But some of them?" she says, her voice squeaky with emotion. "You really believe that I'm desperate for attention?"

"No . . ." I let my eyes drift toward the Olivia Rodrigo poster on the opposite wall. "I'm talking more about how sometimes, it feels like you don't really care about being my friend."

Tears fall down her cheeks. She wipes them away.

"But I *do* care. You're my best—"

"I know you're with Jeremiah," I say, staring at Olivia for courage. When a few seconds pass, and Camila doesn't say anything, I add, "You told me you didn't like him."

"I didn't know how to tell you the truth."

I look at her. She's looking down at her hands.

"You can be really stubborn," she says, picking at a hangnail. "I thought if you knew, you'd force me to end it."

"I wouldn't do that."

She laughs a little, humorless and dry.

"I *wouldn't*," I say again.

"You wanted me to date Shane Duncan," she says. "You didn't care that I didn't like him. You only cared that he was Ethan's best friend, and he fit into your vision of how life should be."

I want to tell her that she's wrong—that I wanted her to be with Shane because he's sweet, and cute, and would treat her well—but I can't. The truth is, I wanted her to be with Shane so we could go on double dates. So we'd be best friends dating best friends. So I'd have plenty of material for *AnaStaysDreaming*. I wanted her to date him for *me*.

"You're right," I say, feeling the tears well up. "But still. We're supposed to tell each other everything."

"We're supposed to." Her eyes lock onto mine. "But we don't."

I nod. She didn't tell me about her relationship with Jeremiah for the same reason I didn't tell her about my Netzine. Sometimes the most sacred things are the hardest to explain. Especially to someone who might try to ruin them.

"When did we forget how to talk to each other?" I say, hugging the pillow tighter. "Like, I used to know everything that happened in your life, and I didn't even have to try."

"That's because we were always together," she says. "We didn't have to tell each other things. We knew already, because we were there when they happened." She laughs through her tears, just a little. "Now we have lives."

"Only you do," I correct. "I'm still the same plain Jane."

She looks at me like I'm ridiculous. "Come on. You were dating Ethan Gray. You're always busy with the paper..."

She trails off. Her eyes lock onto the space between my collarbones. Instinctively my hand goes right to the butter charm.

"You didn't have to wear it," Camila says, her voice cold again. "Since you hate it so much."

I remember the post in the *Grizzly* and groan. "I don't hate it," I say, dropping my hand. "I just, um—don't really understand it."

"You don't?" She sounds surprised. "Butter and croissant?"

I shake my head. "Is that a fresh take on peanut butter and jelly, or something?"

She scoffs. "You really don't remember!"

"Remember what?"

Camila reaches over and yanks the fuzzy blue pillow from me. She hugs it to her own chest. "Two summers ago, when the black-and-white-movie theater was playing *Breakfast at Tiffany's*, and we went to the bakery beforehand to get croissants to sneak into the theater? And you took way too many butter packets—"

"And I kept finding them in my purse for weeks after," I say, cracking a smile. "That's right. I thought you were playing a prank on me." I start to giggle. After a moment, Camila does too.

"And then that one time Leo asked you for a stick of gum, and you reached into your purse and handed him—" She's laughing so hard now that she can barely get it out. "A butter packet?"

We both burst into laughter.

"And he almost ate it!" I say. "He would have if you hadn't realized what it was and slapped it out of his hand."

We laugh so hard, our gasping breaths are the only sounds we make. We laugh until it hurts, and we can't anymore.

"I can't believe I forgot about that," I say when the laughing dies down.

Camila, still hugging her pillow with one hand, starts to smooth down the fuzz with the other. "I can."

I think about what she said in New York: *You're always in your head, absorbed by your own problems.*

Followed closely by what Leo said to me in the newsroom: *You're so selfish.*

And I realize they're right. Both of them. I've been so focused on trying to make my life look like Anastasia's perfect dreamland that I forgot to appreciate what's always been right in front of me: my friends.

Anastasia's life might be perfect, but it isn't real. What's real is the feel of Cami's fuzzy blue pillow. The smell of melted butter in the bottom of my purse. The sound of the shutter release on Leo's camera and the temporary blindness that comes after, when he's using the flash. The way the powdery cheese melts on my tongue when Leo insists on making cheddar popcorn for movie night. The tang of the hot sauce Camila sometimes adds to the bowl when nobody's looking. The sound of their laughter—Cami's high pitched and silly, Leo's low and melodic—and the way it can bring a smile to my face even when everything feels like it's falling apart.

And then I realize Ethan is wrong—about my writing *and* about me. My life is interesting *because* it isn't perfect. Perfection is boring.

"I'm sorry," I say to Camila. "About the Netzine, and about being a crummy friend in general."

"I'm sorry too," she replies. "I should've told you about Jeremiah. I just . . ." She covers her face with her hands. "I never meant for it to happen."

"I know," I say. "It's okay."

She peeks at me over her fingers. "It is?"

"Well." I swipe the pillow off her lap, wrap it in my arms. "It's going to take some getting used to. But if you're happy, that's all that really matters."

She gets out of her chair and tackles me in a hug. The force knocks us backward, and we fall onto her comforter in a heap of giggles.

"Jeremiah," I say when she rolls off me. We're both lying down, looking at the ceiling. "How *did* it happen, anyway?"

She sighs. "I guess it started when we'd hang out in your basement, and you and Leo would go on your tangents, and I'd get bored and go upstairs."

I scrunch up my face. "What do you mean, our tangents?"

She gives me a knowing look. "You guys have so many

inside jokes, it's like you speak another language sometimes. It can be hard to keep up, even for me."

I don't know what tangents she means specifically, but I can understand where she's coming from. My friendship with Leo literally preceded our ability to process language. I guess it's inevitable we still communicate that way sometimes. It hurts to hear it made Camila feel left out, but it shouldn't be that surprising, either.

"It's okay," she says, as if reading my mind. "I'm not upset, or anything. I know you guys have your own bond." She glances at me, and I'm acutely aware of the fact that I haven't extended her the same courtesy when it comes to her cheerleading friends.

"But, um—I'd go upstairs, and Jeremiah would be gaming in his room with the door open, and I'd wander over and ask him what he was playing—"

I can't help but laugh. "And you swooned over the way he slayed all the monsters?"

"*No,*" she says, embarrassed. "We'd just talk, and—I don't know. He surprised me."

I wince. I can't imagine Jeremiah wooing anyone with his words.

"He's so cool, and funny, and like, *mysterious*. But he's got a soft heart, too." She puts her hands on her cheeks and smiles, giddy. It occurs to me that she looks very much like a girl in love.

"Also," she says, looking a little mischievous. "He's an *amazing* kisser."

I cover my ears. "*La la la*, can't hear you."

She laughs and pulls my arm away. "Okay, you're right. That was too soon." Then she props herself up on her elbows and looks at me. "But you know what isn't? You and Leo. It's been a *long* time coming."

My smile falls. "There is no me and Leo."

"Why not? He's not with Brynn anymore, and you're not with Ethan."

The sound of Ethan's name makes me scrunch up my nose. I'll have to fill Camila in later.

"He probably hates me." I sit up. "Things were just starting to go back to normal between us, and then this happened."

"I don't know," Camila says. "You never said a bad word about him. If anything, you did the opposite."

"What do you mean?"

Camila snorts. "Jane, if there's one thing those posts made painfully obvious, it's that you are so completely in love with him."

"What?" I say with a scoff, but inside, my heart flutters. "No way."

"Yes way. You've been virtually ogling him for years. Plus, why else would you go to such great lengths to try and break up him and Brynn?"

"Ugh!" I grab the blue fuzzy pillow and put it over my face. "Just let me suffocate, please."

"Sorry." Camila takes the pillow. "But if you die without resolving this, I'm pretty sure your spirit will stick around to haunt me."

I stare at the light fixture on the ceiling. I don't know, yet, whether it's worth it to tell Leo how I feel. Could he ever really love me after all I've put him through? Could he choose me, and all my messy imperfections, like he chose Brynn?

Chapter 34

When I walk out to Jeremiah's truck before school the next morning, he's already there. I can hear the rumble of his rock music halfway across the yard.

"Morning," I yell over the music when I open the door. He doesn't reply or even turn it down. Once I'm in, and my seat belt is fastened, he shifts the car into drive and takes off.

"You're going to give me the silent treatment?" I shout. "Really? What are we, two?"

No reply. I turn the music down.

"Yo," he snaps. "Don't touch the dash."

"Stop being immature!"

"Me, immature?" His expression is halfway between annoyed and amused. "I'm not the one who wrote a bunch of petty stuff about my friends and published it on the internet."

I frown. I figured he'd heard about the *Grizzly*, but a small, perhaps naive part of me hoped he hadn't bothered to read it.

"It wasn't *all* petty," I say. "Just the stuff Brynn bothered to print."

He flips his hair out of his eyes to shoot me a judgmental glance.

"Doesn't matter. It still hurt people."

"I already apologized to Cami." I reach into the side pouch of my bag to look for lip gloss, but then opt for ChapStick instead. I don't want to draw any more attention to myself than I already have. "Sorry, I mean, your *girlfriend*."

He tenses up.

"She told you?"

"No." I pull out the ChapStick. "But she confirmed it."

He stops at a red light, drums his fingers on the steering wheel to the beat of the song.

"So. Do you hate us forever now?"

I flip down the sun visor, take the cap off the ChapStick. "I did for a few minutes." I apply the ChapStick in careful strokes. "But now I think I'm over it."

He raises his eyebrows in surprise. "Really."

"Yeah. Life's too short." I smack my lips together, satisfied.

"Wow," he says. "Surprisingly mature of you."

I shrug. "I want her to be happy."

"Just her? What about me?"

I close the sun visor and look at him. "Does she make you happy?"

He keeps his eyes straight ahead, but he can't hide his small smile.

"Yeah. She does."

I nod. "Good."

The light turns green. He drives through the intersection.

"While I'm on an apology tour," I say. "I'm sorry for what I wrote about you."

His expression doesn't give anything away. "What did you write about me?"

"You know, that I was an only child."

"Oh." He sort of shrugs it off. "Whatever. It's not that big of a deal."

I'm weirdly disappointed by his reaction. I tell the whole world that my brother doesn't exist, and he doesn't even care? Once upon a time, he would have cared. When we were kids, he'd tell everyone on the playground that he was my big brother, so they better not mess with me. He was proud to be related to me, and vice versa. What happened?

"I only said it because it's how I feel sometimes. Like, I don't know—you're unavailable to me."

He snorts. "Am I unavailable to you every morning, when I drive you to school? Or how about every afternoon, when I drive you home?"

"You know what I mean," I say, feeling my face get hot. I'm nervous to open up to him like this. "We used to hang out all the time. We were, like, friends."

"Yeah. And then you started spending all your time in your room, on your laptop." His expression changes, like a lightbulb has just turned on above his head. "At least now I know what you were doing."

"Only because every time I wanted to do something with

you, you were either gaming in your headset or doing something stupid with Danny."

"Not every time," he says. "Anyway, you could've hung out with us."

"No, I couldn't have," I insist. "You didn't want me there."

He shakes his head. "I never said that. That's just the story you made up in your head to make yourself feel better about ditching me."

I want to laugh. I can't *believe* he's trying to blame this on me. "Whatever, Jeremiah."

"You were always welcome," he continues. "I even used my chore money to buy an extra controller for you."

I blink, stunned. "You did?"

He nods. "It's purple."

All of a sudden, my eyes start to burn. I look out the window so he doesn't see.

"Do you still have it?" I ask.

"Yes."

I wipe my eyes quickly, stealthily. When I'm sure there are no more tears, I turn to him.

"Maybe we could play *Mario Party* after school? Like we used to?"

He cracks a smile. "Sure. But I'm not going easy on you. I'm coming for all your stars."

I laugh a little, feel a wayward tear escape down my cheek, and wipe it away quickly. "Deal."

We pull into the school parking lot. There's an easygoing

sort of energy in the air; everybody's smiling, chatting leisurely, taking their time walking into school. Today is the last full day before finals. Tomorrow and Friday—exam days—are half days.

Jeremiah pulls into his spot and puts the car in park. "By the way," he says. "Who told you about me and Cami?"

"Ethan," I say. "He saw you two after baseball practice."

"Figures." Jeremiah rolls his eyes and shuts off the ignition.

"You were right about him, by the way," I say. "He's a total player."

Jeremiah nods. "Glad you've come to your senses." He looks at me. "Uh. You okay?"

"Yeah." My thoughts flicker instinctively to Leo. "I will be."

I open the door and get out of the truck.

When I walk into the newsroom, Leo is sitting in his usual seat. The desk next to his—my desk that became Brynn's desk—is empty. I only hesitate for a second before walking up to the desk and sitting down.

"You got your desk back," Leo says, not looking up from the book he's reading. I'm secretly relieved that he's the first to speak. "Happy?"

"Yes," I say. "And no."

I take a deep breath, preparing to say everything I spent the last two classes rehearsing in my head. *I'm sorry about what I wrote in the blog. I should never have tried getting in between you and Brynn. I don't know how everything got so messed up. Well, actually, I do. It's because, as it turns out, I'm sort of in love with you.*

"Leo—"

"Hey, Jane," Halle calls out. She's sitting cross-legged on top of a desk at the front of the room. "Can you come here a sec?"

My stomach lurches. Halle probably hates me now. Because of me and my blog, she definitely won't win the leadership award. And now that she can't be editor next year—also because of the blog—she won't get another shot at it. I feel terrible.

"Hi," I say, approaching her desk. I have trouble looking her in the eye, so I look down at my hands instead. There's a chip in the pink polish on my left thumbnail.

"How are you holding up?" Halle asks.

I look at her, surprised. "I'm . . . okay."

She raises an eyebrow. "You don't sound so sure."

"No, I just—um. You're not mad?"

"Oh, I'm furious," she says. "At Brynn, not at you. She completely violated your privacy."

"Well," I say, wary. "What she published was posted on the internet. Not exactly private."

"That's generous of you." She sounds skeptical. "How would she like it if I copy-pasted her most vulnerable Netzine posts into the *Grizzly* for everyone to see?"

I'm stunned. Not only does Halle not blame me, but she's actually on my side?

"I guess I hadn't thought of it like that."

"Yeah, well," Halle says. "As someone with my own private Netzine, I sympathize with your situation."

My eyes widen. Halle has a Netzine? What I wouldn't give to see her profile. "Um, thanks."

Halle adjusts her position on the desk, unfolding her legs and letting them dangle. "As it turns out, there is one good thing that came out of this."

"Really?" I can't imagine what.

"Yep. It's an idea I had. I wanted to run it by you while I'm still editor and have the power to make it happen." She smiles a little, trying and failing to mask her sadness at getting fired.

"What if, next year, you spearheaded an advice column for the *Grizzly*?"

My mouth falls open. It takes me a second to remember how to speak. "An . . . advice column?"

"It would be anonymous on both ends. You'd give advice under a fake name, something bear related, probably, but it would be your column. And then, when you graduate, you can pass it along to whoever you deem worthy."

"I—" I shake my head, dazed. "I don't know what to say."

"Say you'll do it," she says. "I checked out your blog. You give *great* advice. And a column like this could really take the *Grizzly* to the next level. Everyone will want to get their hands on the next issue to see if you've answered their question, or to try and guess who wrote the question in the first place."

She's probably right. There are few things teens love more than gossip, especially if it's about people they know. Something like this could possibly double our readership.

"Okay," I say, feeling reassured. "I'll do it."

She smiles for real and jumps off the desk. "Great. I'll tell Mr. Franklin."

She goes to our adviser's desk, but I stay where I am. I'm too astonished to move. I'm going to have my own column in the *Grizzly* next year. I'll get to help people. And this time, I don't have to pretend to be Anastasia. I can use my own voice.

I look at Leo's desk, a wide smile spreading across my face. I can't wait to tell him the news.

But he isn't there.

"Hey, Kat?" I walk back to her desk, which is next to mine. "Do you know where Leo went?"

"I think I heard him tell Mr. Franklin he was going to the library," she says, not looking up from her sketch pad.

I nod, sit down at my desk in a huff. Did Leo go to the library to avoid me? He didn't seem like he was avoiding me before. He spoke to me first! But why else would he go?

My mind spirals, going a thousand miles a minute. *Just stay calm,* I tell myself. *Leo will come back soon, and everything will make sense. You can apologize like you intended and tell him how you feel, and he can reciprocate—or not. The point is, all this agony will be over soon. Just wait until he comes back.*

But Leo doesn't come back. I only realize, once the bell rings, that his book bag is gone. He was never going to come back.

AnaStaysDreaming

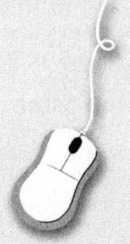

Inbox (772)

Anonymous asked: Anastasia! You haven't posted in four days. Are you okay?

Anonymous asked: Ana, I really need advice. My best friend told me she doesn't want to be friends anymore. She says we have different interests and we shouldn't try to force a friendship that feels fake. But it doesn't feel fake to me—this news caught me completely by surprise. I don't want to lose her. What do I do?

Signed, Bestie Breakup

Anonymous asked: My cousin's boyfriend goes to Brookhill High in PA. Is it true that you're lying about who you are??

Anonymous asked: WHERE ARE YOU???

Anonymous asked: You're a liar and I hope u die xx

Chapter 35

I finish my last final on Friday at noon. When I walk out to the parking lot, the air is warm and still, and the sun is shining bright. Summer is finally here, and just in time for Camila's pool party. Mother Nature must have been in a forgiving mood.

Half the cars are already gone, so right away I spot Camila and Jeremiah waiting for me at his truck. She's sitting in the bed, her legs dangling over the edge, and he's standing in front of her with one hand resting on her thigh. He says something that makes her laugh, and then she drapes her arms around his neck, leans forward, and kisses him.

I scrunch up my nose, wondering when I'll ever get used to that.

Camila spots me first. "Hey!" She pushes him away and jumps down. "How was math?"

"You know. I plotted some graphs, solved for x." I put my tote bag down on the pavement. "The usual."

"I can't believe we don't have to think about polynomials

for three whole months!" Camila says with a squeal. "Only sunshine, swimming, and . . ." She pauses, looks at me. "Another *s* word."

"Sandals?"

"Sandals!" she repeats. "Great. Now I want to go shopping."

"We are going to the grocery store," Jeremiah says. "Party supplies, remember?"

She waves his words away with her hand. "That's not shopping. That's errands."

"Is there anything I should bring?" I ask. "Besides my ravishing good looks and charming personality."

Jeremiah snorts.

"Actually, yes," Camila says. "Can you bring that Polaroid camera you got for Christmas? I'm going to see if I can get a bunch of film at the drugstore."

"Sure. Get some batteries, too. It probably needs new ones."

She nods. "Done. And come to my house early, will you? The party starts at three, but I need your expertise about which bikini-slash-cover-up combo I should wear."

"The red bikini," I say immediately. "That one looks the best with your skin. Plus, you don't want to worry about the strapless one falling down when you jump in the pool."

"See?" She grins and looks at Jeremiah. "This is why she's my best friend."

"Great," he says. "I'll be sure to ask Danny which bikini I should wear too."

"Definitely *not* red," I say. "It'll wash you out."

All three of us laugh, and it feels weirdly comfortable, like maybe I could get used to this after all.

Jeremiah drops me off at home. Dad is at the office, and Mom is out, probably with a client, so I'm alone. I put my bag in my room, let Maggie out into the backyard, and head to the den.

I haven't been on Netzine since Monday, before I got my laptop taken away. This is the longest I've ever gone without posting, and it feels strange. Not because I miss it, but because I don't. Part of Anastasia's allure was that she was separate from me. Now the lines are blurred. Her life is no longer this perfect, untouchable thing. Her life is my life, and my life is *so* not perfect. What's the point in pretending otherwise?

I open the internet and log into Netzine. Unsurprisingly, people have noticed my absence. I see right away that I've lost over thirty thousand followers, which is a blow, but it's nothing compared to what I find in my inbox. There are almost eight hundred messages there, and some of them make my skin crawl. People calling me mean names, wishing me harm. People calling me Jane. I wonder if Brynn knew this would happen when she decided to post the blog in the *Grizzly*, being a victim of cyberbullying herself. I really hope not.

I click the create new post button and stare at the blinking cursor for half an hour. Do I apologize? Explain myself? Act like nothing is wrong at all? There are so many things I want to say, but I don't know how.

I delete the entry and click on Anastasia's profile. I scroll through the posts, studying them like an archivist. A photo of Central Park. A date with Miles. A still from *Pride & Prejudice*. A quote about writing from Joan Didion. In them, I see little pieces of me, surrounded by all the things I want to be.

And then I want to laugh, because all of a sudden it's so obvious. Anastasia was never really separate from me. That was just—what did Jeremiah call it?—a story I made up because I wanted to escape. Leave it to a writer to escape to a place inside her own head.

All the hours I spent wishing I was Anastasia, I was really wishing to live my life to the fullest. The parts of her that I wanted to be—bold, adventurous, free—were already inside me. I just needed to find them.

I lean back in my chair, feeling a new sense of conviction sweep though me. *AnaStaysDreaming* is done. We had a good run, but now, I need to see if I have what it takes to stand on my own, without hiding behind Anastasia's perfect facade. Some of my followers might be disappointed, but the truth is, this blog was never really about them. It was always about me and the person I wanted to be. But I don't *want* to be Anastasia anymore.

I don't want to be anyone else but me.

In the end, I log out of Netzine without writing anything. I'm not sure when—or if—I'll ever log back in again. I don't owe random strangers on the internet an explanation. There's only one person I owe an explanation to, and he's always seen me, and liked me, for exactly who I am.

I leave the den, let Maggie back inside, and go to my room to get ready for Camila's party.

Chapter 36

"Woo!" Danny shouts as he does a cannonball into the deep end of Camila's pool. The splash is gigantic—it reaches a few of Camila's cheerleader friends sitting on lounge chairs. They squeal and jump out of their seats.

"Danny, you jerk!" Cami says when he surfaces. We're sitting at the edge of the pool with our legs dangling in the water. She grabs a pool noodle floating nearby and tries to smack him with it, but he ducks his head under just in time. A few seconds later, he pops up a couple of feet to the left like a whack-a-mole and laughs.

"Hey, this is what you signed up for," I remind her. "They're a package deal."

Camila shakes her head. "What Jeremiah sees in him, I'll never know."

I take a sip of my pink lemonade and look around. There are people everywhere, swimming and snacking and dancing to Sabrina Carpenter on the patio. It feels like the entire freshman class is here—soon to be sophomore class, I realize—plus a handful of older students. My sunglasses have a rosy tint, which makes everything look like a movie.

In a second-story window, I spot Camila's dad frowning down at the party. I point him out to her, and we both laugh.

"He promised me he'd stay upstairs," she says, taking a sip of her fruit punch. "But he wasn't happy about it."

"Cami." One of the soaking-wet cheerleaders walks up to us. "Can I borrow a towel? And, um, some dry clothes?"

"You didn't bring your bathing suit?" I ask.

She shakes her head. "I didn't know I was supposed to."

I blink at her. "But it's a pool party."

"Of course you can borrow some clothes, Meg," Camila cuts in, shooting me a meaningful glace. *Be nice.* I resist the urge to roll my eyes, and force a smile in return.

"Let me know if you need some sea-salt spray for your hair." I look up at Meg, using my hand to shield my eyes from the sun. "I have some in my bag, and it's like magic; it makes the beachiest waves."

"Okay." Meg smiles warmly. "Thanks, Jane. I love your suit, by the way."

I look down at my bathing suit—a lavender one-piece with a crisscross back and plunging neckline, plus a pair of denim shorts on top. Camila assured me I looked irresistible.

I smile back. "Thanks."

"Come on." Camila stands up. "Let's go to my room." She looks down at me. "Want to come, Jane?"

I know she's asking because she doesn't want me to feel

left out, and I appreciate it. But for better or worse, Cami *is* a cheerleader now. It's inevitable that she's going to form friendships with girls on the squad—friendships separate from me—and it doesn't mean that ours is any less important. That's what she's been trying to tell me all along. It took a while, but I'm finally listening.

"That's okay." I give her a reassuring smile. "I'll see you in a bit."

I watch her grab Meg by the wrist and lead her toward the house, and I don't feel any jealousy. Besides, I know we have something none of those girls will ever have: butter and croissants.

My eyes drift left, onto the patio, and land on two familiar faces. Ethan and Brynn, dancing together. Around them, some people whisper and sneak furtive glances, while others stop and stare openly. A new power couple in the making. I take a sip of my lemonade and watch them without bitterness. This is the way it was always supposed to be.

A flash of light catches my eye. I look right, toward the source, and find Leo standing in the grass with a disposable camera in his hand. I wonder if Camila enlisted him as party photographer, or if he just decided to do it on his own. Knowing Leo, it's probably the latter.

Before I have time to second-guess myself, I stand up. My heart is pounding, and my stomach is in knots, but I walk over to him anyway. At this point, the only thing worse than telling him how I feel would be not telling him.

As I get closer, I'm struck, right away, by how hot he looks. His wavy hair is long and luscious, and his cream-colored button-down makes his tan skin look especially soft and warm. I get the sudden urge to curl into him—to feel his arms around me like my favorite cozy blanket. I've *never* felt this for Leo before, and I don't know how to act. I'm afraid he'll be able to sense it coming off me, like pheromones—or desperation.

"Hey," I say when I get close enough. He turns, gives me a nod. His expression remains unreadable.

"Getting some good pictures?"

"We'll see." He holds up the disposable as if to emphasize that he has no way of knowing.

"Oh. Yeah." A beat passes in silence. In the distance, Danny yells, *"Cannonball!"* and lands in the pool with another big splash. Leo's flash goes off right as he hits the water.

"Um." I try again. "So, any luck buying a replacement camera?"

"I'm saving up," he says. "Turns out mowing Mr. Kowalski's lawn hasn't been all bad. He recommended me to a few friends, and they actually pay."

"Nice." I nod. "Got yourself a little landscaping business."

"Yeah. Leo's Luxurious Lawns. Coming soon to a billboard near you."

I laugh. "You have to wear a suit and slick back your hair. For luxury."

He smiles a little, like he wants to laugh, but something is holding him back.

"My parents are going to match what I earn, so hopefully I'll be able to buy a new camera by the end of the summer."

"That's great," I say, meaning it. "Seeing you without your camera is all wrong. Like something's missing."

"Well, something is."

"Right." I laugh uncomfortably, while inside, I'm cringing. I'm totally off my game, and I'm sure he can tell.

I take a deep breath. It's now or never. "Um, can we talk?"

He angles his camera up and takes a picture of Camila's dad in the window.

"Aren't we talking right now?"

"Technically," I say. "But I want to talk about what got published in the *Grizzly*."

If Leo is surprised, he doesn't show it. He takes another picture—of five girls tipping over after trying to balance on a pool floatie—and puts the camera in the pocket of his swim trunks.

We walk to the edge of the yard, where a large yellow hammock is tied tightly between two trees. Leo sits down, fixes his eyes intensely on me.

"Talk."

I put my lemonade down on the ground and sit next to him. I force myself to look at him directly. The sunshine brings out the gold flecks in his hazel eyes.

"Everything got so messed up."

He's quiet, waiting for me to continue.

"I know this is going to be hard to believe, but I only ever wanted the best for you. That's why I did it."

A pause. "Did what?"

"All of it." I look down at my hands. "The blog. The things I said to Brynn. I just really didn't think she was good enough for you."

Leo looks out at the party, runs a hand through his hair, messing it up. "That's not for you to decide."

"I know. I'm sorry."

"I didn't think Ethan was right for you, either," he says. "But I didn't go behind your back to try to break the two of you up."

"I know," I say again. "That's because you're a better person than me."

He shakes his head. "Don't do that."

"Do what?"

"Put yourself down like that. You do it all the time."

"What? No I don't."

"*Brynn is better than me. I'm not interesting enough.* It's like you think the worst of yourself, and you want me to agree with you." He looks at me. "But I'm not going to do that, because none of it is true. You *are* enough. You're amazing just the way you are."

I bite the inside of my cheek. I don't know what to say.

A breeze picks up, blowing his hair back. I have the sudden urge to reach out and touch it.

"Look, Jane. I've known you my whole life. I know when you're mad, I know when you're upset, and I know when there's something you're not telling me. So come on. Just tell me."

I want to tell him. I can practically feel the words leaving my mouth. *I like you. A lot. As way more than friends.* But suddenly I'm terrified. Because what if he doesn't like me back? What if I admit my feelings, and he never looks at me the same way again?

"Okay," he says when I don't speak up. "Answer me this, then. Why didn't you change my name in your blog?"

His question takes me by surprise. "Oh, um. I don't know."

I don't meet his gaze. I think I actually do know, but I'm scared to say. What if—

No. This is no time for fear. Be honest. Be brave.

"I guess," I say, taking a deep breath, "because I wanted you there."

"Wanted me . . . in the blog?"

I watch a squirrel run up a tree. The truth is I never even considered changing Leo's name. When I was building out Anastasia's life, he was always just . . . there. Not a fictionalized version of him, amped up for dramatic effect, but him, completely. I couldn't have imagined it any other way.

"It wasn't just a blog to me. It was . . ." I trail off, searching for a word big enough to encapsulate everything Anastasia was. "My own dream world. When I logged on, I could be a better version of myself, you know? I could take spontaneous trips to the city, go to glamorous parties, watch the sunset over the Hudson River. But you were always part of it."

I look at him. His eyes are already fixed on me like there's no one else around. Like we're the only two people in the universe.

"Do you understand what I mean?" I say, my voice soft. "It wouldn't have been my dream world without you."

He doesn't say anything right away, just looks at me with uncertain eyes.

"Are you saying..."

He trails off, looks away. He's afraid to ask the question, or maybe afraid of the answer; I don't know. What I do know is that from this moment forward, I never want Leo to feel like he has to guard his heart around me. I want to be the one who protects his heart. I want to make him feel safe.

"I'm saying that I love you."

He looks back at me, the surprise plain on his face. For a second, the fear comes back, but I push the feeling away.

And then something amazing happens. Leo smiles, small but sure. He shifts his body in the hammock so he's facing me.

"I love you, too."

A tingle runs down my spine.

"You do?"

He nods. "Yeah."

"Since when?"

He looks down at his lap, suddenly shy. "Since always."

I open my mouth, close it. Is this really happening?

"But what about Brynn?"

"What about her?" he says, looking toward the dance floor. "Have you seen her over there with Ethan?"

I stifle a laugh. Inside, I feel so full of adrenaline that I'm about to burst. "I think everyone has."

"I only went out with her because you liked Ethan," he says. "I thought I'd never have a shot with you. So when you told me she liked me, I—I don't know. I guess I thought it was a sign. To move on with my life, already." He laughs to himself. "I should've known it would never work."

I shake my head. "I can't believe it. I thought you really liked her."

"I wanted to," he says, looking back at me. "But she wasn't the one. I knew it when we kissed."

"How?"

Leo shifts closer to me. My breath catches in my throat.

"Because," he says. "All I could think about was that I'd rather be kissing you."

That's all I need to hear. I close the gap between us and press my lips to his. For a moment I can tell I've caught him by surprise, but then his mouth relaxes, his hands move to the sides of my face, and he kisses me deeper.

Who finds their soulmate at fifteen?

As we kiss, I breathe him in. I smell sandalwood and musk. The soil in Mom's garden, damp from rain.

A soulmate is someone who feels like home.

Leo is home. He's as sturdy as the foundation, as comfortable as the couch in the basement, but he's exciting, too. He's the feeling I get when I step into the garden at sunset, and the sky is pink, and the light is coming through the trees just right, casting orange-gold rays onto the azaleas, and I wonder how something so beautiful can be real.

We kiss until we can't breathe, and then we look at each other and laugh.

"That was kind of amazing," I say, breathless.

"Kind of," he says. "Let's do it again." He starts to lean in.

"Wait." I reach into his pocket, pull out the disposable camera, and turn it so it's facing us. "So we remember this."

"Oh, I'm going to remember this," he says, but he wraps his arms around me and looks at the camera anyway. I lean into him, smile, and take the picture.

Then we kiss each other again, and it's better than a dream. It's real.

New post from JaneInRealLife

Sunday, June 22, 12:00 p.m.

Jane in Real Life, Online

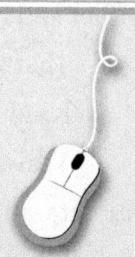

If you're reading this post in your feed, and you're confused because you never followed an account called *JaneInRealLife*, allow me to (re)introduce myself.

My name is Jane, but you probably know me by a different name. I used to run a blog called *AnaStaysDreaming*, where I pretended to be a girl named Anastasia. She was popular, confident, adventurous. She took spontaneous trips into New York City with her friends, just because. She had a perfect boyfriend and perfect hair. But she wasn't real. She was just a character I created. An idealized version of me.

The real Anastasia—me, Jane—is far from perfect. She's self-conscious, moody, and clumsy. Her parents would never allow her to travel to New York City unsupervised. She *does* have a perfect boyfriend, Leo, but it's a pretty recent development. For a while, she was pining over a different boy, who didn't know she existed (and who, it turns out, isn't as great as he seemed). She does not have perfect hair—yet. But she's still begging her mom for highlights!

Anyway. Maybe you can understand why she preferred to be Anastasia.

I used *AnaStaysDreaming* as an escape from my own life, and it was fun—for a while. Unfortunately, I was so busy living in dreamland, feeding off the attention of strangers, that I neglected the attention of the people closest to me. It took nearly losing them for me to realize that dreamland isn't all it's cracked up to be. Sure, it's pretty, but pretty is superficial. Yes, it's perfect, but perfect is boring. Most importantly, dreamland isn't real life. You always have to wake up at some point.

This is that point. From this day forward, my blog will no longer exist in dreamland. I'll be archiving all my *AnaStaysDreaming* posts and shifting to a new project. *JaneInRealLife* is a place for me to write about—you guessed it—my real life, all the good, bad, and in-between. If that's not interesting to you, feel free to unfollow. But if you like the messiness of reality—high school drama, sibling spats, suburban ennui—you should stick around. Maybe you'll even learn from my mistakes.

Here's the biggest one. I used to think I needed popularity, a perfect boyfriend, and fancy things to make my life special, but now I know that I was wrong. I'm enough the way I am. My life is special already, just because it's mine.

Talk soon,
Jane

Acknowledgments

When I came up with the concept for this book, I was home for the holidays, lying in bed with my laptop on my stomach, daydreaming. It was a position that felt familiar to me, since it was how I spent so much of my time as a teenager. I'd spend hours in my room scrolling Tumblr, looking at pretty pictures of New York City, and reblogging quotes about love, wishing that my life even slightly resembled the exciting, dreamy world I'd built for myself online.

Now that I'm older, I've moved to New York City, and I've fallen in love, I wish I could go back and tell myself to savor every moment of my "boring" adolescence. One day I *would* grow up, and things would change—for better and for worse—and I'd never again get to be that teen girl in her room, full of big dreams. This is what I was thinking about when something occurred to me: what if I could be?

And so, Jane Scott was born.

This book wouldn't exist without the support of Jessi Smith Dobies, editor extraordinaire and my dear friend. Thank you for believing in me and always encouraging me to dream big. As always, Jazz and Liz forever.

To my agent Uwe Stender: thank you for your dedication, your words of wisdom, and for talking me out of naming this book *Peaches and Dreams*. You were right!

Thank you to everyone at Aladdin and S&S Children's for championing me and this story. Special thanks to Heather Palisi for once again giving me the prettiest cover on the shelf.

To my mom: my inspiration, my biggest cheerleader, my TV buddy. Love you always. And to the rest of my family, my Gore family, and my friends: thank you for your love and support.

To my partner, my chef, my home: Eddie. Thank you for being my person in this life and the best dog dad to Audrey. I love you.

Finally, the biggest thank you to my readers. Without you, none of this would be possible. I feel so lucky that I get to write these stories for you.

Read on for a peek into Britnee Meiser's

TRACK ONE

"We're Going to Be Friends"—The White Stripes

This one's obvious, isn't it?
From the very beginning, you were there.
I never stood a chance.

My name is Imogen Marie Meadows. I'm seven years old.

I can do long division and spell "facade" and "rutabaga."

I love to draw pictures and collect taxidermy butterflies.

I know all about in vitro fertilization.

I do not know anything about my father.

This is what I'm ready to tell the boy who's zooming toward me on a skateboard—this, and nothing else. I'm used to people asking questions about me, because my mom and I move around a lot, so I've come up with a script that perfectly *encapsulates* me. (That's a word I just learned—"encapsulate": to express the essential features of something succinctly.)

Then he falls off his skateboard and into my front yard.

I stand still on my porch, watching and waiting. But the boy doesn't get up. He doesn't even move, just lies there with his face in the grass. Did I just witness someone *die*? Now *that* would be an interesting addition to my script. I look around for Mom, or one of the movers, but everyone is inside the house, unpacking our furniture. Guess it's up to me to investigate.

I take a sip from the glass of lemonade I'm holding, then slowly walk toward him.

"Hey," I whisper.

No answer.

"HEY! Are you dead?"

Finally, he turns his head to look at me, squinting through the bright light of the summer sun.

"Not dead," he says weakly.

"Hm." So much for my fun new anecdote. "Okay. I guess that's good."

"You guess?" He pushes himself off the grass to sit upright and takes off his helmet, revealing a shaggy head of bright blond hair. He looks at the glass in my hand. "Hey, is that lemonade?"

"No," I say quickly, tucking my long black hair behind my ear.

"Can I have some?"

I make a face. "You can't just ask strangers for lemonade."

"Sure you can," he replies. "Haven't you ever seen a lemonade stand before?"

"Do I *look* like a lemonade stand to you?"

"Okay, okay. Jeez." He stands up, dusts himself off, then looks around for his skateboard. It's in the neighbor's yard. He sighs.

"You better go get that," I say, trying to urge him along. I'm ready to get back to reading my book and drinking my lemonade in silence.

"Yeah." He doesn't move, just stares at his skateboard wistfully. "You know, I think I'm done with skateboarding. I stink at it."

I nod. "You can say that again."

"Okay." He cups his hands around his mouth. "I STINK AT IT!"

A giggle escapes my lips, surprising both of us. He cocks his head at me, smiles a little.

"It's okay. You can laugh," he says. "I laugh at myself all the time." Then he looks back at his board. "I don't even like skating, anyway. I only do it because of my older brother."

"Is he as bad as you?"

He shakes his head. "No, he's good. Michael is good at everything." A pause. "He's not going to like it when he finds out I busted his board. Maybe I can blame the new scratches on our cat Tina."

"What did Tina ever do to you?"

He gives me a knowing look. "Have you ever had your sister put catnip in your pocket when you weren't paying attention?" He winces at the memory.

"I don't have a sister," I say with a frown. "Or a cat."

"Consider yourself lucky."

He goes to the neighbor's yard to get the skateboard, and I see my chance to get away. I walk around the side of my new house, cut across the backyard, and step past the tree line. There are woods behind my house, which Mom already said I can't explore alone. She didn't say anything about hanging out on the edge, though. That's where, earlier today, I found the Tree.

The tree has these huge, exposed roots that I can crawl under like a dugout. It's the perfect place to disappear. Under the tree, I try to get back to reading, but I can't focus. I keep thinking about what that boy said: *Consider yourself lucky.* Is it lucky to be lonely? It's never really felt that way.

"So what's your name?"

The sound of his voice makes me jump. I look up to find him with his skateboard in his hands, grinning at me from the other side of the roots.

"How did you find me here?"

"I followed you."

"That's creepy."

His smile falls. "Was I not supposed to? I thought we were talking."

"We *were*. And now we're not," I say, returning my attention to my book.

He lingers there, not saying anything. I sigh and put the book down.

"You're distracting me."

"Sorry." He crouches down. "But come on. You're really not going to tell me your name? We're practically neighbors."

"Fine. My name is Imogen Marie Meadows. Happy?"

"Imogen? That's a weird name."

"My mom calls me Immie."

"That's a weirder name." He puts the skateboard down by the trunk of the tree and crawls under the roots to sit next to me. "I'm Jack."

"Well, Jack, you're being kind of rude about my name."

"Oh." His eyes widen. "Sorry, I didn't mean to be. I just meant that I haven't met anyone named Immie before."

It wasn't the first time someone made fun of my name. Kids at my last school called it a grandma name, which is funny, since I actually *was* named after my grandma. Once, Timothy Kline said Imogen sounded like "emoji." I responded by hissing at him and stomping on his foot, and I got sent home early. I still don't regret it. Nobody disrespects Grandma Imogen like that.

"I forgive you."

"Hey." He points to a doodle of a butterfly in the notebook by my feet. "Did you do that? It's really good."

I feel my cheeks heat up. "You ask a lot of questions," I say, flipping the notebook closed. "I don't even know you."

"Not yet," Jack says. "But we're going to be friends. I can tell."